THE TIME TRAVELERS ACADEMY

The Time Travelers Academy

First Edition

Copyright © 2006, Reginald Williams
All Rights Reserved
ISBN: 978-84728-926-1

Visit the Time Travelers Academy website:

WWW.THETTACADEMY.COM

For information or correspondence:
The Academy
PO Box 201352, Arlington, TX, 76006
contact@thettacademy.com

MANUFACTURED AND PRINTED IN THE UNITED STATES OF AMERICA

Dedication

This book is dedicated to my wonderful wife Maria, for inspiring me to write *The Time Travelers Academy* and for being there through the long nights I stayed up typing the book.

Acknowledgments

Thanks to all my family and friends.

Special thanks to my editor Arlene Robinson, for working so hard on *The Time Travelers Academy* and helping to make a dream become a reality. Arlene may be reached via e-mail at BettyBoopWrites@aol.com.

THE TIME TRAVELERS ACADEMY

By

Reginald Williams

The Time Travelers Academy Manual, Page 37, Section 1

There are over 100 billion galaxies in the current universe. Only one of those is the galaxy where Earth resides. We have learned that many civilizations throughout the universe tried to perfect time travel. To the future, they found, is comparatively easy. Just go at or near the speed of light; you will go into the future due to relativistic effects and time dilation. But time travel to the past— beyond the universal timeline—while possible with today's technology, is extremely dangerous.

The fact remains that there is more than one universe, each having its own laws of space and time. But ours is a fragile, 15 billion-year-old universe. If someone or something travels into the past and successfully causes a dramatic change in the past timeline, our universe will collapse upon itself at the point of the disruption and restart time again in a massive explosion, destroying the universe.

While still theoretical, the universe's only known defense against tampering with a past timeline is the time eliminators. Nothing can survive them; they attack anyone or anything that has gone back in time and attempted to cause a severe change in an already-set timeline. Time eliminators attack on a molecular level, absorbing all molecular activity until the person or thing causing the anomaly is literally absorbed out of existence. The time eliminators' main purpose is to stop time travelers from going past the universal timeline and changing the past. Once they appear, someone or something will be no more.

1

It started, as so many things do, with the best of intentions. A comet from deep outer space was heading toward Earth, but on a trajectory that could be intercepted.

Under the guidance of the United Nations Space Administration, two nuclear missiles were prepared. The first shot, from the red-colored missile codenamed Unicorn, was plotted to push the comet's trajectory by two degrees. The second missile, codenamed Horseman, would push the comet another two degrees. If the mission was successful, the comet would miss Earth.

"Are there any holds?" asked UNSA Mission Control.

"Negative," the UNSA space station replied. "We're ready to launch the missles."

There was silence, then the crackling voice replied, "Launch."

"Affirmative, payload launched."

Horseman launched without incident, but Unicorn misfired. After a few seconds, Unicorn managed to free itself and launch, but off course and out of sync with Horseman.

"What is the status?" asked Mission Control.

The answer came, and the messenger's voice was tight. "Sir, we're going on visual data. Preliminary evidence shows the comet appears to have split into two parts. One portion has veered away from Earth, toward Pluto. The other comet portion . . . it might have a close approach with Mars."

"Come again?" demanded Mission Control. When there was no answer, the speaker said, louder this time, "Repeat your last message."

"It . . . Something's gone wrong. The comet's in two parts, and one's headed for Mars."

The Mission Control commander considered the segment's trajectory, knowing what the space station's commander surely realized, but couldn't bring himself to say: If the renegade comet fragment missed Mars, it might get Earth.

A few weeks later, the world watched the 55-mile-wide mass approach, holding their collective breath. Their hopes came true; the comet struck Mars, leaving Earth safe and its population breathing again.

The comet's impact left a crater 80 miles deep in the Martian planet, hurling a massive number of small meteorites into space toward Earth in the process. Those on Earth had been warned this might happen, so they only watched, entranced, while hundreds of thousands of meteorites created a spectacular, worldwide shower that resembled July Fourth fireworks.

Many of the projectiles vaporized on entry, but an estimated five hundred thousand landed on Earth. Scientists determined that some of the meteorites contained a nanobacterium. Fossilized versions of the bacteria had been found in Antarctica many years before, in rocks that had come from Mars. Because the bacteria were fossilized, though, researchers couldn't conduct an accurate examination. Yet now, with live bacteria to study, they were able to conclude that it was harmless. Eager collectors continued to grab up the meteorites and use them to decorate their gardens or homes, or as souvenirs or even paperweights, unaware of the danger to come.

2

From a balcony in Russia, soft music playing in the darkness, the meteorite shower looked like a rainfall of stars. Two couples stood on the balcony, wearing formal dress and holding cocktails contained in slender glasses. One of the men, John Richards, held up his glass and turned to his boyhood friend. "Antonio, it's almost like heaven is smiling down on you and Natasha getting married. And celebrating, complete with fireworks."

Antonio clinked his glass with John's, then looked at his new wife, who stood on his other side. She smiled at him but continued talking to her sister, who stood beside her.

He turned back to John. "Someday," he whispered, "I hope the same happiness for you that Natasha and I have. And if you find that happiness with Bonita, so much the better."

John felt his face grow warm and quickly held up his glass. "A toast to the newlyweds!"

Bonita caught his eye and beamed at him, then held up her champagne glass. "Yes, a toast to Antonio and my sister. May they have fun always, and remember that Mother Russia brought us all together."

When Natasha and Antonio's kiss lingered, Bonita walked to John and took his hand, then retuned her gaze to the sky. "How beautiful, huh?"

"Yes. And the meteorite shower is also beautiful."

Bonita giggled. "That is what I meant, silly man."

The smile left her eyes, and she looked down. "I . . . I just wish this could go on forever. . . . That you didn't have to go. That I could come with you to America tomorrow. I—"

His finger on her lips stilled her. "I hate it that Antonio and I have to leave too. I'd like to have more time . . . for *us* to have more time. But—"

"You have to go."

The sadness in her voice hurt him. When he came to Russia to celebrate his best friend's wedding—Antonio had fallen instantly in love with Natasha after they met, first on the Internet, and later in person—he'd scoffed at the idea of falling so quickly for any woman. But now, knowing Bonita, his vow to remain single seemed . . . less important than before. Still, he had to be careful. It wouldn't be fair to make someone he loved carry his burdens. Even if that meant spending the rest of his life alone.

He tried but failed to hide his sigh, and hoped she would believe it was of frustration, not doubt. "Yes, I have to go. I'll be back in six months, about the time Natasha's visa's ready. And your student visa, too. And you said yesterday that you were glad for the delay."

She nodded. "Yes, but only because I want to give the children plenty of time to prepare. Leaving them will be my only regret."

John understood. Bonita was well educated, but jobs were scarce in Russia. She'd been lucky to snag a plum job as nanny to the US ambassador's three children, whom she'd grown to love.

The sadness on her face became unbearable, so he said, "We'll e-mail every day, and by the time we come back . . . well, I don't know what will happen then. But I'd like to think we'll know more then than we do now. About us."

She nodded. "Six months is too long, but I will write. And I will phone. And you must phone me too!"

Still not wanting to raise her expectations too much, he simply had to touch those lips again. And then he had to kiss them, just once more. . . .

⁘⟫⟫⟫⟫⟫⟩ ❀ ❀ ⟨⟪⟪⟪⟪⟪⁙⊢

They arrived at the Moscow airport two hours before their flight. Natasha and Bonita had come with them, and John almost wished they hadn't. On the drive, the normally stoic Russian women whispered to each other, and occasionally, one or the other would burst into tears.

He wished he could have shared more of his past with Bonita, in the rare times they'd been alone the past two weeks. But every time he drew up the courage to do so, either he backed down, or Antonio or Natasha entered the room.

Bonita wiped her eyes with a tissue and handed him a cloth bag. When he opened it and retrieved what was in it, he looked up at her, befuddled, hefting the palm-sized object in his hand. "A rock?"

"A meteorite." She sniffled. "It fell near my apartment. I want to give it to you for good luck."

Then, he remembered. "From the Mars blowout?"

She nodded. "That is what makes it lucky. Good luck for Earth, good luck for . . . you."

She wanted to say 'us,' he thought, but pushed the thought away.

Their flight was called, leaving them only time for a hasty goodbye and last kiss before he and Antonio rushed to board the plane. *It's better this way,* he decided, stowing the meteorite in his jacket pocket. Six months would give him time to decide if he could trust his heart to this woman, and if his feelings for her were greater than the risk of possibly putting her in danger.

3

Curtis opened his eyes but closed them immediately, willing the cabin's ceiling to stop spinning. Then, he sniffled. The *Luminaria*'s end-of-cruise party was great, even though he'd gone a little overboard on the champagne. But, except for the colds it seemed like every passenger had caught, including him and his wife, it had been a great vacation. When he returned to his job in Chicago, he would have no complaints about the luxury liner's service. Their colds would be a faint memory by then. As well as the hangover.

He opened his eyes again. The pain in his head made him groan, but this time, the cabin's ceiling stayed in place. Blinking, he turned over in the bed and saw his wife's sleeping form. He reached out and touched her arm. "Honey? You were right. That champagne'll sneak up and bite you on the butt."

She didn't move. Which was odd, since she was a light sleeper. Besides, being smarter, she had limited her own champagne intake to a couple of glasses.

A coughing fit overtook him. When it eased off, he reached out and gently grasped her bare shoulder. It felt . . . funny. Cold.

Groaning, he pushed himself up onto one elbow. "Honey? Honey? Wake up."

Five seconds later Curtis was outside his cabin, screaming for help. There was no answer to his plea, even from the nearby cabins, who surely must hear him. But pounding on their doors brought no reaction, only silence.

He raced down the hallway and up the stairs until he saw a steward.

"You have to help me," he begged. "My wife won't wake up and her nose is bleeding!"

The steward listened, and coughed before he replied. "I'll call for assistance right away. Please return to your cabin."

Curtis nodded, then stumbled back down the hallway.

The steward tried to raise the ship's infirmary. When he received no reply, he tried the head steward, then the purser, and reached two more dead ends. His next action was to head for the ship's bridge.

There, he found the entire crew either dying or dead, most of them bleeding from the nose and mouth, just as the passenger had told him his wife was. The captain had just enough time to radio a distress call before losing consciousness.

⊹〉═══ ❄❅ ═══〈⊹

The Secretary of Defense listened to the ringing on the other end, staring out the window of his office, his face a mask. When the person answered, he didn't bother with hello, instead saying, "What happened out there?"

The Navy admiral sighed heavily. "Sir, our country's been attacked by terrorists using a biological agent. It's the only thing it could be. Every person on the *Luminaria* is dead, both passengers and crew. Nearly 2,000 souls. And the captain barely had time to notify us before he died too."

The Secretary leaned forward, his face a mask. "What's next?" he said, knowing what the answer would be.

Another heavy sigh. "Investigations are continuing as we speak, Mr. Secretary. I'll give you another report as soon as I have it."

"See that you do. If this is terrorists, we're about to have a busy, busy day."

4

The one hundred students of the Rockville Academy of Martial Arts watched a practice duel between John Richards and his part-time instructor, Chen Lee Kahn. Each man held 13-inch knives, and used the knives to both block and to simulate an attack. Antonio watched from the sidelines, making sure all the students paid close attention.

The school's main classroom was huge, something John still counted himself lucky about. When he and Antonio started looking for a place to open their school, they were short on cash, so didn't expect anything more than a small storefront building. As it turned out, a friend of theirs had heard of a warehouse/office combo available. "It's not on the best side of town," he'd said, "but for the square footage, you're paying next to nothing in the purchase price."

Even cheap, it was still more than John had planned to pay for the school building. Antonio had talked him into it, and sure enough, the warehouse was perfect. Even with part of it divided into smaller classrooms, the main classroom easily fit the hundred students watching the match, plus had plenty of room for the stage and podium at one end, where John gave out awards and spoke to students and the younger students' parents. What had seemed only a foolish dream five years before turned out to be a satisfying and lucrative reality for both business partners.

After the match, John walked to the podium on the room's small stage. The chatter-filled hoots of appreciation ceased.

"When you're being attacked by a weapon," he said, "never take your eyes off your opponent. As you've learned, you can use your knives not just for offense, but also defense. Your knives can also be used to block, as we've demonstrated here. As you saw, Sensei Kahn's knife never touched me. I didn't have to use offense to stop him. Rather, I used defense to block his knives."

As he took his place behind the podium, his eyes fell on the meteorite Bonita had given him. He picked it up for a moment, felt its heft—much heavier for its size than a rock on Earth. He looked back up and was pleased to see the students' still-awed expressions.

"We'll start tomorrow at noon with kickboxing," he said. *And if I'm lucky, one of you will be as rare and substantial as this rock I'm holding, and you'll win at nationals next year.*

"Tomorrow," he added, "one of you might be chosen to spar with me. *If you're worthy.* Class dismissed."

Calls of "All right!" and "Cool!" accompanied the students' exit from the room. Antonio and Chen Lee Kahn remained behind. Seven months ago, John had hired Kahn as a janitor for the school, there being no other positions open at the time. Kahn had been reluctant to talk about his background, but John's gut told him that the reserved man would be an essential addition to the school. Kahn still made sure the school was clean and well-maintained at all times, but when their other instructor was called for National Guard duty, Kahn was able to seamlessly fill in. John had no qualms about asking him to look after the school while he and Antonio were in Russia. His only regret was that Antonio and Kahn seemed to get along as well as oil and water. The hostility didn't come from Kahn, who never complained, but from Antonio's continued distrust of the quiet man.

He looked again at the meteorite, considered how long its journey had been, and what a miracle it was that the object survived until landing on Earth. He picked it up, gave it a reassuring toss in the air, and resolved that if a meteorite could make it to Earth, perhaps someday his best friend and his best teacher would bond as friends.

At his wave, they headed into the school's office. The previous owners had used the warehouse's office for their sales, and had gone to great lengths to make it luxurious. Instead of a cramped, industrial-looking space, it was paneled in light oak, with recessed lighting in the ceiling. The plush, dark green carpet absorbed all sounds from the busy classrooms, making it an oasis of quiet whenever he or Antonio needed a break from the hustle.

He took his usual spot behind his desk. Antonio and Kahn remained standing.

"Good class," he said, and grinned at Kahn. "And hey, you're really coming along."

Kahn gave him a small smile. "Thank you. And oh, I need the keys to lock the building after I check the parking lot."

"Oh, sorry, I forgot." He opened his middle desk drawer, drew out the keys and tossed them across the desk.

"Thanks." With a nod at Antonio—a nod that wasn't returned—Kahn tossed the keys gently into the air and left.

Trying to ignore the tense exchange, John reached down to close the drawer. As he did his thoughts returned to the meteorite, and his gut clenched harder. In the past six months, he and Bonita had e-mailed every day and phoned each other at least once a week. The more he knew about her, the more he knew she was everything he'd been looking for in a woman. If only he had met her before . . . before everything he was certain was right turned out to be wrong. Before things became so . . . muddled. Would the same miracle he hoped for with Kahn and Antonio happen for him and Bonita?

He noticed Antonio peering at him. His voice rushed, he said, "Kahn's one of the best instructors I've ever seen. He's done well in all areas since we hired him, don't you think?"

"Yeah. Maybe."

He sighed. "We've had this discussion before—"

Antonio placed his hands on the desk and leaned forward. "Look, I trust your judgment, just like you trust mine to do the books. You know that. You've made this school one of the best in the state, no lie. But . . . he's never mentioned any family or friends. And he's so quiet. He's never talked about his personal life. Not once. And why is someone who's clearly not a janitor willing to work as a janitor? I didn't get it when you hired him, and I still don't. And I still don't trust him."

John sighed, leaned back and put his hands behind his head. "Talking about his personal life isn't in his job description, and I don't require that. We hired him to clean up the place and help with classes when we're short. In spite of what you think about maintenance crew also being masters, that's not uncommon in martial arts schools. And he does an exceptional job at both. And *that's* what matters. Some people are just quiet by nature. Maybe he doesn't want anyone in his business."

Like me.

He jerked his left arm down and looked at his watch. "It's getting late. The jewelry store closes at six. They're expecting me today."

The worry left Antonio's face, replaced by a smile. "Getting ready for our trip back to Russia? Buying something special for your *girlfriend*?"

He allowed himself to smile back. "Yeah, you might say that. When the time's right, I want to be ready. And who knows what kind of . . . gifts they have in Russia?"

"Just remember to take your time," Antonio said. "As much as I love Natasha, things don't usually happen that way for most people. Make sure it's right. I mean, you two were only together for two weeks when we were there. It's been six months since you even laid eyes on her."

He peered past Antonio's right shoulder, then his left. "Hey, I thought you were my risk-taking buddy. What happened to him?"

Antonio shrugged. "I guess now that I'm married, I've got a different take on some things. Like women." He grinned. "But that's the only thing. With everything else, I still like to jump over the cliff *and then* wonder what's down there."

With a chuckle, John said, "I value your opinion, but I'm in no rush. I'll know when the time's right."

Antonio's smile faded and he looked at John, measuring his face. "Well, you better get going. Remember rush hour traffic."

"You're right. And unlike you, *I* don't drive like a maniac."

Leaving a laughing Antonio, he exited the school by the front doors, calling a goodbye to Kahn, who was raking up leaves that had fallen from the massive oak trees lining the edges of the parking lot. Kahn looked up and greeted him, then returned to his work.

5

Thanks to the unseasonably cold and rainy Texas day, they were able to wear dark suits, raincoats and even hats to shield their features without risk of attracting too much attention on the quiet city street.

"We can't let him get away this time," the older man said. "But we've gotta make it quick, easy and painless."

The other man scowled. "Yeah, we deserve quick *and* easy. It took forever to trace him here." He gave a small wave. "Jewelry store, middle-of-nowhere burg? We got him as soon as he leaves the place!"

They approached the jewelry store, but didn't enter it. Instead, they stood outside, pretending to look inside the nearby display windows, glancing away when the occasional passerby gave them a curious look. Neither noticed the man behind the jewelry store's counter, peering at them with narrowed eyes.

They kept up their ruse of deliberate casualness when John arrived at the store. The older man had hoped John would be the only customer. He was, but the store clerk was still in there. He gave his partner a quick, low wave with his index finger, indicating they should wait until John exited. The other man kept his hand in his pocket, but nodded slightly. Now that they were so close, the waiting would be easier.

It didn't take long for John to choose just the right ring for his soon-to-be—or not—fiancée. Thankfully, with Antonio and Natasha's help, he knew Bonita's ring size, and Natasha had been thrilled to advise him on all the various styles. He decided on a solitaire diamond set in gold, with tiny sapphires on each side.

By then, the store was officially closed, leaving him the only customer inside. Judging from the way the salesman was acting, he wasn't comfortable with customers inside the store after quitting time. *Or maybe he has a hot date waiting,* John thought, hiding a grin. *Yeah, he just wants to get through taking my money, get me out the door, and then he'll call up his sweetie.*

John pulled out his credit card to pay for the ring, but noticed it had just expired. He winced, said, "Hang on a second," then slowly drew another card from a hidden section of his wallet, making a mental note to talk to Antonio first thing in the morning. Antonio, the school's bookkeeper, knew all about his personal finances. Except this part.

He looked up when the salesman said, "Hey, don't look at the window, but two guys have been hanging around outside since just before you got here."

John willed himself not to yank his head around, and managed, just barely, to keep his eyes on the man across the counter from him. "What do they look like?" he said.

"Dark suits, overcoats, hats. Two peas in a pod." The man trained his eyes on John. "Not too obvious, but . . . different enough to bug me. We've had some burglaries lately on this street. I saw these two the minute they walked up to the store window next door. One guy keeps putting his hand in his coat pocket, like he's checking to make sure his cell phone's there or something. And he keeps checking his watch, like he's really worried about the time. They haven't done anything yet, so I didn't call the police. But . . . still, I thought they looked funny."

"Maybe you should call the police anyway," John said.

"Nah. They've been out here a lot already. I don't want them to think we're crying wolf. But don't worry. When I saw them, I alerted my father and brother— we're all part-owners of the store. They're in back, watching the security cameras. I mean, it could be nothing. Maybe they're just waiting for someone. Just be careful when you leave, okay?"

John wondered if he should offer to stay. He wasn't carrying a weapon, a decision he'd made five years ago but for the first time regretted. At the least, he could tell the man of his martial arts training to reassure him: that he could at least help defend the store until the police arrived. And he could agree with the man that yes, the suspicious men might have their eye on the easy money they'd make by cleaning out a jewelry store. But what he couldn't tell the man, or the police, was that those men might be after him. That they might be yesterday's shadows, which always returned in the light of the next day. Or the next.

But, if his suspicion turned out to be more than simple paranoia, he would put the salesman at greater risk if he stayed. He gave the man a careful nod, said, "Okay, thanks. Hope it all works out for you," then left the store.

As soon as he exited, the men moved into the neighboring doorway, out of sight. Even worse, one of the men was slipping his hand inside his jacket, just like the salesman had described. But in that split-second glance, he only appeared to be patting something inside the pocket. When the man withdrew his hand, it was empty.

He turned and kept walking toward the parking lot, depending on his instincts to tell him what was happening at his back—instincts that, with one exception, had never failed him before.

With his heightened senses, he heard them fall in behind him. When he got to the store's parking lot, he began walking faster.

"Ivan Godunov?"

The question had come from behind him, but he was transported back to when he and Antonio were in their first year at the U of North Texas. They both loved military thrillers, and Antonio always got a kick when the captain or major or general, when faced with danger, ordered his troops to do a "rapid retrograde movement."

Stupidest thing I ever heard, Antonio said once, chuckling before tossing the book he'd been reading on the floor between their dorm-room beds. *'Rapid retrograde movement,' my butt. Why not just go ahead and say 'Okay, men, run back the way we came!'*

John had laughed too. Then. But now, a rapid retrograde movement was the only choice he had. Not panic. Not attacking the men. *Definitely not attacking them. Not without a weapon.* No, his only choice was running. Which likely wouldn't do any good. But he had to try to save himself.

It was after seven by then, but the jeweler's shared parking lot was covered with cars. He kept walking, keys in hand, never slowing his stride, and turned down the lane where he'd parked his car. If he could make it there, he could jump in the car and get away under the cover of the rush-hour-shopping crowds roaming through the parking lot.

Ten feet away, he hit the blue sports car's automatic door lock on his keys, hoping those following wouldn't hear the sound. They did. The feet behind him made pounding noises now.

He raced for the car and yanked open the door. No arms grabbed him, no taser was shoved into his side. He risked swiveling his head around. A couple and their child had walked in front of the men . . . who had turned completely around and were now walking away.

Not understanding why they'd stopped their pursuit, he took his chance, started the car and pulled out of the parking space so fast he startled the couple. With a quick apologetic wave, he wheeled the car around and burned rubber again, this time to the parking lot's exit.

He risked a glance in his rearview mirror. The older man was patting his chest. Neither man was moving toward him. He turned onto the highway, his thoughts scrambling. *Totally out of character. If they wanted me dead, why didn't they chase me?*

They don't want witnesses came the gut-punching realization.

He glanced again at the rearview, then side-view mirrors, but saw nothing that appeared to be a backup surveillance vehicle. Now, he was more certain than ever: they didn't attack because the couple they'd nearly collided with had a child with them. Many hired killers wouldn't touch a child. *At least they have that much of a conscience.*

"Ivan Godunov," he whispered, thinking how long it had been since he'd last heard that name. And then, like an unwelcome blow, came the memory of the mess he'd nearly made of things the last time he heard it. While in Special Forces, under the name Ivan Godunov, he conducted many successful operations, the last going undercover in a large black-market operation in Russia. Several of the high-level black-marketers, who'd been secretly selling nuclear materials to foreign nations, had threatened him with retribution. After his service was finished, the military secretly discharged him and assured him that all traces of his missions were buried under his codename. That his civilian identity and address would always be kept secret. Even then, John knew what scant protection those measures were against a determined foe.

Now, it appeared that one of his enemies had found him. He gave a weary sigh and patted his shirt pocket, where the ring he'd just bought remained. *Yeah, they just didn't want any witnesses.*

He should have listened to his gut when it told him that, no matter how much he cared for Bonita, it was too risky to pursue the relationship with her. Now, four days before heading to Russia, his decision had been thrust at him. His thoughts bitter, he sped down the highway toward home, trying to consider everything that had just happened—and why he was still alive.

6

He spent the next two hours driving around Rockville, trying to decide if he should risk going home. The men were after him. But did they know where he lived?

"Of course they do, dumbass," he muttered, and gave a sour chuckle. If they knew when he'd be at the jewelry store, they already knew where he lived.

A slow ride down his street revealed no strange vehicles. And from the outside, at least, there were no signs that anyone had been near his house. The garage doors and front door were closed, just as he'd left them. Everything else looked the same, too. With a sigh, he pulled into the garage. Nothing happened, so he turned off the car and prepared to head inside.

Like the school, the house had been another fortunate find. He'd been willing to rent an apartment at first—or, as he'd jokingly told Antonio, bunk at the school until they got their financial feet wet. In reality he planned to stay with his parents, who lived within driving distance of the school. But when his father died right after the school's opening, his mother insisted that John take the trust fund left as his inheritance. With that, he had enough money to put a down payment on a real house that, from attic to floor, was a place he could be proud of—and someday, perhaps, raise a family with the right woman.

That was then. Now, he unlocked the door leading from the garage, locked the two deadbolts, then checked every room for signs the two men might have already been there. He reached for the phone and called 911. Within seconds, the police dispatcher came on the phone asking, "What is your emergency?"

John thought for a second, then said, "I'm sorry. I was trying to call 411 for information. I must have dialed the wrong number."

All these years, he'd been successful in keeping his past secret. Now wasn't the time to reveal his alternate identity to the police.

Upstairs in his bedroom, he rummaged through the closet until he found the box he was looking for. He always called it his bad-memory box, and laughed when he said it. But now, looking at the scarred wooden lid bearing a tiny plaque with the Russian words for "Don't Sweat the Small Stuff," he found himself fighting a lump in his throat. He opened the box and retrieved what was inside.

In spite of looking like a regular Glock, the gun was undetectable in most electronic searches, constructed as it was from a special, stronger-than-steel plastic. Another difference: this gun held 400 rounds in its clip. The bullets were much smaller than regular bullets, yet more lethal, since they would explode on contact. This, and the credit card, was all he'd kept from his time in Special Forces.

Looking over it, he wiped off imaginary dust and muttered, "I never thought I'd need you again, but I might need you now."

He inserted a full magazine and chambered a round, then peeped out the bedroom window at a strange noise. Nothing but an old car going down the street. He then fell onto his bed with gun in hand, looking up at the ceiling. "I was so careful," he whispered. "How did they find me? How?"

Thanks to the two men in the long coats, it took little effort to remember that day. Right after college, he joined the military. He could still remember the thrill that permeated him when his commanding officer asked him to join the United Nations Special Forces, an elite group made up of the best from all countries. He gladly accepted the transfer, took the name of Ivan Godunov, and went through their specialized training.

Even though he'd served in the US Special Forces, his new assignment was tough at first. His enduring interest in Russia helped, especially his college classes in the Russian language. He had his father to thank for that. From childhood, his dad had envisioned that, one day, the Cold War would end and Russia would become an ally. Still, from time to time, John was sure he'd been made when he used a word he thought was right, but wasn't.

Over time, the missions came easier, until his last assignment: trying to catch corrupt Russian officers who were selling Russian nuclear material on the black market. Posing as a Russian military officer, he'd infiltrated an abandoned nuclear enrichment plant. As soon as the deal went down, he was able to call in his backups. Together, they netted the arrests of 15 crooked officers and their assistants. Yet one of them had been better than usual at hiding a gun on his person. John nearly died from the blood loss, and the scar on his back returned him to that day every time one of his students landed a successful punch or kick there.

Yet there were other memories. Even injured and near death, he could never forget what happened when the police were taking the highest-ranking officer away.

"You are a traitor, Ivan Godunov!" the man had screamed. "I should have known you were an American dog! One day, I will find you and kill you. I'm bigger than what you think. I know Foxhound1, and someday, you will as well!"

"Ivan Godunov," who'd been threatened before, managed to smile before losing consciousness, and the United Nations military police added making terroristic threats to list of the charges already against the man.

That was five years ago. In those five years, he'd never been able to find out Foxhound1's identity. He did learn enough to believe that the corrupt officer was capable of carrying out his threat, even from inside the Russian prison where he lived now. That was why, as glad as he was to see Antonio so happy, he dreaded ever returning to Russia, where the man's network spread wide and deep. But now, it seemed the man's network had jumped the Atlantic and found him anyway.

He looked at the window, saw the moonlight streaming in, and was surprised to discover that thoughts of the upcoming reunion with Bonita gave him the courage to face what he couldn't alone.

⊹⟩⟩⟩⟩⟩⟩⟩⟩⟩╍ ❀❦ ╍⟨⟨⟨⟨⟨⟨⟨⟨⊹

The restless sleep did little good, and the two-mile run the next morning only heightened his tension. He kept looking around and behind him, wondering if *this* jogger or *that* person at the corner was only waiting until he got a good shot at him.

He returned to the house, showered and shaved, and went into his closet. He stood there a moment, then, sighing, took down the bad-memory box. What he wanted to do was walk over to the bay window in his bedroom and fling the box as far as he could. But, that would do no good. Instead, he retrieved what he came for from the box, placed it in the pocket of his jacket, and got dressed.

He arrived at the school at 11:00 a.m. After a quick greeting to Kahn, he approached Antonio, saying, "I have to talk to you."

They both walked into the office and closed the door. It had been a difficult decision. He never wanted to think about his military service again, and never wanted even Antonio, his best friend, to know. But he had to tell Antonio about the credit card transaction yesterday, and that would lead to more he'd have to explain. "Uh . . . I didn't get much sleep last night," he said.

"Hey," Antonio replied, "it's not like you to complain. Anything wrong?"

In spite of his worries, he smiled. "You can always tell, huh? Yeah, I think there's something wrong. I think I was followed yesterday. Sent by someone I ticked off when I was in Special Forces."

Antonio leaned forward. "Okay, dude, spill it."

John told him what happened, and his suspicions, then finished with, "I can't help but think the black-marketer finally found someone—or got enough funds to pay someone—to follow through on his threat. I didn't want to tell you this, but I don't want you caught up in this without at least knowing what I'm facing. And I had to tell you that I used my old credit card to pay for the ring anyway."

Antonio leaned back in his chair with a small whistle. "Wow. But look . . . if you came out of a jewelry store, they might have been trying to rob you. Might not be any sort of Russian connection at all. Relax, my friend. I'm your lifelong buddy, and you never even told *me* what you did in the military."

John sighed. "I didn't think there was any reason until I was followed. But now, you have to know. Small chance, but they might use you to get to me. They

—19—

might change what they wear, but just so you'll know, they were dressed in all black yesterday: trench coats, and they both wore black hats."

He gave Antonio a dark smile. "It isn't paranoia if they really are trying to get you. But I'm not going out without a fight, or because I wasn't paying attention." He handed Antonio a small revolver. "Keep it in the school in a safe place. It shoots six rounds."

Antonio's eyes widened at the sight of the gun. "But I—"

"Don't give me any crap. I know you know how to use it. I'm the one who made you go to the firing range with me, remember?"

Antonio took the gun with reluctance. "Look, do we have to get so . . . official? I still think there's a chance they were just casing the jewelry story. And look, maybe you're overworked. Stressed out. Take your mind off this and concentrate on our trip to Russia."

John looked out the window. "Yeah, it'll be a relief to get away. But I'm a little worried about leaving everything with Kahn this time. And not just because of what happened yesterday."

"You mean the fire last week?"

He nodded. "That's part of it." Just the week before, a gang-fight down the street had ended up in a business burned to the ground. And the local gang kept putting pressure on all the neighborhood businesses for "protection" money. Just like the Mafia of old, gangs had become an increasing problem in all cities, not just the big ones anymore. As if that wasn't enough, the person Antonio laughingly called "their corporate neighbor" had increased his pressure to buy them out.

With a sigh, he said, "One business burned down, and three have shut their doors because of the gangs. But I'm not afraid of the gangs, *or* Gary Collins. I just don't know if I should warn Kahn. Seems unfair to lay this on him."

Antonio got up, walked around the desk and put the revolver into a drawer. "Well, there's nothing we can do about any of it right now."

This statement turned the conversation to other things. They briefly talked about the upcoming trip, and finally, John smiled.

"Man, I still can't believe it," he said, shaking his head and making a *tsk-tsk* noise. "I spent most of my time in the military in Russia, and you'd never even been. So what do you do after I finally get away from Russia? You put an ad in some Russian newspaper, and one month later, you've met yourself a Russian mail-order bride."

"It was a marriage agency on the Internet, Bozo, not a newspaper," Antonio said, grinning because he knew John was joking. "All on the up-and-up. And hey, we knew each other for a year and I visited her *numerous* times before we got married. Eighteen months now, that's how long we've known each other. Heck, that's longer than most Hollywood marriages last."

"Yeah, I know," John said, grinning back. "And as soon as she gets here, you and she will have that white picket fence you've always wanted."

He thought of the meteorite on the podium. He wasn't smiling now. Antonio was happy because of the choices he made in life—to go straight from college and follow his passion to crunch numbers for a living. Now, with Natasha's visa approved, his wife was about to join him and help him continue his American dream. In spite of his dedication to martial arts, John chose the military after college. A decision he was still proud of. Even when the black-marketer threatened him, he'd felt only pride mixed with disgust for the tragedies black marketers created because of their greed.

Not even the men following him were enough to shake that sense of recalled triumph. But he couldn't let the consequences of his decision, years ago, cause Bonita a broken heart she didn't deserve. Right now, he couldn't even guarantee he'd live another day, or that he could protect her.

Yet he couldn't stop the plans Bonita had either. In the six months since Antonio's wedding, Bonita had applied for and been accepted to a graduate program at the University of North Texas. She would travel back with them on a student visa.

And after that? Until yesterday, he thought he knew. If the magic they'd felt in the past six months was still present, he would ask her to marry him when he saw her in person. *But now . . .*

"It takes forever just to process a visa," Antonio said, as though hearing his dark thoughts. "And even though Natasha's a licensed cosmetologist in Russia, she'll have to practically start all over again once she's here. Maybe it won't be like that for you and Bonita. I mean, when she applies for her permanent visa, she'll already be here in the States." He sighed and leaned back in his chair. "It was so hard to kiss Natasha goodbye for six months."

"You had to follow the immigration rules," John said.

"Rules, rules, rules, who needs them!"

John laughed. "You never follow rules. Ever since I've known you. One day it's going to catch up with you. Rules were made for a reason, no matter how simple or stupid they might seem." *And no matter how many hit men are following you.*

"I follow rules only when I have to," Antonio said. "There are rules for everything. Too many rules. Over half of them just don't make good sense. If I don't think they're important, then I don't obey them. Anyway," he grinned at John, "only four days to go."

John reached into his pocket again. "I have something to show you."

"What, another gun?"

Smiling, briefly forgetting about the two men following him, he pulled out the ring.

"Wow, it's beautiful," Antonio said, then grinned at John. "Are you proposing to me?" They both laughed at that.

John took a deep breath. "I finished college, got the military behind me. Now I have a successful business and good friends. All I lacked was a lifetime partner.

A wife and children. Then, I'd have the perfect life. Six months ago, I knew it was love. But after what happened yesterday—"

"You have to quit worrying about yesterday," Antonio said, and waved his hands in the air, then used them to punctuate his next words. "If they didn't go after you right then—heck, you said they ran away!—then they're not going to do anything else. Who knows? Maybe that guy just sent them here to scare you. Maybe he wasn't happy with his prison breakfast that day, and said, 'I'm annoyed, so maybe I'll just send a couple of my friends to harass old Ivan. Yeah, *that'll* make me feel better.'"

He stopped waving his hands, leaned forward and placed his elbows on the desk. "And you know what? Those two guys probably already left the country. Yeah, they're back in Russia now, telling that guy, 'Yeah, we scared old Ivan real good.' And the guy gave them their money, and now they've forgotten all about you and gone to the next job."

John looked at him, wanting to believe him.

7

Charlene Vaughn loved her job, but today, she was a frustrated woman. It was six p.m. and the lab was closed for the night. Her coworkers had already left. As soon as she finished doing her computer backup, she'd be gone, too, back to her tiny Washington, DC apartment and the brown Pomeranian she had a love/hate relationship with—a gift from her parents last Christmas on her brief trip back home. Even so, she stole a longing glance at the electron microscope across the room, wondering if her boss would yell at her if she snuck in a couple more hours of work tonight.

She shook her head, muttered, "Nope, better not risk it," and continued her backup.

Sometimes she wished she could have worked for the old Centers for Disease Control. That had been her dream. But by the time she earned her doctorate from Baylor University and snagged this job three years before, there'd been big changes in the wake of heightened terrorist activity. Washington dismissed the United States' worldwide public health mission, and the CDC was absorbed into a new department dubbed the US Department of Nuclear, Biological and Chemical Deterrence, or the NBCD. The NBCD's primary mission was to stop terrorists from the making, manufacturing, distribution and use of nuclear, biological and chemical warfare.

She'd loved her job even more when a career-making assignment had practically landed in her lap. In Antarctica, long before the spectacular meteorite shower on Earth, scientists found meteorites from Mars that contained fossilized microorganisms. But, they couldn't conduct an accurate examination on fossils that old. But with the recent fall of meteorites—meteorites *teeming* with organisms—they were working with live specimens. And Dr. Charlene Vaughn was one of the few who had the pleasure and privilege of comparing those ancient meteorites to those that landed six months ago.

Single, 28, and with a passion for her work, Charlene was in the perfect time and place to make a huge name for herself in science. But that's when the second boom fell. Congress decided that the Mars fossils project wasn't connected to terrorism and cut their funding. Charlene's boss fought it; Charlene was convinced the nanobacterium wasn't completely harmless. But his protests were in direct opposition to the party line now being bandied about in the press. If the announced cuts really came, she'd have to give up on her research on the nanobacterium and concur, at least on paper, with the NBCD's official stance. And Charlene Vaughn never liked agreeing to anything she didn't feel 100% good about.

She left her backup busily transferring from the computer to the CD and went back to the latest samples, still under the electron microscope. *Something's there, I just know it,* she kept thinking while she peered at the images. *Something the team has overlooked*

But with the funding about to end and short of a lightning bolt from above, she wasn't likely to find it before she was reassigned.

That morning, two men talked by telephone. One of the men was Charlene's boss at the NBCD; the other was speaking from a remote hospital in North Dakota.

"Look, I told you ten days ago and I'll tell you now . . . My patients are dying, Dr. Davies. Their symptoms are like nothing we've ever seen before. No one is living past seven days. The military has just quarantined our city, but they still won't tell us anything!"

The man's voice lowered, became more desperate. "Some of the patients are members of my hospital staff. You need to get down here now!"

Davies knew there was little he could tell the frantic hospital administrator. Sure, he could speculate. Charlene Vaughn didn't believe the new organism was as benign as the other researchers did. But she was a lone voice. Kind of like him. The Pollyanna attitude about the organism's potential danger had pervaded all departments, all the way to the President. Even the report of the almost-instant annihilation of thousands of cruise-ship passengers hadn't swayed them. But the way this man was talking, the strange new disease at one North Dakota hospital seemed identical to the one that had taken 2,000 lives on a cruise ship thousands of miles away.

How could this have happened? he thought as he listened to the voice at the other end of the phone. But perhaps *how* it had happened was less important now than how to stop the disease from spreading. Twenty patients at this one hospital had already died from it, and ten patients now had the symptoms. And this time, there was no cruise ship to serve as a natural containment.

"They're all in quarantine, of course," the administrator was saying now. "And we've taken blood samples from every patient in the hospital, and every one of their visitors we could locate. And what's growing out of them doesn't match anything we've got on the books. Nothing!"

Unfortunately, no matter how strong his suspicions, there was little Davies could reveal to the hapless administrator now. "We'll fly out tomorrow with our team," he said. *And we'll pray that we can find out enough to keep this from spreading all over the world.*

⊹≻═ ❀❧ ═≺⊹

Six o'clock turned to seven without Charlene realizing it. Her frustration had led her to going back and pulling the original slides from the set of those taken from the meteorites six months before, hoping that another comparison would yield a new insight. Just about the time she decided it wouldn't, after all, she heard a knock at the lab door. Without getting up or looking, she yelled, "What do you need?"

"I need one of my best employees to put down her microscope and pack her bags, that's what."

She looked up to see Davies. At nearly six-and-a-half feet, she had to look *way* up to see his face in the dim light. She grinned at him. "Hey, tall, dark and handsome."

Davies grinned right back. Even though he had the swarthy complexion and dark hair of his Black Irish ancestors, he'd still have to get an unbelievably deep tan to match his lead researcher's deep-copper skin. And there was no way his blue eyes would ever match the depth of her soft brown ones, which were meeting his now with confusion, but also her customary eagerness.

"So what's up?" she said. "What upcoming mission? I checked the schedule and the fieldwork's already been cancelled because of the budget—"

He held up a hand to stop her. "We got a phone call from a hospital in North Dakota. People are falling out all over the place up there. Patients *and* staff. We've been authorized funding to assemble a team to find out what's causing it." He paused a moment, then added, "Whatever it is, it's working fast. From first symptom to death within seven days."

Her eyes widened. "Man, that *is* fast. Heck of a lot faster than hantavirus, but not nearly as fast as—"

"Yes, I know. The military's already quarantined the area, and they're waiting on us. We leave tomorrow at oh-eight hundred. You'd better wrap up what you're doing, go home and get some sleep."

She nodded. "I'd better call that high-priced kennel and make arrangements for my mangy little dog too."

He grinned and nodded. "Somehow, you don't seem upset."

She shrugged. "Hey, he'll eat better than me and get walked three times a day while I'm gone. He'll think he's in dog heaven."

With a final nod, Davies turned and left the room. After the door shut, she reached out to pick up the phone, intending to call the kennel first, then her neighbor to ask her to housesit. Instead, she decided to pack up her research materials first. Goodness only knew what they had for equipment in North Dakota. As far as she knew, the nearest electron microscope was in Wyoming, at the former CDC facility in that state.

But, she'd worry about that when she got there. For now, she would take her small microscope and hope that was all she'd need up there.

Fifteen minutes later, she had her equipment ready to be loaded onto the plane the next morning. She picked up the folder holding her notes and the CDs, but at the last minute decided to just shove the folder into her roomy purse. No need to risk losing them in the plane's cargo hold tomorrow, or forgetting them.

She flagged down a taxi to take her to her apartment. Once home, she fed the yapping Pomeranian and then grabbed her cell phone to call the kennel, mostly to quell her rising excitement. In her past three years with the NBCD, she'd spent most of the time in a lab. She hadn't even been invited to the cruise ship where the passengers fell out and died. This was her first serious field mission, and she couldn't wait.

8

The suit felt stuffy and confining, even though she knew there was plenty of air-flow—as a student microbiologist at Baylor University, she'd had the honor of helping test this particular design. Even so, her racing heart and fast breathing had already fogged up the suit's visor. *Note to self,* she thought, *tell the next set of unfortunate undergrads to work on fixing the fog-up problem . . . and be glad it's not me this time.*

She had to stifle her giggle when her teammates heard it though their head-sets and turned to her, confusion on their faces.

Aside from that, the only hassle had been getting her equipment on the plane. She was glad Dr. Davies was there to sweet-talk the Homeland Security screen-ers into not putting her microscope through the X-ray machine. Or her research CDs. And, when she protested, he kept them from giving her one of those body-intrusive pat-downs.

Now, she listened while the hospital's medical staff briefed the NBCD agents. "Even though my staff took full infection precautions," one of them was saying, "some of them have died also. We believe this . . . whatever it is, has a communi-cable rate between 90% and 100%. Gloves and facemasks don't work."

Listening to the symptoms, Charlene's excitement grew. Organisms that took months or years to develop outward symptoms, like AIDS, were harder to track. This one, which moved so fast, was devastating for the victims, but would give them much more information, and quicker, to find a cure.

"Certainly, that's troubling," Dr. Davies told the man. "But remember, that's why we're here."

After a moment, the doctor nodded. The worry didn't leave his tired face, though.

✦ ❀❀ ✦

Three days later, Charlene was still frustrated. She and the rest of Dr. Davies' staff had examined the organisms invading the dead and dying patients' bodies, but remained clueless as to what the new life-form was and why it was resistant to treatment. But there were now twenty new cases, and she knew the situation was urgent.

Yet that night, in her makeshift office in the hospital's basement, she finally picked up the pattern.

"*Two* DNAs?" she whispered, looking at the report she just received. "That can't be!"

But no amount of double-checking, or verifying with her team and then the top brass in DC, changed her discovery. What couldn't be, *was*. Two organisms—the virus that caused avian flu, and the bacterium that caused bubonic plague—had merged to form one.

Her mind began flying, and soon, she became queasy when the next realization hit her: Their very merging should have been impossible. But it seem that both organisms had used each other's strengths to prove the Darwinism survival-of-the-fittest theory: the rapid-destruction power of the bubonic plague bacterium combined with the incurability of the avian flu virus had formed one quasiorganism . . . one that was killing people in North Dakota, and with no way of stopping it from creating a worldwide pandemic.

"My god," she whispered. "This is like Darwin's worst nightmare." *And a microbiologist's worst nightmare come true.*

No, she thought. *Not just mine, the* entire planet's *worst nightmare. Dear God, this is a setup for an apocalypse!*

Then something else hit her. There had surely been some mutation since the organism had been passed around between humans. But the bond *between* the two morphed organisms had eerie similarities with what she was looking at right now—the CD images of the nanobacterium found on the Mars meteorites.

She jumped up from her seat and ran down the hall, heading for Davies's makeshift office.

Her coworkers were in awe and disbelief, since the Mars organism had been deemed harmless. "Yes, harmless," she replied. "Harmless *by itself*. But look what it's done . . . it literally merged DNA to create another life-form. Its bonding protein is an *exact match* to the Martian nanobacterium. And . . . if it's doing this to one-celled animals and viruses, what's it doing to people? We've theorized that some of us here might have the Martian nanobacterium from our drinking water, but not this . . . this avian plague."

Davies sat back in his chair. "Avian plague?"

"I gave it a name, taken from both diseases."

He leaned his head back, closed his eyes, and stayed that way for so long, she thought he might have fainted. Just as she was about to ask him if he was all right, he lowered troubled eyes to meet hers.

"If everything you've just said pans out," he said, "we have a monster on our hands. I . . . I haven't wanted to say anything to distract you, but . . . I received reports a few days ago from other countries, asking us to help them. The symptoms they describe match the patients' here. Because of the funding cuts, I told them the only thing I could. I said we couldn't help them. That international assistance was the old CDC's mission. That ours was to protect only this country. That we couldn't go visiting every country each time someone cries wolf."

He leaned his elbows on the paper-cluttered desk and put his head in his hands.

Charlene leaned toward him and patted his shoulder. "Well, boss, you'll just have to tell them . . . this time, the little boy's right."

9

Chen Lee Kahn heard the knocking, but only peeked through the heavy blinds covering the school's front windows. When he saw who was outside, he didn't go to open the door, but instead headed for the office.

"Gary Collins is outside," he said. "Should I let him in?"

John looked at Antonio, his mouth grim. "Well, he's ready for his next volley at us. You up for it?"

Antonio grinned. "You know it. Think he'll try the sob story this time, or start yakking about eminent domain again?"

John shook his head. "Maybe both. According to him, if we don't cave in and accept his *extremely generous offer*, he'll only have half the parking lot he really, *really* needs, and he'll be out of business." He shook his head again and gave a mock groan. "Are we evil, or what?"

"Yep. Evil John and Evil Antonio, that's us."

It was nice to joke about it, even though Gary Collins had the weight to put behind any of his implied threats, and both of them knew it. The eminent domain mention had worried John the most, enough to contact the city council. As it turned out, the karate school, being a business, too, wasn't vulnerable to eminent domain laws. And he got a good feeling when the city councilman he'd talked with said that their well-run business was one the city was glad to have—had actually called the school a "godsend for the youth of this city."

But Collins had strong connections in the city as well. And if what John had found out about the man was true, he had connections with other people who could make their lives miserable.

John looked at Kahn. "Open the gate, my good man, and let the rodeo begin."

They made it to the lobby as the 6′9″, 300-plus-pound man trundled himself through the door and removed his Stetson from his head. Collins was dressed as he always was, in a hand-tailored suit and cowboy hat that matched his country-western accent. An outsider would never guess that he owned a huge store that sold and manufactured electronics. At Twin Sky Electronics, a customer could find everything from a handheld kid's video game to the most sophisticated electronic surveillance equipment costing many thousands of dollars. Of the latter, John and Antonio suspected that, somewhere in the back of his huge store, Collins sold surveillance equipment that probably wasn't sanctioned by the government for private use. Judging by the number of shady types slipping in and out of his place, many of them with out-of-state tags on their expensive-looking vehicles, he probably did as much business on the sly as through the store's public access. But, they'd agreed that if Collins stayed out of their business, they'd do their best to stay out of his.

In spite of appearances and what they suspected, Collins was unfailingly polite, with that rare and enviable gift of building a successful local business to national prominence. That was where the trouble started for the karate school. Twin Sky Electronics grew so large, there were no more spots for its employees to park. And so they parked at the businesses next door, leaving those business's employees with no place to park.

So that's why, for perhaps the dozenth time, Gary Collins was taking a seat across from John and beside Antonio. But just before he lowered his massive self into the chair, he noticed Kahn in the corner, holding a dust cloth.

"Oh, excuse me, son," Collins said. "Would you like this chair?"

"Thank you, but I prefer to stand," Kahn said. "I'm just here to take care of some unfinished business."

Collins gave John a questioning glance. John nodded, indicating that anything he had to say, he could say in front of Kahn.

With an unlit cigar in his mouth, only taking it out to talk, Collins cleared his throat and said, "I don't think there's any reason not to get right to my point. My lawyer told me you refused my last offer. I'll tell you, I think that was a more-than-fair offer for such an old building in this part of town. And I believe I've made it clear that you're holding me up, putting my business in jeopardy. But still, I'm a reasonable person."

After talking, he flashed a smile, showing his slightly yellow teeth from smoking, then put the cigar into his mouth before taking it right back out. "But this time I want to approach you directly, man to man. I'm willing to double my previous offer. I say again, I'm doubling the amount. With that kind of money, you could relocate and expand your business and have plenty left over."

John shook his head. "As I told you before, I'm not interested in selling. I'm happy right where I am." He leaned forward, the smile still on his face. "Pardon me if I sound harsh, but . . . what part of no don't you understand?"

Collins bit down so hard on the cigar, John feared he would bite off a piece and choke on it. Instead, he pulled the wet stub from his mouth and said, "Look, don't tell me you're stalling because you like this area. Why, it's a wonder any business can survive here, what with the surge in crime and gang activity. I'll ask you again to take my generous offer and relocate to a safer area."

THE TIME TRAVELERS ACADEMY

John bowed his head a few seconds, as if in deep thought. Then, raising his head, he said, "Your offer is good, but we have no plans to move or relocate. From the sound of it, moving might benefit *you*, though. *We* don't have any problem with the crime, or anything else. And I have no intention of seeing my life's work bulldozed and turned into a parking lot. I say again, what part of *no* do you not understand?"

Collins stood, and so did John, who walked around the desk, placing his 6′2″ height next to the larger man's. Amazingly, Collins stepped backward.

"Temper, temper," Collins said. "This is only business. I'm not here to fight."

Putting his cigar in his mouth and taking it out again, he turned and walked through the lobby to the front door. Holding it open, he swiveled his head back to them. "Expansion is the key to a successful business. I intend to expand. You all have a nice day."

He then stepped out, never taking his eyes off John through the closing door.

John locked the door behind him, muttering, "Just in case he decides to come back." Then he rejoined Antonio and Kahn. "Nice guy. Obsessive, compulsive and arrogant, but *nice*."

Even Kahn cracked a smile at that.

⊹⟞⟝ ❀❀ ⟞⟝⊹

Outside the school, the big man pulled out his cell phone and made a call. "They refused to accept my offer," he said when he heard the other person's greeting. "Looks like we'll have to go to the next option on our list."

⊹⟞⟝ ❀❀ ⟞⟝⊹

Two hours later, there was another knock on the door, this one much louder. Kahn was outside now, raking the school's side yard, so he didn't see them. But he heard the knock, as well as the laughter and profanity. And he remembered that, when he came outside, he'd left the door unlocked. John and Antonio were alone inside the building.

He put down his tools and rounded the front to see about 15 young men entering the front door. Walking quickly, he got there just as the last man entered and followed him in.

The men clearly belonged to a gang; they were all dressed like lowlife thugs, complete with tattoos. Some were smoking, clearly disregarding the signs posted both inside and outside the lobby.

Kahn saw John and Antonio enter the lobby and approach the men. After a quick glance at Kahn, John said, "May I help you all?"

One of the gang was dressed in all black, and the name "Mal-A-Dies" was emblazoned in red on his shirt, along with a skull and crossbones. He was sucking on a lollipop. Kahn hid a smile, thinking, *Does that punk even know he's wearing a combination of gang and martial arts attire?*

"Mal-A-Dies Shirt" seemed to be the leader. "Can you help us?" he said, pulling the lollipop out of his mouth. "Yeah, you can help us. Where is da paycheck? You all runnin' very late on our pay, and we don't work for free. We come to collect our money!"

John laughed first, but Antonio soon joined in. Kahn's chuckle was characteristically restrained.

Their mirth ended and Antonio stepped forward. "I'm the co-owner and the accountant. You're not on my payroll, and you need to get out of my business."

Mal-A-Dies Shirt started talking again, showing not fear, but anger. "Oh really? We been working here for a few weeks. Been *protectin'* you. And now we come to collect. Your building has not been vandalized, your employees have not been harmed, and your students have not been bothered. But," he shrugged, "that can all change if you don't pay up."

John grabbed the man's arm. "Listen to me and listen to me clearly, punk, because I'm only going to say this once. I'm giving you until now to get the hell out of my business, or I'll disassemble all fifteen of you right down to your blueprints."

All the gang members tensed, and a few pulled out knives from the sheaths hidden under their floppy t-shirts.

Kahn was standing by the door. Seeing them take out their weapons, he reached in his shirt and pulled out his karate knife, which he never let out of his sight. He moved toward the front and stood just behind John.

John glanced at Antonio and nodded, then nodded at the office door across the lobby. Antonio walked nervously backward toward it.

As soon as the office door's lock clicked, John let go of the leader's shirt. The leader backed off and started walking toward the door; the other gang members followed him. But then, as though by a silent order, the gang suddenly stopped, turned, and charged John and Kahn. Between their superior martial arts skills and Kahn's knife, they were able to fend them off. Soon, one punk after another began racing for the front door.

Antonio hating leaving Kahn and John like that, but he remembered what John had told him after Gary Collins's first visit: *Since you're not skilled at martial arts, if there's ever any sort of trouble, I'd rather you be away from it. Then, I don't have to worry about accidentally hurting you.*

But still, he felt he had to do something. He reached for the telephone to call the police. Once he made contact with them, he slammed the phone down, opened the desk drawer and grabbed up the gun. He didn't intend to use it. As much of a risk taker as he was, the idea of using a gun against another human being was too much. *But maybe I can threaten them with it.*

Turned out, his threats weren't needed. By the time he emerged from the office, holding the gun in shaking hands, the leader was racing toward the door,

THE TIME TRAVELERS ACADEMY

bellowing, "We'll be back! We're going to teach all of you not to ever screw with us again!"

John yelled back, "And we'll be ready!"

The punk slammed the door behind him.

Antonio looked at Kahn, then his best friend. "You two okay?"

John gasping, replied, "Yeah, but you look like hell."

Antonio looked down. His hands were shaking like he'd overdosed on caffeine.

Seeing that, John endured his biggest personal crisis in recent memory. Likely, the gang had been sent by Collins or one of his cronies. But that small doubt still crawled at the back of his mind: What if the two mysterious men who knew his undercover name had sent them? Or even worse, what if they'd been sent, as a warning, by those men's higher-ups? What if this was just the beginning? What if the minute he and Antonio left for Russia, the gang came back to torch the place? Could he really ask Kahn, an innocent employee, to stand in his stead under these circumstances?

With a big sigh, he walked over to the door and locked it, then turned to Kahn, "Did I tell Antonio the truth? *Are* you all right? Did any of them hurt you?"

Kahn held up his knife. "I might have a sore wrist tomorrow. Otherwise, I think I might have caused *them* a few more sore muscles."

"I want you to be careful while we're in Russia. If you see them again, call the police. And . . .I don't feel good about leaving just now."

Kahn's face turned serious, and he crossed his arms and bowed slightly. "On the honor of my ancestors, I will protect what belongs to you as if it belongs to me." He raised his eyes to meet John's. "And yes, I won't hesitate to contact the police."

Antonio stepped between them. "Ah, as for calling the police, they're on their way." He looked at Kahn and added, "We also have a firearm if you're not able to call the police in time. It's a revolver. Before I leave, and with John's okay, I'll put it in the safe, and you'll have the combination."

Kahn bowed again, then straightened, holding the knife at eye level. "Thank you, but no need. This is my revolver."

Antonio gave him a nervous grin. "Yes, but don't ever match a 13-inch knife against a gun. The one with the gun'll come out on top. I guarantee it."

Sirens interrupted them.

⊹══ ❀❀ ══⊹

Sergeant Kim, a detective with the Rockville Police Department, gave John a careful stare through almond-shaped brown eyes. "We got a disturbance call."

Antonio said, "Yes sir, we just had 15 gang members come in here, trying to extort money from us."

Kim turned his gaze to him, saw how shaken he still was, pulled out a notepad and began writing. "Did you get a description?"

"They were all dressed in martial arts and gang member attire," John said. "The name 'Mal-A-Dies' was on their t-shirts. I saw tattoos like dragons on one of them. It really happened so fast." Then, reluctantly, he added, "We had a brief fight in here."

Kim gave them a small grin. "And I assume you won?"

This brought relived chuckles from all three men.

"Seriously," he said, "are any of you hurt?"

When all of them denied any injuries, Kim closed his notebook and looked at each of them in turn. "We've had a recent increase in gang activity. Your business is one of many they're terrorizing." Another smile. "It seems you're the only ones that stood up to them, though. Everyone else is afraid to talk. If they come back, call us at once. You don't want to mess with any of the gangs, but the Mal-A-Dies have been particularly vicious."

Before he left, Kim gave each one of them his calling card, then said, "No matter how silly their name sounds, be careful."

10

Vincent Goff, like many 19-year-olds, had a generational problem. His father had just laid down the law: Get a paying job, go to college, or get out.

Thing was, Vincent had a job. One he'd dreamed of since he was a kid: using giant telescopes connected to the Hubble Space Telescope. The team he was a part of was trying to discover new planets by determining how much of a gravitational pull a suspected planet had on its sun. The observatory's director, himself a highly educated man, suggested that he wait about college. "After all," he'd once told Vincent, "you already have more knowledge and on-the-job training than most full-fledged astronomers."

Basking in that praise, Vincent ignored all the scholarships he'd been offered and stayed at the observatory.

So, Vincent did have a job. A great job. But it was a volunteer job, and his father, a decorated former Marine, didn't understand his son working for no pay. And he couldn't understand why his own flesh and blood, who'd earned a perfect score on both the ACT and SAT tests, and had received full scholarships in every state and in 20 countries, turned all that down just to do what he loved the most.

A year after his graduation, his father's patience ran out. "You have a brain, don't waste it at that lab, or whatever you call it," he'd said. Then he showed Vincent his old military uniform and awards, saying, "I got nearly every ribbon in the military except for one, but I had to work hard so my family didn't have to work so hard. Son, please use your intelligence to become a doctor, or an attorney, or even a researcher for some private company. Anything but spending your life as an unpaid stargazer!"

This argument wasn't new, and neither was Vincent's reaction. "Dad, that's just it, I don't want to be a doctor, or any of those other things! I want to be a scientist. It's my life-dream to be astronomer. I want to discover planets. And

I'm doing that right now, *without* college. That's a lot more exciting than doing surgery or curing incurable head colds."

His father sighed, then put the wooden box containing his medals back into the trunk and closed the lid. "Son, if you don't have a *real* job, or at least enroll in college by the end of the day, your plate will be broken today and you can no longer live in my house."

Vincent had heard that once or twice before. The "broken plate" was an old boot-camp threat: If someone's behavior was unacceptable, their parents or loved ones told them, "Your plate has been broken." Meaning there was no longer a place for that person at the family's table. Meaning that the person couldn't go back home, and had to make it on his or her own.

But, since Vincent heard that before, he had his answer ready. "Yeah, right," he said. "Broken plate, whatever. I would *love* to talk more about your old boot-camp stories—they're fascinating. But I have some planet observing to do."

He grabbed his backpack, raced outside, jumped on his bike and pedaled to the observatory.

At the telescope, he monitored his instruments. Technically, he was looking for new planets, but he was intrigued by the Big Bang theory and wanted to discover proof. No one had proven how the universe began, and he'd been playing with the idea of making that his life's work.

As he rotated the telescope to another area, he heard a tiny blip from one of the displays. Moments later, he discovered the signal had come from a galaxy five billion light-years away, near a black hole. What was so odd about this noise was that it didn't seem to be a natural occurrence. "More like a bomb, maybe set off by an advanced race," he muttered. *Wow, I'm the first person to ever discover a planet that once had life on it.*

⊹⟜ ❀❁ ⟞⊹

That day turned out to be a banner one for him, and for the observatory. The other scientists reviewed his findings and concurred. They also agreed that this planet, being five billion light-years away, no longer existed, and had perhaps been swallowed up by the nearby black hole. They named the planet "Planet Peligroso," meaning "Dangerous Planet" in Spanish, partly because it was near a black hole, and also because the inhabitants might have destroyed themselves.

Vincent's only disappointment was that they didn't name the planet after him. *But,* he told himself, *'Planet Vincent' just doesn't sound very jazzy. And 'Planet Goff' sounds way too much like 'Planet Goof' anyway.*

He went home early to tell his father the good news—that his dad could finally be proud of him. What he found was his clothes neatly packed in his luggage sitting on the front porch and the house locked up. An envelope stuck out from one of the bag. Inside the envelope there was some cash, and a note. On top of the note was a broken plate with a spoon, fork and knife, and another message: *Your plate has been broken. Get a job.*

—37—

"Boy, I guess Dad *was* serious," he muttered, then reached for the envelope, counted the money, and read the contents of the note.

> *Son, I love you. I took care of you for 19 years, and I've done all I can. You're an adult, and now you must make a man of yourself. Your mother and I are on vacation for the next two months, so you won't be able to contact us. Goodbye and good luck.*

11

Kahn stuck his head inside John's office door. "I finished vacuuming and putting up the equipment, I'm calling it a day."

John walked with him and unlocked the door. "We appreciate everything, and I guess we'll see you in two weeks."

Kahn smiled. "I guess when I see you again, you'll be a married man."

"Not. I'm not even engaged yet. But who knows what the future might bring? I'm just putting my trust in God."

Kahn left and John locked the door behind him.

Back in the office, Antonio said, joking, "How's your soon-to-be mail-order bride?"

John's face lost its happy expression. "She called me last night. Said she won't be able to meet us at the airport tomorrow. But Natasha will. And oh, I forgot to tell you . . . I have a date tonight."

Antonio had been leaning back in his chair. This brought him upright. "Huh? You bought an engagement ring for Bonita a few days ago, and you're still seeing other women? What gives, John?"

John was quiet a moment, then said, "Remember when we had that talk a few days ago? About the ring? About the way I feel about Bonita?"

Antonio nodded.

"It's just that . . . It's hard to explain. Those punks haven't been back, and sure, I haven't seen those guys around again. But . . . it's more than that. I figure that sometime in the next two weeks, I'm going to have to decide. And when I do, I want it to be the right decision. So I figure I owe it to myself—and Bonita—to be sure. And I think going out with Amy will help me that way. Can't really explain why, but it might." He shrugged. "And anyway, I'm still enrolled in Match.com, and Amy seemed nice enough on the phone."

"Just make sure you get plenty of sleep," Antonio said, watching John's face. "The flight leaves at seven a.m. We need time to get to the airport and check in. Don't let *Amy* cause you to miss our flight in the morning."

They chatted about less-emotion-charged things, and after John left the school and drove home to prepare for his date, Antonio stayed, finishing that day's books.

⸻ ❦❦ ⸻

John came out of his house in a rush, as if he was late for a fire, puffy-eyed. He stumbled over to Antonio's car with his luggage, and Antonio helped him manhandle the luggage into the backseat.

"Did you get much sleep last night?" Antonio said. "Or did your *beautiful lady* keep you up all night?"

John laughed as he closed the back door and got in the front seat.

"What's so funny?"

"You *don't* want to hear about my date."

"If I didn't before, I do now."

"I went home, got dressed, and met her at the restaurant. I arrived first, and after five minutes, I noticed a beautiful woman looking around who seemed lost. So I walked up to her and asked her could I help her find something. She said, 'Yes, I'm looking for my husband. Could he be you?'"

Antonio laughed. "Elaborate."

"I ordered the food and paid the bill. Well, that made her angry. You see, she's into the women's lib thing. To make a long story short, we had dinner, found out we didn't have chemistry, and went our separate ways."

"That's it?"

John's face fell. "After the date, I saw those two men again. Looking at me from outside the restaurant. Just . . . looking through the window. After we finished dinner, I walked with Amy to escort her to her car. I saw them, they saw me. But they just looked at me and walked away."

Antonio swerved to miss a jogger. "Man, that *is* weird."

"Yeah, *weird's* one thing to call it." He leaned back in the seat, and his expression turned hard. "I don't understand what's going on, but no more running. When I get back from Russia, if I see them again, I'm going after them. If it's me they want, it's me they're going to get. But . . . seeing them did help me make up my mind about Bonita. I'm glad she got her visa, and I do really care about her. But . . . until this situation is finished, there's no way I'll put her in harm's way. I'll tell her to get busy with school, and I'll see her whenever I think it's safe. But . . . as far as any long-term thing, well . . . it'll have to wait."

Antonio looked at his watch. "Well, I can't tell you what to do with your life, but we're running late." He increased his speed to 75 mph, even though the speed limit was 60. Soon, he was frustrated because he couldn't find a space in airport parking.

"Calm down," John said. "We have enough time. You're going to see Natasha. But with the way you're driving, you'll probably land both of us in the city morgue."

"We're running out of time. I'm going down that lane."

John looked where Antonio indicated. "That's one-way!"

"Watch my fancy driving. Besides, no cars are coming."

"That's not the point. You can't break the rules of the airport. You're nothing but a risk taker."

Antonio chuckled and whipped the car into an empty slot. "I'm so hurt you called me that."

"Next time, I'm driving," John said in a huff. "You can't go around breaking rules and doing what you want to do. You almost got us both killed."

"No, I got us here on time."

They gathered their luggage and rushed toward a waiting airport shuttle. They managed to catch their flight just in time.

During the flight, their joking got back around to the way Antonio and Natasha met. When John invoked the "mail-order bride" joke for the nth time, Antonio said, "You're full of it, and you know it. I visited Natasha four times and had known her for a year before we got married. And she was worth the wait. And just to prove that, after we get back to America, we're going to have another wedding. Bigger and better than the first one!"

"That's all good, but be careful after she gets her green card," John couldn't resist saying. "She doesn't need you anymore after that."

"Be careful, John. I know karate . . . and ten more Japanese words."

They both laughed, then John said, "Since we're talking about family, how's Mario?"

Antonio beamed at John's mention of his twin brother. "He's okay. Great, in fact."

"Which one of you is older? I forgot."

"He's younger, but just by seconds."

"We'll, if you keep taking trips to Russia, he'll be older than you."

Antonio looked at him, perplexed. "How's that possible?"

"Simple. Say you and Mario are running a race that should take 30 minutes. Then suddenly, *you* could run at the speed of light—186,000 miles per second. Of course you'll beat him in the race. But what if you keep running? When you get to the Atlantic Ocean, you'll run right over it. Then right through Africa and Australia, then to the moon and around the sun, and maybe to Jupiter, Saturn and Pluto. You finally get tired and head home, and finish the race.

"But here's why you'll end up being younger than him. A few seconds after you cross the finish line, Mario finishes the race right behind you. You say to him, 'I won, and you'll never guess where I've been in the past 30 minutes.'

"He looks at you and says, 'I'm not concerned where you've been in the past 30 minutes. I'd like to know where you've been in the past *20 years*.'"

Antonio shook his head. "I still don't get it."

THE TIME TRAVELERS ACADEMY

"It's because you ran at the speed of light and he didn't. In the 30 minutes you were running around the solar system, 20 years on Earth has passed. But to you, running at the speed of light, it was only 30 minutes. Essentially, you just went into the future. Time travel."

Astonished, Antonio said, "Okay, I get it now. But how would I get back? Is there a way to go backward in time?"

John thought for a second. "I heard that Einstein discovered a way to go backward, but something about it scared him to the point that he abandoned it. Even destroyed all his notes about it."

"Huh? What could have scared him so much?"

"Fear, maybe. You know he helped develop the nuclear bomb. A group of scientists took his work and developed the first atomic bomb—the Manhattan Project. It was used to end World War II. But all through his life, he felt uneasy and worried about helping develop something so powerful and destructive. I guess he didn't want to make the same mistake twice. Or maybe he *did* develop a time machine, and used it, and discovered something he was afraid of anyone else finding out."

Antonio leaned back in his seat and looked out the plane's window. "But . . . just think of all the possibilities. If you could go backward in time, what would you do different?"

"I'd buy my mom the winning state lottery tickets. So what about you? What would *you* do if you could go backward in time?"

Antonio looked away from the window and back at John. "I'd save my grandfather. He was in the Navy. On December 7, 1941, he was in a hangar, working on a plane, when we were attacked. Died when one of the bombs hit the hangar. If I could go back in time, I'd warn him to not be there at that time and date."

"I'm not an expert, but if you did that, wouldn't that change history?"

Antonio shrugged. "Sure it would—his, and mine. He'd survive the attack and I'd have had my grandfather to grow up with."

"That's not what I'm getting at. If you go back in time and just . . . okay, for example, what if you picked up a piece of paper, and wrote, 'Dear Grandfather, the Japanese will bomb this airport hangar at 7:00 a.m.' Your grandfather reads it and doesn't show up for work that day. So he survives Pearl Harbor. And then, maybe he's promoted. Maybe now, he's in charge of ordnance and weapons on the *USS Hornet*."

"So what's wrong with that? He gets a promotion. That's good, right?"

"Not necessarily. The main reason the Japanese lost the battle of Midway Island was because they couldn't locate the three American carriers. The *Hornet* was one of them. But what if your grandfather, who's now on the ship because you saved him, inadvertently gave the position of the *Hornet* on the radio, and the Japanese heard it? Now, they're able to win the battle of Midway Islands, and so they eventually win the war. Just because of your grandfather's one simple error, the victors in World War II changed. And *your* message to your grandfather made it all possible."

"Wow," Antonio said. "I guess in my letter I should have added, 'By the way, don't get promoted!'"

Both of them burst out laughing.

"Actually," John said, "I'm not really sure how I feel about the grandfather clause. I mean, I studied it in school, but it's just a theory. And until a theory is proven, it's still just a theory."

"Yes, and I have a theory, too."

"What's that?"

"If we don't get any sleep, we're going to be zombies when we land in Moscow."

They continued picking at each other, occasionally causing enough noise to garner annoyed stares from the other passengers, until they fell asleep.

12

"You are here today because of a recent discovery," the President told the group. "And because of the dilemma that we as a nation face. This is, of course, classified top secret."

Charlene glanced at her boss and received a reassuring smile in return. It helped, if only a little. When the news of the incurable avian plague reached the President, he called a meeting of his staff and advisors, along with the NBCD team. Dr. Davies appearance was a given, but when Charlene's was ordered too, she stayed on pins and needles the entire flight back from North Dakota. Even now, trying to settle into the thickly padded chair in the Cabinet Room, she was having a hard time sitting still.

The President turned to Davies and said, "Who wants to speak first?"

Davies rose from his chair and introduced himself, then said, "Mr. President, we are glad to be speaking to you today. I very much agree with your need for urgency. So, I will allow one of my staff to take the floor in my stead. Dr. Charlene Vaughn is not only one of my top researchers, she actually made the discovery you're interested in right now."

He lowered himself into his chair and made a small upward wave to Charlene, who suddenly felt herself freeze in her seat. She froze even more when the Secretary of Defense glared at her, as though not believing she could offer them anything of use.

A couple of more waves and one stern look from Davies unglued her from the chair. After clearing her throat, she introduced herself, then said, "I've been studying the organism discovered in meteorites found in Antarctica . . . *and* the ones that landed on Earth six months ago, also on meteorites. I was able to confirm that it is, in fact, the same organism. What is unusual is that this organism seems to have the ability to join other organisms . . . to create a morphing of both. Very unusual, to put it mildly."

"This is all interesting," the President said, and gave her a fatherly smile. "And I'll admit that no matter what you say, I'd otherwise be happy to allow you all the time you wanted to say it."

The response to this was many chuckles and a few head-nods. But the mirth ended when the President fixed his staff with a no-nonsense look, and then turned back to Charlene. "As I said, I would be happy to hear more about the background of this discovery. But, we seem to have a disease that is killing people right and left. And Dr. Davies has assured me that your discovery holds the key to stopping it. If you could get to the point quickly, we would appreciate it."

"Ah, yes, Mr. President, of course," she said, and took a deep breath. "But unfortunately, I'm afraid just a bit more background is required."

He nodded. "So be it, then. Continue."

"Thank you, sir." Another deep breath, and then she said, "I believe it's possible that this—conjoined organism is what might have caused the Martian people to vanish."

The President's eyes narrowed, and he glanced from Davies to Charlene. "The Martian *people?*"

Davies whispered to Charlene, "You'd better quit while you're ahead."

She bit back what she wanted to say: *You did say to hurry it up, didn't you?* Instead, she said, "Pardon me, sir. Now, the organism—"

The President held up his hand to stop her. "No, Dr Vaughn, that's fine. Continue what you were saying about the Martian people. Vanishing, did you say?"

She looked at Davies. He gave a nearly imperceptible shrug of his broad shoulders and a rolling gesture with his hand.

Another deep breath, and she continued. "Sir, three billion years ago, Mars had advanced life. Many of the recovered meteorites in Antarctica contained fossilized evidence of that."

She was stopped by a snuffling laugh from the Secretary of Defense. In the long silence that followed, she struggled to remember his name even as she forced back her rebuke. *V something,* she thought. *What is that a-hole's last name?*

The President of the United States saved her the effort, saying, "Secretary Lanti, we have no time to engage in frivolity. Once we have some inkling of how the hell *we're* going to deal with this crisis, you can laugh all you like. Until then, I suggest you pipe down and give this young woman your full attention. Is that clear?"

Lanti wasn't pleased, but was in no position to express his unhappiness. "Yes, Mr. President. I must say, this has been very entertaining, though. Quite entertaining."

The President ignored him and turned back to Charlene. "Continue."

Charlene had never been good at the politics required to convince people of something they didn't want to believe in the first place. So she decided to fall back on the strategy that had always worked before—she would tell the truth.

"Sir, whatever destroyed the Martian civilization is now here on Earth. This organism is harmless by itself, but it has the ability to merge two or more basic life-forms together by matching their DNA patterns to form one new life-form. In this case, I fear that it is also a deadly life-form. With the permission of the NBCD, I have termed this organism the 'missing link,' or the ML-20. Again, the ML-20 has the ability to connect molecules, viruses and/or one-celled animals together to form another, separate life-form. Essentially, it has the ability to cause an organism to jump to its next adaptive stage.

"Again, we don't know how and cannot prove this beyond question . . . but a careful study of our records and after consultation with National Institutes of Health as well as other institutes worldwide among our allies, we believe this organism arrived here ten to twenty times in Earth's history, each time changing life on Earth radically. We believe this is only the organism's latest visit.

"But there is a problem this time, one that wasn't present on previous visits. This time, there is advanced life already here. Us. And in us, apparently, the combined organism is causing the full-blown plague—the avian plague mentioned before. If the organism continues to spread, and to behave as it has so far, we believe that humanity will soon meet the same fate as the Martian civilization. Annihilation."

In spite of the President's earlier warning to Secretary Lanti, the Secretary of Health jumped to her feet. "How can this be? You can't just say something like this without some heavy-duty documentation—"

"Which, Ms. Secretary, I have brought with me," Charlene said. "There was no time to prepare it for the meeting, but I assure you, as soon as possible after we adjourn, I'll have a copy of the team's research on your desk. But please, since the President said time is short, please let me just give you the summary now."

She glanced at the President, ready for whatever rebuke she surely had waiting from him. To her amazement, he was smiling at her. No, *beaming* at her, as though she was a long-lost daughter who had just done him proud.

The Secretary of Health saw his face, and lowered herself into her chair. "Very well. But I expect to see your proof immediately. What you're proposing is going to be a hard sell to the public."

"Yes, I'm aware of how it must sound," Charlene said, "but in the smallest nutshell I can contain it, the nonfossilized form of the ML-20 organism recently landed on Earth. Once on Earth, it conjoined two other organisms—ones with which we're familiar. One of those is the virus that causes avian flu. The other is the current mutation of bubonic plague bacterium."

She ignored the babble of voices and continued speaking. "The ML-20 somehow fused these two organisms together—caused them to merge as one. This happened only a short time ago. But in just that short time, I believe this *super organism* has continued mutating and becoming more virulent. I'm basing that on our study of the most recent victims. Our study also tells us that ML-20 is resistant to every drug we've tried. And because there's no way to eradicate the ML-20, our present avian flu and bubonic plague treatments are useless. The combined organism quickly becomes full-blown avian plague, and the person who has it dies shortly thereafter. Only those with a natural immunity—and there are always at least a few—will avoid catching the plague."

She bit her lip, wondering if she should just stop there and not reveal her latest findings of only the day before. She glanced at Dr. Davies, saw him nod, and knew that she had to. "We've used the former CDC's computers to project the progression of the disease. Every computer model says the same thing: This disease will bring humanity's reign on Earth to an end in an estimated three years." She looked at the President with troubled eyes. "Sir, we'll soon become like the dinosaur, extinct."

The Secretary of State spoke. "I'm not so sure about all this talk of morphing, but I'll have to agree with Dr. Vaughn's last remark. According to our own projections, this . . . this ML-20 will reach pandemic levels in six months. Russia, China, and Southeast Asia have the largest reported outbreaks so far, but there have been cases in every country." He shrugged. "Not surprising, considering what Dr. Vaughn believes is the cause: The meteor shower pretty much got the entire Earth. But except for those three areas, the outbreaks are still containable." He sighed. "Even so, it's all we can do to keep it out of the press."

Secretary Lanti said, "The first outbreak we're aware of in the United States was on an American-based cruise ship on the last leg of a Caribbean cruise. Ten days ago. Within a few days, nearly everyone onboard had symptoms. Now, there's no one left alive to man it. We have it quarantined."

He glared at Charlene. "But with all due respect, Dr. Davies, Dr. Vaughn, what you've just reported is bullshit."

Lanti turned to the President. "Sir, I don't believe this disease is spread through benign means, like they're saying it is, and I request permission to go to DEFCON 3. I believe this is a biological weapon made by terrorists. I'll be willing to accept that they *might* have used the Mars nanobacterium, or bacteria, or whatever the hell it is, to create their weapon. They could have gotten hold of it through the meteorites. But that's as far as I'll go to accepting all these ridiculous speculations from a department that, until a few days ago, couldn't even hold on to its funding."

Davies opened his mouth to speak, but Lanti wasn't going to let it happen. "The outbreaks we're dealing with are a series of terrorist attacks from some as-yet-unknown group. Most likely Al Qaeda, since they're the only group right now that has even near that kind of funding and reach. But that can be determined later. Most important, this has to be recognized as a terrorist attack from the get-go. That the first known outbreak was against citizens of the United States on that cruise ship should be enough to convince anyone of that."

"But Secretary Lanti, the pattern of the outbreaks is almost identical to the pattern of sightings of the meteorites—"

Lanti's bellow cut Davies' rebuttal in half. "We've got a cruise ship with 2,000 passengers and crew that is literally dead in the water. And now we're getting reports of the same thing happening on a few of our military bases. You say you have hundreds of cases in North Dakota? I have reports of *thousands* in my military infected. The cruise ship was just the test case. It was out on the water, easy to get to. Clearly a dry run, with the plan to attack military personnel next. *Our* military personnel."

He turned to Charlene, glaring. "You're talking about a civilization on Mars that died millions of years ago. Well, I've got bigger things to deal with. Soon, I'll have to contact 2,000 families and tell them that their loved ones are now permanent residents of a floating morgue. And based on the weak theory you've given here, the only reason I can give them is that the . . . what did you call it? . . . that ML-20 did it by creating the avian plague. Things they've never heard of. How do you think they'll take it, Dr. Vaughn? How am *I* supposed to take that?"

He turned back to the President, his face brilliant red. "Sir, again, I implore you to consider allowing me to go to DEFCON 3. If the public knows we're taking it seriously, we'll have only half the panic we might have otherwise."

The President, frustrated, replied, "That's crazy talk. DEFCON 3 is just two steps from launching our nuclear missiles. Even if it were terrorists—and I'm heartily inclined to disagree on that—who are we going to attack?"

"Sir, I'm just requesting to have the entire military at stand-down and quarantine. I believe terrorists made this . . . this *superbug* that is attacking our military. And we should take military action. At once."

"Nonsense," the President said. "You heard Dr. Davies talk about the requests for help he's getting from every county on the planet. If terrorists were going to make a disease as a weapon, they wouldn't infect themselves!"

Lanti said, "I don't know about that, Mr. President—"

"I can't believe this is a biological weapon. I believe my scientists that it's not of this Earth."

The Surgeon General spoke up. "Sir, my scientists have managed to examine this organism, and have been in constant contact with Dr. Davies's team. Our finding corroborates that of Dr. Vaughn's. The organism means us no harm, it's just doing what it was meant to do—evolve life. That harmless organism just managed to bond the avian flu virus and bubonic plague together. But as Dr. Vaughn said, the problem is, there is already advanced life here . . . life that can be killed by either of those diseases."

"So what do you make of this, Madame Secretary?" the President said. "What is our next step, and what do you think are our chances of beating it?"

The Secretary of Health thought a moment, then said, "Avian flu is deadly, but difficult to transmit at present. In fact, we've had no reports of human-to-human contact at all. The bubonic plague is deadlier, but very easy to transmit. The problem is, based on the reports, that combined organism has a 90% transmission rate. If a person just sneezes or coughs, anyone standing nearby will acquire the mutated organism. Death will occur within seven days. And we have no vaccine or cure for the combined organism, or even the, as Dr. Vaughn aptly put it, the missing link organism that brought them together. Essentially, there is no cure, or any way to prevent the avian plague from happening."

His face thunderous, the President slammed his fist on the table. "I will not accept this! Any of this! There *is* a cure out there. Humanity will not come to an end like the Martians. I'm the President of the United States, and we'll find a way. We'll find a way. Secretary Lanti, there will be no DEFCON 3. Put the military on a worldwide quarantine."

Lanti opened his mouth to protest that quarantine wasn't enough, but he closed it because the President had already turned away from him.

The President made his next remarks with lightning speed. First, he ordered the Secretary of Transportation to stop all international flights. The he said to the Secretary of State, "I appreciate your efforts to keep panic down, but we need to alert our citizens, and those of other countries. We'll contact as many leaders as we can, but we can't delay."

He turned back to Lanti. "Have your people prepare a press conference for two hours from now, stipulating a national and international emergency."

"What good would that do, Mr. President?" Lanti said. "All I can offer them is a quarantine, for goodness' sake! That's not military! For all they'll care, you might as well let the Secretary of Health do the press release—"

But the President was no longer listening to him. Lanti could only watch while the President asked two of his aides to accompany him. Both were generals; both had briefcases handcuffed to their arms. Lanti recognized one as the briefcase holding the codes to launch nuclear weapons. At first, Lanti didn't recognize the other one. Just as they exited the room, he did, and rose from his chair to follow, eyes turned into slits.

—⊹≫⊱ ⊰❀⊱ ⊰≪⊹—

He found them in a small room off the Situation Room, just as the President was picking up a red phone receiver from the second briefcase. The President didn't dial the phone, just spoke into it, saying, "Thank goodness you're there, Jones. And get hold of Adams as soon as you can, tell him and his crew to be ready. We've got a problem."

Lanti strode past the Secret Service agents and into the room. "Mr. President, you're making a mistake, sir. Terrorists caused this. We should concentrate our resources on fighting terrorists, not looking for extraterrestrials. The funding for that . . . that *preschool* has already hampered my nuclear program goals. And Congress' plan to make it the sixth branch of the military will never happen. Not on my watch, not in my military!"

The President said into the receiver, "Hold on a moment, General." Then he leveled his gaze on Lanti. "Apparently, you didn't hear me when I said I've made my decision. So I'll repeat this once more, and once more only. I'm against the use of nuclear weapons unless we're attacked. I don't believe we've been attacked. And as far as the Time Travelers Academy? Whether Dr. Vaughn is right or not about our three-year demise, the Academy might be our only hope. You are dismissed."

Lanti stormed out of the room.

A few minutes later, the President returned to the meeting and told Lanti to cancel the news conference. "I realize this is sudden, but . . . I've received some new information. We'll notify all heads of state, but not the public. Not yet. We need some time to prepare." He swiveled his head toward Charlene, held her startled gaze for a moment, and opened his mouth. But whatever he might have said was drowned out by the entire Cabinet asking questions at once.

+}━ ❀❀ ━{+

"Man, after *that* meeting, even that mangy Pomeranian's starting to look good!"

After ten minutes of listening to one Cabinet member after the other bellowing to be heard, the President had finally noticed her unease and dismissed her and her boss. Dr. Davies had offered to drive her home, but she had him drop her off outside the gates of the White House. She needed time alone—to think, and to wonder what the President had meant about needing time to prepare. And what wasn't he able to tell her before he was distracted?

She'd walked for a while, but now stood on a street corner, thinking about flagging down a taxi. That's when she noticed that someone she'd seen three blocks ago was still following her. No, not one guy. Two. Both dressed in dark clothes. One kept looking at his watch.

"Damn," she muttered. "I know Secretary Lanti was mad at me, but can even *he* work that fast?"

Deciding the best course was to do nothing, she waved for a taxi, which pulled up immediately. The men increased their speed, walking straight at her, intense looks on their faces. She jumped into the cab as soon as it stopped moving, yelling "10001 Candice Park Lane. Hurry! There's someone following me!"

She glanced behind her. One of the men was reaching into his suit jacket. "He's reaching for a gun!"

Hearing that, the driver forced his way into the heavy DC traffic, leaving the men behind.

+}━ ❀❀ ━{+

It was well after dark by the time Secretary Lanti prepared to leave his office, still fuming about the private chat he'd just had with General Jones. When Charlene Vaughan predicted the three-year timeline for the end of humanity, he had allowed his hopes to soar. At last, he thought his pleas for the return of his nuclear-defense funding would be granted. But then the President had turned lily-livered. No, even worse, he'd turned to the most wasteful, useless agency in the country, as though they could possibly hope to help with the problem of the plague.

I'm your boss, he'd said. *As such, I don't see why I can't be involved in hand-selecting the people who will undertake your crazy plan.*

To which Jones had replied, *I'm sorry, Mr. Secretary, but the President's word is final on this. If you want the procedure changed, you'll have to take it up with him.*

Just as he was bidding his exhausted secretary goodnight, his cell phone rang. He completed his goodbye, told her he would see her in the morning, and answered the call. When he heard whose voice was on the other end, he barked, "Under the circumstances, you're the last person I thought I'd hear from. Building the Time Travelers Academy for us apparently wasn't enough. The President wants you on the decision team for this mission. So you and General Jones will have your little clique, and there's absolutely nothing I can do about it."

"I just wanted you to know I had nothing to do with the decision, and I'll do everything I can to keep you in the loop," came the smooth answer. "You have my word on it, Mr. Secretary. And I hope you'll feel the same about me. Call it a sharing of information. Isn't that what the military and private businesses are supposed to do?"

Lanti leaned back in his chair, beaming now. Finally, someone had the sense to realize that he, the Secretary of Defense, must be informed of what was going on at the TTA, at all costs.

13

The man boarded quickly and took a seat on the back of the bus. He was one of the last to board before the bus headed across the bridge, with a final destination of the trains that would take them home.

The man had been sick for a while, but it was just a cold. Just like everyone in his office had been fighting for a week. He felt like hell, but there was no need to stay home, he'd decided. Especially since everyone else on the bus was coughing and sneezing too.

He held a napkin over his runny nose and coughed. But when the sneeze came, it happened too quickly for him to cover his mouth in time. Millions of invisible organisms emerged. Once they hit the air, they spread, unseen, everywhere on board.

The man looked around, but saw no annoyance on any of the other passengers' faces.

But what would they get pissed about? he thought. *Some of them look sicker than I am. What's gonna happen? They'll catch my cold?* He chuckled at his joke and settled back in his seat.

The made its ponderous way through the city. Within minutes, it was headed for the bridge. By the time the driver guided the bus to the bridge's midpoint, the man who had sneezed minutes before was dead.

The driver glanced into his rearview mirror, saw the man slumped in his seat, blood pouring from his nose. Another glance showed several other passengers, all at various levels of consciousness. One grabbed the seat in front of him, tried to rise, but couldn't. He fell back into his seat, and a gout of blood began pouring from his nose too.

Panicking, the driver jerked at the wheel, intending to pull into the emergency lane and get off the bus. The swerving bus hit cars in the next lane, causing a chain reaction. A fuel truck, one of the vehicles caught in the chain-reaction wreck, flew from the bridge and exploded; its fuel burned the suspension wires and supporting structures on the bridge, causing the metal bridge-supporting systems to melt from the intense heat.

Hundreds of cars on the bridge fell, one by one, into the water below. Mass panic erupted. Many who were caught on the bridge emerged from their cars and tried to run to the opposite shore. Before they could, the bridge's supporting structure broke and, in one horrific instant, the bridge turned completely upside down, throwing them into the water below. Many that survived the fall tried to swim to the shore, but the bridge itself landed in the water, crushing and drowning nearly every survivor. The scene was repeated, in one form or another, around the world.

14

As soon as the plane landed, Antonio and John grabbed their luggage from the overhead compartment and walked to the exit. Antonio's wife, Natasha, squealed as soon as she saw them and began waving.

While John watched, Antonio dropped his carryon bag and grabbed her into his arms. John noticed that she was wearing blue jeans and a red cashmere sweater, items very difficult to find or afford in Russia. Antonio had sent them to her as gifts a few months before.

When the embrace ended, she turned to John and held out her hand. "It's nice to see you again, John. Bonita is so sorry she couldn't be here. But she asked me to bring you to her. After you unpack at your hotel, we will go to the embassy."

John nodded. He had purposely booked a hotel near the US Ambassador's residence where Bonita worked.

Three hours later, still jet-lagged but showered and dressed in fresh clothes, they accompanied Natasha to the hotel's entrance. "I called Bonita," she said. "She will meet us at the park across from the ambassador's home. It is such a nice day. Why don't we walk? It's not far."

The men agreed, and ten minutes later, they were at the park.

Natasha noticed John looking around. "Bonita must have been delayed," she said. "I'll get her and be right back." She pointed to a nearby bench. "Have a seat and enjoy this nice warm day."

John grinned at her and shrugged his jacket closer to his shoulders. "Hate to tell you, but in Texas, 50-degree weather is a cold snap."

She laughed and gave Antonio a loving glance. "All the more reason I'm happy to be going there." A moment later, she became a flash of red and blue in the crowd outside the park.

Bonita's blond hair fell loosely around her shoulders and her blue eyes were shining. The jeans and sweater John had sent her last month, the sweater blue to match her eyes, made her look more beautiful than the last time he'd seen her, six months before.

He stood from the bench and reached out his arms, happy to realize that his doubts had faded into the background of his mind.

"I missed you," he said, and they embraced.

At that moment, looking over her shoulder, he saw the two men, clearly Americans by their clothing, looking at him.

It can't be.

Bonita felt him stiffen and pulled away. "Is everything all right?"

The men faded into the crowd, and John gathered every bit of his will not to show alarm when he met her eyes. "Yeah . . . Yes, it's fine. Just thought I saw someone I knew." He forced a grin. "Silly, huh?"

She smiled back. "Yes, silly. You only know Natasha and me here."

"Yeah." He put his arm around her shoulder and glanced at his watch. "Say, how about getting something to eat? Any good restaurants around here where we can have lunch?"

Laughing, Natasha said, "You guys. Always hungry. This way," and they left the park. As they walked, John looked nervously around, but saw no more familiar faces.

After their meal, the two couples parted ways, Antonio and Natasha intending to return to the hotel.

"Why don't we leave the lovebirds alone and head back to the park?" John said. He told the truth—he didn't want Antonio and Natasha, in the hotel room next to his, to be distracted. But he also wondered if the men that had followed him in America would show up again at the park.

The men weren't there, and he was relieved. His mind now free, he gave Bonita the necklace and small teddy bear he'd purchased for her at the airport back in the States. The bear had a small heart stitched onto it. He'd been hesitant to give it to her, in fear she might think it cheesy. But in delight and surprise, she gave him a hug and kiss. Soon, they were talking about their lives.

"I'm so sorry I couldn't meet you at the airport," she said. "The ambassador's children have the sniffles, and they didn't want me to leave them."

"It's okay. Meeting here was better, don't you think?"

She looked around at the park. "Yes. So peaceful. So . . . romantic."

"Do you think you'll miss it when you leave?"

She looked back at him and shook her head. "No. This is my home, and I love my job. But you must know that Russia isn't a safe place to live."

A sudden image of the black marketer who had threatened him long ago leaped into his mind. "Ah, yes," he said quickly. "I've heard there's a lot of crime here. Texas has crime too. But not as much, I'd think."

She sighed and looked at a mother and child who were walking through the park. "All my life, I have dreamed of living in such liberty as you have in America.

And to finish my education in such freedom? What a privilege! The ambassador's wife was very sad at my decision, but her entire family supports me."

She turned her head to look at him. "And there are other things I look forward to in America. Happy things."

He looked away, uncomfortable, wondering what Antonio might have told Bonita's sister about his mixed feelings. About the ring he had in his luggage. About his own desire to be happy, but also his fears. Until seeing the two men, he'd almost resolved to give her the ring today. But now, all his past anxieties came to the fore. If those two men indeed worked for the black marketer who had threatened him, there was still much danger to him, and to anyone he cared about. And if they didn't know before, the men had just seen him with Bonita. Had he put her into danger by just being in her presence?

He noticed her questioning eyes. "Don't worry. There are many happy things in America. And it's safer there than here." *I hope.*

She giggled and made small chopping motions with her hands. "I forget you're a martial arts expert. Likely, I am safe with you no matter where I go."

He managed a smile.

⊹⊱ ❦ ⊰⊹

That night, they rejoined Antonio and Natasha, then spent the next several hours enjoying the Russian nightlife and restaurants. On the way from the restaurant, John saw the two men again, standing half in and half out of an alley, watching him. Using jet lag as an excuse, he saw Bonita back to the ambassador's residence and spent the taxi-ride back to the hotel downplaying what he'd seen, and what he feared most. Only his sudden fatigue allowed him to sleep that night without dreams.

⊹⊱ ❦ ⊰⊹

On the second afternoon there, they emerged from the movie theater, laughing and talking about the American movie they'd just seen.

"Steve Martin is so funny," Natasha said, giggling. "But I can't believe there is actually a movie called *Cheaper by the Dozen*. Who could possibly afford twelve children? In Russia, a family that large is unbelievable."

"Hey, that's true in the States, too," Antonio replied, "so don't go getting any ideas."

His remark brought a flurry of giggles from both women.

"Hang on, I'll hail a taxi," he said.

"No taxi," Bonita said quickly. "I've been sitting for hours. Let's just walk to that coffee shop at the corner."

Antonio shrugged. "Walking on a Russian city street? Just the kind of danger I love."

She playfully slapped her brother-in-law's arm, and they headed off.

Their route took them by a hospital. In front of it, they saw people wearing plastic suits.

"What in the world is going on?" Bonita said. "Why are those people dressed like that?"

John peered at the group, willing himself not to show his thoughts. He said only, "Hey guys, wait here, I'll try to see what's happening."

Running in an easy lope he hoped didn't look too rushed, he approached the group. As he neared, he saw that all of them were wearing facemasks. Then, he saw what the others couldn't have seen because of the angle—police had set up a barricade to prevent people from coming close to the building's emergency entrance. A crowd of the curious had gathered outside the barricade, and he joined them.

Past the barricade, he saw ambulances arrive, taking people into the hospital. He watched for a few minutes, his focus so intent, he was startled by Bonita standing beside him.

"What has you so curious?" she asked.

"I . . . I just find it strange to see so many ambulances at one time, and health care professionals all draped down from head to toe in those . . . uniforms." Especially since they were clearly biological or chemical-warfare suits. Something he hadn't seen since his Special Forces training days.

One of the patients suddenly screamed. John focused on the man, who was lying on a stretcher being wheeled inside the building. The man's neck appeared swollen, he had red spots all over his arm, and his eyes were bulging and yellowish-red. Blood poured from his nose. The man leaped from the stretcher and tried to run away, bringing a gasp from Bonita. He was caught by the hospital staff just as he collapsed to the ground.

A policeman stood nearby, and when his radio squawked, John and Bonita turned their heads to look at him. The officer listened, then strode toward the crowd behind the barricade.

"All right, you all need to go," the officer said. "We have an outbreak of . . . of whooping cough, and you don't want to catch it."

John glanced back to where the man had fallen. Now, he was in a body bag, which was being zipped up by one of the people in the suits. His unease growing, he said, "What's really going on? That man didn't have whooping cough. I didn't hear him cough even once."

Others in the crowd heard him and began asking, then shouting questions at the policeman. He didn't answer; he was busy speaking into his radio. What seemed like only seconds later, a paddy wagon arrived, accompanied by an entire squad of policemen. Before John could protest, he and Bonita were pushed into the paddy wagon.

As soon as it was confirmed that John was American, they took his passport and separated him from Bonita. Tired of pacing in his jail cell, he looked out the window. He wished he hadn't. From the window, he saw what at first appeared to be a construction excavation project. Moments later, he saw a small flatbed truck piled high with bodies, which were summarily dumped into the hole and covered.

No one would answer his questions about where Bonita had been taken. He told them repeatedly that she was with the US Ambassador's staff, but it didn't seem to matter.

What seemed like hours later, two guards appeared, flanking a well-dressed American who introduced himself as Bonita's employer. With the group was a Russian officer who introduced himself as General Vladimir. All of them wore facemasks.

"You're lucky," the ambassador said. "If you agree to say nothing about anything you've seen, I can get you and Bonita out of here and on your way to the States."

"Where's Bonita?" John said quickly. "Is she all righ—?"

"I'll say this again. You need to stay quiet. I need you to cooperate so I can get you both out of here."

Too angry to comply, still suspicious that his arrest had something to do with seeing the two men just prior to it, John grabbed the metal bars of his cell and glared at the Russian general. "For your information, I come from a democratic country called the United States, and *we* don't go around arresting people just because we feel like it."

"Calm down, John," said the ambassador. "You're not under arrest. Under quarantine, yes. Under arrest, no."

John let go of the bars and stepped back. "Quarantine? Does it have anything to do with what I saw?"

General Vladimir chuckled and turned to the ambassador. "So much for keeping quiet, eh? But," he shrugged, "is just as well."

Then he turned to look at John. "You seem fine now. Perhaps you are immune. You will be examined before you leave. But again, anything you might have seen is none of your concern."

A doctor came in with an escort. Both were draped in surgical gowns and facemasks. The doctor held a test tube and swab.

"We just need to briefly examine you," the doctor said. "A simple test of your saliva."

"What if I refuse?"

General Vladimir sighed and looked at the ambassador. "Oh, these Americans and their American attitude. The same *attitude* that led to your country's refusal to help us in this . . . situation." Another sigh. "But soon, I suppose, your country will be struggling under the same burden."

He turned back to John with narrowed eyes. "You are not in America. But as an American citizen, you have the right to refuse a routine examination for your own benefit. If you do, however, you will be here in jail for at least a week. And if you have what we think you might have acquired by standing next to the hospital, then one week is all that you have left to live." His eyes turned menacing. "Now, I advise you to let us do our jobs."

The doctor took the sample to another room. Thirty minutes later, he reappeared. "You are lucky. Your test is clean. You can leave now."

John looked at General Vladimir and the ambassador. "Where's Bonita?"

Vladimir reached up and pulled the mask from his face. "Unlike you, she had common sense and didn't resist. She's in the lobby awaiting you. If you decide to stay for your entire trip, I won't interfere. But I advise you to leave as soon as possible. Have a safe trip back to the United States, Mr. Godunov."

A pained smile spread across the man's face, and he leaned forward and whispered, low enough so the ambassador couldn't hear, "And be sure to give Foxhound1 my regards."

"Who the hell is Foxhound1?" John whispered back, but Vladimir had already begun talking to the ambassador again.

Hearing the general call him by his codename confirmed his worst fears. The black marketer had ties to the Russian army, and had, probably gleefully, blown his cover thoroughly enough that General Vladimir knew about him five years later. But who the hell was Foxhound1?

Holding a terrified Bonita by the arm, he emerged from the detention area and began searching for a taxi. The two men were waiting, this time standing about twenty feet down the street. Not looking at him. Just standing. *Probably wondering how I got out alive,* he thought bitterly. *Probably had it all arranged with good old Vladimir to off me while I was in there, and the ambassador screwed with the plan.*

He leaned close and whispered, "We have to get your sister and Antonio and get out of here." He told her what the general had implied—that there was some sort of epidemic in Russia, one they were trying to hide from the public. And that soon, whatever disease it was might jump to other shores, including America's.

In response to her volley of questions, he held up his hand. "I'll tell you everything I know, but for now, let's catch a taxi and get away from here." *And away from my two shadows, too.*

In the tiny apartment she kept for her days off from her duties, they talked about their ordeal, and he finally revealed more than he'd ever told another living soul about his covert identity in the military. He thought about telling her about the two men and Vladimir's strange mention of Foxhound1, but ditched the idea. She already had to deal with so much street crime living in Moscow, he didn't want to make her more nervous.

During their talk, he called the airport and changed their tickets. No flights out were available, but the reservations clerk assured him that the first four available seats belonged to him and his group.

He hung up the phone and looked at Bonita. "I hate to leave you here alone, but I have to find Antonio and Natasha, let them know. How long will it take you to pack?"

Her face resolute, she replied, "I will be ready to leave as soon as you return. If I only take the clothes on my back with me, it will be enough. Just that I can get away from this horrible place with my sister and . . . our lives. That is enough."

She looked at him with hard eyes that softened after a moment. "John, I just want you to know that I love you. But I realize you have . . . what do they say? . . . mixed feelings about our relationship. That no longer matters. If you don't . . . want me as your wife, I will make my peace with that somehow. The most important thing is to get to America. The rest will . . . how you say? . . . the rest will take care of itself."

He gave her a tight smile. "I couldn't have said it better myself."

As he entered the hotel he saw the two men, far up the quiet street but still clearly following him. Could one of *them* be Foxhound1? They obviously knew he'd be on the street in front of the hotel around this time. Could they have had something to do with getting him freed? If so, why?

He had the quick urge to confront them, force them to try whatever they were planning. He no longer even cared about who they were. He was tired of being watched, tired of having every cheerful thought about the future smeared with the dirty memories their presence brought him. And he dreaded the idea that, when he left, they would follow him back to America, now or later, continuing to threaten his chance at happiness with Bonita.

No, I'll just let them be, he finally decided, then he grinned. *And hey, what if I'm lucky? Maybe they'll stay here long enough to catch whatever old Vladimir's so scared of.*

And if he had to confront them, it was better to do it on his own turf anyway.

He knocked on Antonio's room door, hoping he was there. Natasha answered.

"I need to speak to Antonio," he said. "Now."

"Where have you been?" she said, her voice a near-scream. "We looked everywhere. Where is Bonita—?"

"She's fine. This is very important. I have to talk to him in private."

Antonio emerged from the bathroom and an instant grin appeared on his face. The grin faded when he drew close enough to see the worry in John's eyes. He followed John to his room without resistance. There, John quickly explained his ordeal with the Russian police, and that he'd seen the two men again.

"We have to get out of here, and today," John said when he finished.

"I don't see what the problem is," Antonio said. "Why should we blow our entire vacation because of some stupid general and some . . . some bug that we obviously haven't caught? And those two men? Do you know how many people dress like that in the world? They only looked at you. They never came near you. It could be two completely different men. So please stop being so paranoid. And what happened at the hospital? Let the Russian government handle that. It doesn't concern us, and it's not our problem."

John glared at him. "Bonita and I are leaving on the next flight out of here. I've also made arrangements for you and Natasha. If you want to stay, fine. But after what I've seen and heard, by the time our vacation's over, we might all be dead if we stay here."

15

They waited in the airport lobby. Antonio's reluctance was still with him, but after hearing what Bonita had to say, Natasha's decision was easy. And with Natasha leaving, there was no reason for him to stay in Russia.

Bonita looked at John to see him wincing.

"What is wrong?" she said.

"I just . . . I have to use the restroom." The same restroom the two men just disappeared into.

The reaction that had boiled inside him when he spotted them in Russia had finally made up his mind. No way was he going to let this go on a moment longer. It was now or never.

Bonita followed his gaze. "You'll have to come back through security. The only restrooms are outside of security." Her eyes widened. "Oh! Just wait, and you can use the one on the plane—"

"I know," he said, keeping his eyes on the restroom's doors. "But I have some unfinished business to take care of."

"Just be quick," she said, and patted his arm. "I would hate for you to miss your flight. If you did, I wouldn't leave, and we would both be stuck here. All for a bathroom trip."

⊹⊱ ❀ ⊰⊹

The men's room appeared deserted, but he knew better. He had also decided against trying to kill the men, even if they attacked him. He didn't want to leave that kind of memory for Bonita. No, all he wanted, and today, was the truth.

Certain the men were hiding, he stood quietly for a moment, then said, "I'm here. Whatever your business, I'm ready to listen."

Stalls at the very end of the room opened and the men emerged from them.

"Are you alone?" the younger one said.

"Yes, but I don't know for how long. And I've got a plane to catch. If I'm still able to catch a plane. Whatever you're planning, let's get it on."

–62–

The men began walking toward him, and the older one reached into his overcoat. John braced, ready to evade a loaded gun. But when the man's hand reappeared, it was holding a large yellow envelope.

When the men were close enough, the man handed it to John, who noted the words "Top Secret" printed on it.

He looked up at them. "Well . . .it's been a while since I've seen these words. So you guys are from—?"

"Pursuant to the United States laws of Selective Service Registration, you've just been drafted," the man said. "Your country needs you. Again. You're a hard man to find, John Richards. Actually, that was part of the problem. Seems that all your records were destroyed after you left the service. Took us forever to connect you with your codename. If you hadn't used your old credit card at the jewelry store, we might never have. But after that?" He smiled with pride. "It was easy. And your passport told us you'd be in Russia at this time and date."

"I—I thought you were from my past," John said. "What I did in the military . . . that you were out to get me."

The man gave a tight smile. "Yes, we *were* out to find you. But not to *get you.* Not in the way you're thinking. And we're not from your past. We're from your future. From exactly one month in your future."

John took a step back. "My *future*?"

The man nodded. "Yes. We couldn't start the class without you."

John looked at him, then back down at the envelope. "What class?"

"What's inside will tell you what you need to know. Nice meeting you finally."

John kept his eyes on the envelope, trying to decide if he should open it now. Then he remembered, and looked up. "And hey, have either of you ever heard of Foxhound—?"

The two men had vanished.

"Hey, John, come on. Hurry!"

He whirled around to see Antonio at the restroom door, gasping.

"They just called our flight," Antonio said. "Bonita and Natasha are already onboard. If we don't get our butts on that plane in five minutes, it'll leave without us."

John looked at the envelope, then at the nearby trashcan, overflowing with discarded cups and paper towels. The temptation to toss the envelope there peaked, then subsided. With a sigh, he slipped the envelope into his jacket pocket while racing after Antonio on his way back home.

As they boarded the plane, Antonio tapped his shoulder, "Hey, look. Four first-class seats nobody's sitting at. Let's take 'em."

After they settled in, he grinned at Antonio. "You know we only paid for coach. You're breaking the rules again."

Antonio smiled. "Some rules are just made to be broken."

The flight was long, but made shorter because of Bonita's presence beside him. Once she was asleep though, he spent most of those hours wondering what was inside the sealed envelope, which he could feel against his chest like a silent-but-threatening hand.

Charlene stepped into the morning sun outside her apartment building, wishing for the hundredth time that the Capitol's public transit system was more reliable. When she reached up her hand to flag a taxi to work, she gasped. The men she'd seen just the day before were there. Again. They approached her just before a taxi pulled up. She reached to open its door, prepared to scream . . . until one of the men went to the driver's side, threw a $20-dollar bill at the driver and said "Beat it."

The driver did, nearly tearing Charlene's hand off in the process.

She opened her mouth, this time to confront the men, but the one who'd been so free with a twenty spoke first, pulling a large yellow envelope from his jacket.

"Dr. Charlene Vaughn, pursuant to the United States laws of Selective Service Registration, you have just been drafted."

She looked at the envelope for a long moment, then took it from him and slipped a wary finger under the flap. As the paper tore, she asked, "If these are really draft orders, *which I doubt*, then who are you?"

"Humm. Good question. What's inside the envelope will explain some of it. For now, I'll just say that we're time-recruiters, but from your present."

With the envelope halfway open, she looked up. "What the heck are time-re-cruiters?" But the men were gone.

"Where are you going? What could possibly be more important than the work you're doing here?"

Vincent Goff looked into the face of his distraught boss. "I don't know," he said honestly. "I want to go to college, but all my scholarship deadlines for this year have passed. I have no place to live. Dad kicked me out. And I need a job to support myself. A paying job." He shrugged. "I talked to the manager at one of the fast food restaurants. He offered me a job until school opens in September."

The observatory head, realizing that he'd just come to the end of the budget-sparing free ride Vincent had given them as a volunteer, offered to pay him. Then offered to allow him to live in his own house, if that's what it took.

"Thanks," Vincent said, "but I think it's better if I just . . . get on with my life. My dad left me a little money. I'll stay in a hotel until I get my first paycheck. Then I can find an apartment somewhere."

Pedaling his bicycle with one suitcase piled heavily on top—he'd left the rest with a neighbor until he found a place to live—he left the head of the biggest observatory in the United States near tears, begging him to come back.

He pedaled a while on the dirt road heading back toward town, thinking that his father was probably right. He *had* used his family for free rent and board for too long.

He heard a car revving its engine behind him, and pulled over for it to pass.

Instead of moving on, the car pulled up on his right side, the window opened, and a man in a suit said, "Vincent Goff?"

Vincent peered past the driver and saw another man in the passenger seat, also dressed in a suit. *Man, has he already sent a team of negotiators after me?*

"Uh, yeah, that's me," he said. "Look, I really loved working at the observatory, but please tell my boss that I'm really not interested in—"

"We need to talk to you. Hang on."

He waited while the men emerged from the car. One of them held what looked like a big yellow envelope.

"Vincent Goff."

"I already said that. Aren't you guys from the observatory?"

The man handed him the envelope. "Pursuant to the United States laws of Selective Service Registration, you have just been drafted."

He looked at the envelope, noted the "Top Secret." *Wow, just like in the movies.* He looked up at the men. "Drafted? I mean, I registered for the draft when I turned 18, but I didn't think you guys were so hard-up you had to go chasing people down."

"Your country needs you."

His eyes narrowed. "Who *are* you two?"

"We're time-recruiters, but we're from your present time."

He glanced back at the envelope. His next question was going to be about why anyone in government would draft a kid his age and hand them a top secret document. But he never got the chance to ask. When he looked up again, the men who called themselves time-recruiters were already driving away.

⊹≓— ❧ ≓⊹

The same two men and other teams of time-recruiters were seen in other cities together, handing out the yellow envelopes. Luckily, they'd only had to go back in time once, to locate John Richards, a.k.a. Ivan Godunov. Because his records were destroyed, had they not risked the time-travel, they wouldn't have located him in time to deliver his draft orders.

The time-recruiters knew that going backward in time was technically difficult and extremely dangerous. But out of all possibles, the computer had picked only 800 people with the special skills and high success-probability to complete training. Of those 800, only ten would be selected to complete a critical, extremely dangerous mission. John Richards was at the top of that list.

The envelopes each draftee was handed contained their orders, tickets to a New Mexico airport and simple instructions, followed by a warning to tell no one where they were going or that they had received the missive. Any of their questions would have to wait. Now, they were only to obey.

–65–

16

"Well, folks, I hate to say it, but I'm bushed," John said. "Let's all get settled tonight, get a good night's sleep, and then get together again tomorrow when we're all rested, okay?" He punctuated his suggestion with an exaggerated yawn.

The group had gone to John's house straight from the airport. Bonita had already planned to stay with Natasha and Antonio until she could find housing at the university's dormitory. When he made his request, she simply gave him a goodnight kiss, saying, "I understand."

With Antonio's help, he unloaded his luggage, waved goodbye and stepped through his front door, shutting it behind him.

As they drove off, Bonita said, "Ever since he was at the airport in Moscow, he's been acting different. He didn't even show us around his home. As though he was in a rush for us to leave." A long moment passed, then she said, "Antonio, is he seeing anyone else?"

Antonio smiled at her in the rearview mirror. He wished he could tell her of John's secret worries—about his fear of being followed. So she would know that it wasn't her, but his past that was keeping him from committing to her, or to any woman. But he couldn't tell her. Some risks, he wasn't willing to take.

"I can tell you care a lot about him," he said. "Know why? Because you're showing your jealousy. But remember, I've known him all my life. He's very serious about you, and you have nothing to worry about."

She sighed. "I . . . I told him that it didn't matter what happened with us. That I am here in the United States to go to college. But . . . I hope for more. I would be very hurt if he found someone else before he gives me a chance. These past six months have been the happiest of my life."

"Not to worry," he said. "Maybe he's just tired and needs some sleep. Heck, all of us are jet-lagged. Tomorrow morning, I bet he'll be at our house with a handful of roses, ready to take you out on the town."

She nodded, as though wishing Antonio's words would make it so. He hoped so too.

Looking closer under the light of his desk lamp, John noticed that, in addition to the top-secret stamp, the envelope also bore the Presidential seal. So it was likely genuine. What worried him was the way he'd received it. Sure, when he was in Special Forces, he'd gotten orders in some pretty bizarre ways. But he'd been out for over five years. And not only did those men stalk him before even approaching him, if he could believe what they said, they'd traveled from the future to his present to hand-deliver the order. He'd joked with Antonio on the airplane about time travel, but no way was technology that far advanced.

Yet now, he was forced to wonder.

A bit paranoid that it might be booby trapped, he was careful opening the envelope. Inside it, he found $2,500 dollars in US currency and official orders. No surprises there. In previous packets, he'd received money in the currency of the country or countries he would be working in undercover. And he'd already been told he was being drafted into a new assignment. But instead of his real name, or the alias he'd be operating under—what he was used to seeing—both John Richards and Ivan Godunov were on the forms.

"Like they couldn't make up their minds," he whispered to himself. But then, they had implied as much when they explained why it took so long to find him.

The order was simply to board an airplane to the Albuquerque, New Mexico airport. There was no end date for the mission—whatever it was. *That* was unusual. Also odd was that he had only one day to report or be considered AWOL. This stunned him. How could they have known the exact day he'd be back in the United States? And why only one day to report? What could be so urgent that he'd have to leave without even saying goodbye to his mother?

"Oh, hell." He glanced at the front door, where he'd just waved goodbye to Bonita. How could he possibly break the news to Bonita? Antonio wouldn't be a problem; his friend had even joked, from time to time, that he wouldn't be surprised if John was called back in someday. Had even sounded a little envious whenever he said that. So Antonio would be cool with it, and between him and Chen Kahn, would do a fine job of keeping the school going. Antonio would also be willing to help his mother in any way she needed, no matter how long he was away.

But what would he say to Bonita? *Hey, I know we have a relationship to figure out, and you just arrived in a completely new country yesterday, but now I've got less than 24 hours to dump you and leave. And no, I have no idea how long I'll be gone, or if I'll ever be able to come back.*

"Yeah, I can see *that* going over like a big load of manure hitting a pothole," he muttered. The chuckle he tried just wouldn't go past his lips. So he forced his mind away from that and went back to the envelope.

There was a small map of New Mexico inside, with Albuquerque highlighted. He didn't need it. Thanks to a rare vacation a year ago, he knew that Albuquerque was less than a day's drive away from Rockville, Texas.

Until then, it hadn't occurred to him that he would rather drive than get on a plane there, like the order instructed. But if he took his car, and things turned sour, at least he'd have a ride out of . . . wherever he was being assigned. If he could get back to his car.

With to many what-ifs rolling in his mind, he looked at the $2,500 dollars, and then the clock. Ten p.m. He dashed upstairs, took a quick shower and shaved, and then packed a small bag, enough for four or five days. The order had said to pack for longer than that, but he wasn't worried; he was used to making do with few possessions on assignment, and that included clothes. Being a guy helped.

Once downstairs, he reviewed the mental list he'd made while in the shower. First, he went to the jacket he'd worn on the flight and retrieved the engagement ring. Giving it to Antonio to lock in the school's safe wasn't an option. The fewer chances he gave Antonio to ask questions about his intentions toward Bonita, the better. Sure, he had no idea where he'd end up, but no sense leaving it for some random burglar to find either.

Next, he called his mother. This brought a few tears, but lifted his spirits when she told him how proud she was of him for being willing to return to service of his country.

Buoyed by her words, he now had the courage to call Antonio, who reluctantly agreed to let Kahn take over the classes for a couple of months. "But only because I just know eleven Japanese words," he kidded. "Otherwise, I'd do the classes too."

"Yeah, I understand how you feel about Kahn. But I know you'll work together. And . . . look, we've talked about this before, but . . . if you don't hear from me for a couple of months, assume that my . . . assignment took longer than I thought, and go to the emergency plan we set up."

"Yeah, I know," Antonio said, his voice deliberately light. "After two months with no word, close up the house, hire another instructor, and start transferring your part of the profits to your long-term savings account. And if I don't hear from you for six months, assume you're on some tropical island somewhere whooping it up, and don't plan to come home. In that case, put the house on the market, contact your attorney, transfer your savings account to your mom's name, and just keep watching your part of the profits pile up in it—"

"Okay, okay, you remember already!" John said, chuckling.

"If *you'll* remember, bud, I'm an accountant. Everything we talked about is written on a scroll and kept in a hermetically sealed safe deposit box. Your wish, in your absence, will be my command. But there's something even more important, and you haven't even mentioned it."

He tried to steel himself. "What's that?"

"Bonita."

A long moment passed. "Yeah, I was getting to that. I know I'm imposing but . . . can you just tell her that something unexpected came up? Something extremely important. Something to do with my Special Forces background. She knows about that. And tell her that as soon as I can, I'll be in touch?"

"Chicken."

"No, it's not that. It's that . . . I just think it'll be better this way. Come on. Be a friend."

A sigh, then, "Okay. Okay. I'll take this volley for you. But you owe me."

"Thanks. And I mean that."

"One more question. . . . Are *you* okay?"

"Yes. I'm fine." He gave a weak chuckle. "Very fine, actually. Duty calls again."

"Just like I said it would someday, my man. As always, I was right."

⊹≻ ⟡⟡ ≺⊹

Upon hearing the news, Bonita broke away from Antonio's embrace and ran for the telephone. She heard John's voice, but when she realized it was only his answering machine, she hung up the phone and strode to her bedroom. Moments later, Natasha and Antonio heard her sobbing.

"Well, as you say in America," Natasha said sadly, "*that* went well."

"Yeah," Antonio replied. "And John Richards owes me. Big time."

⊹≻ ⟡⟡ ≺⊹

He couldn't leave Texas without a last stop. He placed everything in his car and drove to his mother's house. After receiving a huge hug, she said, "Are your friends with you? I've baked cookies."

"No, Mom, everybody's at Antonio's. I'm heading out tonight . . . to beat the traffic."

She studied his face. "I thought I'd get to meet your girlfriend tonight. Is everything okay?"

"Yes, Mom, everything's fine. And . . . about Bonita. We decided to take things easy. Just until I know how long I'll be gone. But if you get a chance, could you . . . I don't know, kind of keep an eye out for her? No pressure, I just think that will make the time pass faster for her."

Her eyes flew open with delight. "Oh, honey, I'll be happy to! Why, the poor thing's just gotten here, and I just know she'll be lost at first. I'll call her first thing in the morning and invite her to lunch."

John's smile was genuine. "Thanks, Mom. I can always count on you."

"Don't be silly, sweetheart. I'm happy to do it. You always have been very thoughtful."

He hoped she would feel that way after she found out he never told Bonita he was leaving. Holding a bag filled with enough fresh-baked cookies to feed an army, he gave her a hug and then headed for whatever awaited him in New Mexico.

–69–

He arrived in Albuquerque at 10:00 a.m., parked his car in the long-term parking lot, then, at the direction the parking-lot attendant, boarded a shuttle bus for the drive to the airport.

Once he arrived, he called the number given to him in the envelope and was told to go to Gate 12. Within minutes, he was picked up in a black limousine. He'd scanned the limo, inside and out, for official markings, but found none. And to his question, the driver only said, "I've been instructed that your orders are awaiting you, and that you need to direct your questions to the person who gives them to you."

He'd heard that before. With a sigh, he settled back against the limo's plush seat and waited to learn of his mission.

17

When the limousine neared the tarmac, he saw what he was pretty sure was a private plane. This surprised him; he'd expected a military transport of some kind. His curiosity even higher now, he boarded the plane at the direction of an unsmiling and silent attendant's wave. The pilot, too, was quiet, and John only knew they were traveling north, judging from the mountains capped by snow.

Later, he regretted not keeping track of time. The small airport where the pilot put down had no landmarks he could identify. But even though he didn't know which airport, he easily recognized where he was dropped off a short while later. Not its location, but it was definitely a military base of some kind.

At the security gate, he asked the armed sentries, "Gentlemen, I've already been through boot camp, and I have no plans to become an instructor. Where am I, and what do you want from me?"

"Sir, we're only instructed to tell you to be patient, and that all your questions will be answered in due time."

"I kind of figured that," he said, and passed them in the direction they pointed, toward a large building. In its anteroom, his luggage was taken. Two unsmiling sentries escorted him into the building, where several hundred people were already sitting.

When he entered the auditorium, a man in uniform at the front door asked his name, then pointed to a series of desks, telling him, "The seats are arranged in alphabetical order."

He headed to where he thought the R's would be, but couldn't locate "John Richards" in that row, or the row in front of or behind it. He wandered a bit, looking at all the seats, and solved the mystery—one seat nearer the front displayed his codename, Ivan Godunov. He took the seat, knowing he could correct the problem later.

The desk held a large book and some other papers.

"Do not look at or touch anything on the desk!"

His head jerked up, but then he realized that the man at the front of the auditorium was talking to everyone in the room, not just him.

Within minutes, the last of the attendees entered and took the desk in front of him. He remembered the name on that desk: the man sitting there must be Vincent Goff.

But he's so young, John thought. *He can't be over 18 or 19 years old. What the heck is he doing on a top-secret mission?*

He looked around, convinced that, like in his case, there'd been some sort of mix-up. But what he saw convinced him otherwise. Some of the group appeared to be military or ex-military, like him, but others didn't have the bearing or appearance. Some were as young as Vincent Goff. Others had to be pushing retirement age. He did a quick headcount. *There's got to be at least 700 people sitting here.*

Confused now, he sat quietly, not touching the book on his desk, even though now the urge was great. He was even more perplexed when he saw who joined the civilian on the stage. By his insignia and uniform, a four-star Army general. Tall. African American. John tried to remember if he'd ever seen him before, but couldn't. This didn't surprise him too much; most of his time in the military was spent in covert operations, so he wasn't expected to know the top brass on sight.

Once Vincent Goff took his seat, the civilian said, "This is General Jones, who will explain why you're here."

Jones moved his six-foot, four-inch frame to stand behind the podium, glad that he wasn't the kind of person who showed his feelings. If he did, they might radiate as an aura that encompassed the entire room. When he turned down the position of Secretary of Defense, it was for this day. He'd freely shared a reminder of his goal with the President when he called.

But there were other things he would never share. He was the only one who'd ever used the Academy's time machine to travel forward. When he did, he'd seen three years into Earth's future. That, he also freely shared. But even when the President and other high-ranking officials demanded to know what he'd seen, and Secretary Lanti threatened him with a court-martial for not answering, his only reply was, "We're in serious trouble."

And now, what he'd seen was coming to pass. The Academy held the only hope—and it was a faint one—to prevent it from happening, and Jones knew that Secretary Lanti would fight him each step of the way. It was Lanti who had fought for the Academy to be built by a civilian contractor, the Ascendia Corporation. And Lanti, as Secretary of Defense, had given Mike Adams, Ascendia's CEO, authority equal to Jones's when it came to the facility and the time machine. Those two things, Jones could live with. With the current push to save money by privatizing military operations, he couldn't have prevented it from happening at any rate. And Adams built the Academy and designed and built the time machine, knew it inside and out. They needed Adams involved. But Lanti had also led the charge to court-martial Jones, accusing him of lying about his trip just to keep the Academy going as a military operation. Since then, Lanti had come near to convincing Congress that the Academy wasn't only unneeded, but was being run by a lunatic.

As he took his place behind the microphone, he gave a quick glance to the man who had introduced him. While Jones didn't see Ascendia's CEO as a direct threat, he kept a watchful eye on the man. Jones had no doubt that whatever he did, Mike Adams took careful note of as well. He was doing that now, giving a smile meant to be encouraging but that seemed to peer into his soul. Jones wasn't surprised by that. After all, if Lanti's efforts to disband the Academy failed, Adams would naturally begin his own push to place the Time Traveler's Academy under a private company's control. And Ascendia would be the first to bid for the contract, he had no doubt. In the same situation, he'd do the same thing.

But now at least, with the threat of human extinction imminent, Secretary Lanti had no choice but to allow the Academy to continue. And now, Jones had to take these raw recruits and show the President, Secretary Lanti, and everyone else that the Time Travelers Academy was vital to national defense. And he had to do it far faster than he'd ever imagined.

"Good morning, students," he said into the microphone, then gave a smile he hoped would reach to the back of the room. "Or, depending on where you're from, I should say good afternoon. Some of you have been here for the past couple of weeks, others have just arrived. As I mentioned on my greeting, you are all students from the moment you arrived here. We have waited to begin your training until everyone was here."

He smiled again, and fixed his eyes briefly on John. "I'll admit that some of you were very hard to contact, but we managed. No doubt, you're all wondering why you're here, and why you are students. In essence, here's why: My name is General Jones, and I'm the director of what is called the Time Travelers Academy. The man who introduced me is Mike Adams, who built the entire Academy.

"You have never heard of the Time Travelers Academy, because its very existence is top-secret, and for reasons that some of you will soon understand. Here's what you need to know now. Our computers selected 800 individuals who were most likely to complete this Academy. You are the 800."

The room broke into a buzz of whispers, then several hands went up. Jones held up his own hands, and the room was soon quiet again.

"I'm sure you have many questions. So let's get started. But be aware that many of your *answers* must wait until you sign a confidentiality agreement and take an oath."

More rumblings, and he held up his hand once more.

"I realize that taking an oath is serious business. But it's necessary, because of the . . . uniqueness of what I must tell you. Please understand that the only requirement you'll have, at first, is to keep confidential everything you hear and see in this room."

When the rumblings didn't return, he continued. "First, the rest of those on the stage will introduce themselves to you. Then we'll ask you to tell something about yourself to the others. And remember, everything said here, stays here. Even though you aren't yet under oath, I will call upon each individual's ethics on this.

"I have been with the Army for over 20 years. As director of the Academy, I am directly accountable to the Secretary of Defense. Put simply, the Academy is my mission in life, and my hope for our future."

Jones then stepped to the side, releasing the microphone to a man in Navy officer's dress. This man was much shorter than Jones, but no less imposing.

"I am Admiral Suarez," he said. "I am in charge of the Academy's security. I have been with the Navy for 17 years. I started in the enlisted ranks and," he swept a modest hand across his heavily decorated uniform, "the rest is history."

Chuckles greeted his introduction, John's among them. The only person not warming up to the comment was Vincent, he noticed.

He had no time to wonder why the young man's reaction was so odd. After Suarez, each person on stage introduced themselves to the group. General Chin, a Marine general in charge of training and development, had come here as an immigrant, graduated from college and then officer candidate school. Next was General Wayne, in charge of the Academy's missions. Before joining the Air Force, he taught at a university, and his specialty was astrophysics. John noted this with interest. The first mention of "Time Travelers Academy" implied that a great deal of science would be needed.

The next speaker wasn't wearing a uniform, unless one counted the typical professor's attire as such. "I am Dr. James Rubiano," he said. "As you've noticed, like Mr. Adams, I'm not in the military."

His statement brought more chuckles, then he said, "I am in charge of all the educational training. I am a graduate of MIT, Harvard and Oxford. I am also a Rhodes Scholar. Not that you'll remember it now, but I have PhDs in astronomy, psychology, physics, quantum physics and nuclear engineering."

Another scientist, John thought, intrigued. Both of the last two speakers were scientists, whose specialties led him to believe that the mission, whatever it was, would involve space travel, not time travel.

Rubiano returned to his seat and General Jones returned to the microphone. "You are a select group, each with the highest probability to make it through this course and the mission that follows. It is only fair to tell you all, now, if you are chosen for the mission, there's a chance you might not be coming back."

Eight hundred apprehensive faces finally returned their attention to the podium, and Jones said, "That's why we'll ask that you accept employment with us on a volunteer basis. Yes, all of you were drafted. That was to get you here. You still have the right to refuse."

This was met with silence. Undeterred, he continued. "You will go through some hard training, including academic training on a pass/fail basis. If you fail once, you will get another chance. A second time, you will be sent home."

He paused for a long moment, scanning their faces, then said, "If any of you feel this is not for you, please raise your hand. If you're not confident you're up to it, now is the time to say so."

Five students raised their hands. Moments later, the five were walking to the side door, where a sentry stood waiting to escort them out.

Without warning, the kid named Vincent stood, and John heard him mutter, "I know I can't make it. I'm going home. Let someone else do it, not me."

He began walking to the door, his head down, to where the other five students waited. But after three steps, he stopped and stood still.

Come on kid, John thought. *It's a simple question. Are you in or out?*

As though in direct answer, he heard the kid mutter, "I have to at least try." Then he turned back around, walked back to his seat, and lowered himself behind his desk.

Knowing how tough any military mission was, and having an inkling of what all the students would face, John wondered how long Vincent Goff would last.

18

General Jones nodded at Vincent, and John saw relief pass over the general's face and wondered why. Generals never, ever showed emotions. If they did, they couldn't lead effectively. This planted a suspicion in his mind: that this kid, however sloppy-looking and rebellious, was someone Jones had hoped wouldn't walk out the door.

"We started with 800," Jones now said, bringing John's attention back to the stage. "Now we have 795 brave men and women. Thanks for staying. Before anything else, you will be sworn in. Will all of you please stand and face the American flag, raise your right hand and repeat after me: I do solemnly swear to protect and defend the Constitution of the United States and its people from any enemies, foreign, domestic, and interplanetary, of the United States, past, present and future. So help me God."

As *So help me God* filtered through the room, then faded, Jones said, "Congratulations, you are now Time Travelers Academy cadets, members in the newest federal organization. Please take your seats."

By the time they returned to their seats and looked up again, the benevolent pride on Jones's face had disappeared, replaced by a look that John could only interpret as worry. Jones's next words confirmed his suspicion.

"The urgency of our mission gives us little time to prepare you. You will be sent through an accelerated eight to nine-week course in physical training, physics, science, and quantum theory. After that, you will go through one week of Time Clauses 101—that will be explained later. You will also go through a briefing on what we have learned about time travel and the laws that govern us all. Much of this will be covered in your Time Travelers Academy Manual, which you will be expected to read, and then commit to memory."

Jones looked over the group, and John thought his eyes seemed to be searing into each person's soul, including his own. Then Jones said, "Of those who pass the course—and no doubt, many of you won't pass—we'll then pick the top ten to go through one week of additional training on the time machine. After that, the mission."

John could hear shouted whispers of "Time machine? What's that?" and "He's got to be kidding, no one has invented a time machine!"

But then Jones lifted his hands, and as before, a hush settled over the room. The next half-hour consisted of the filling-out of employment documents, forms that John had seen many times during his military service. Once finished, Jones said, "Place all the documents in your book and close it."

As soon as the paper shuffling ended, he began speaking again. "Now, to your questions. Who's first?"

A young man with a military-style haircut and an expression as serious as General Jones had, asked, "Sir, no one except you has answered any questions at all. What is this place?"

"We're at TTA, short for the Time Travelers Academy. The Academy was established as a secret military facility five years ago, when we discovered technology that could send someone to another galaxy by traveling beyond the speed of light. To planets that were once unreachable. To time periods that were once unimaginable."

Eyes wide, the young man almost fell back into his chair at the general's matter-of-fact answer.

When the chatter receded, a young woman, asked, "You call it an academy. Have there been any graduates?"

"No. You will be the first. The course is actually four years. You're being sent through an accelerated course because of one reason. That reason is time. And the fact that we're running out of it."

"Sir, can you elaborate on that?" the woman said. "That sounds like we're in some sort of emergency." She smiled. "Like the world's coming to an end."

"Cadet, you couldn't have said it better," Jones replied. "The world *is* coming to an end, and you and everyone in this room is being called on to save humanity."

He held up his hands, but this time, it took longer for quiet to prevail. When it finally faded, Professor Rubiano stood. At Jones's nod, he said, "Can anyone in this room explain the bubonic plague?"

John raised his hand. "That's the disease that killed over half of Europe around the year 1300."

"Very good. The bubonic plague first came from fleas that lived and fed on infected rats. The bacteria multiplied inside the fleas' stomachs. When the infected rats died, the fleas began to starve, so they changed hosts. The fleas vomited blood tainted with the bacteria back into the bite wounds in their new hosts. That infected the new host. That's how the bacteria that causes the plague jumped from rats, to fleas, to people. Once bitten, most people were dead in four to seven days.

"There are actually three ways to get this type of plague. The one we're concerned about is the one transmitted through the air when a person coughs or sneezes, like a person does when he or she has the common cold. The bacteria enter the lungs through the windpipe and start attacking the lungs and throat."

"Sir, what's to worry about? There's a cure for the plague."

Rubiano nodded at the cadet. "How right you are. There *is* a cure for the plague. But I'm not finished. Now, can anyone explain influenza?"

Another young man raised his hand. "I'm a medical student, Professor, so I think I can answer. What's called influenza is really a group of diseases caused by viruses. But three times in modern history, one of that group reached such pandemic levels, millions died from it."

"Very good," Rubiano said. "Back then, they had no way to prevent this from happening. So, based on what you've learned in medical school, what are our options now if faced with a similar situation?"

The young man thought a moment, then said, "There's no cure for any viral infection. But, with the flu, there are vaccines. After the flu infects a certain number of people, it usually stabilizes. Scientists can now make a vaccine in anticipation of that. That's what's happening with H5N1, otherwise known as the avian flu or bird flu. It hasn't yet mutated to transfer from human to human, only from a human contact with birds. Even so, that's likely to eventually happen, so scientists are already working on a possible vaccine."

Rubiano nodded. "And actually, although the public doesn't know it yet, science already has an avian flu vaccine nearly ready. But . . ." Sadness passed over his face. "It's just as well that you mentioned avian flu. That's why all of you are here today. Six months ago, a disease that has the characteristics of both avian flu *and* bubonic plague emerged. We call it the avian plague. The numbers aren't yet in the millions, yet it's already reached pandemic levels. That is, it's already present in every country in the world."

The medical student gasped, and the other students looked at him, befuddled. Except for John. John was remembering what had happened in Russia. Now, he finally understood what he had seen, and the Russian general's mysterious words. At least some of them.

"You will soon learn how this happened," Rubiano said. "But for now, the bond that caused these two diseases to merge is our main concern. Thanks to its bubonic plague characteristic, this new disease can be transmitted from human to human by something as simple as a cough or sneeze. And just as rats once carried the bubonic plague, birds are speeding the spread of the avian plague."

Rubiano paused to let the implications sink in, and the medical student said, "Professor, if it's already pandemic, what do we do about it?"

"First, you have to understand our difficulty in even trying for a cure or vaccine. You see, by themselves, the avian flu is preventable and the bubonic plague is curable. But the bond that caused them to unite has made them incurable. That bond is not from Earth, and apparently, it's unstoppable. We predict that within three years, 99% of the world's population will be infected."

The young woman spoke up next. "Okay, so this is the Time Travelers Academy. If you have a time machine, why don't you just go back in time and stop it before it happens?"

Rubiano sighed. "Another good question. Simple. The plague was meant to be, and you can't change what's meant to be."

"I don't understand," she said. "You tell me you have a time machine, so you can go back to stop this and refuse to do it?"

Another sigh, this one directed toward General Jones. "The general could probably explain it better, but with his permission, I'll give it a go."

A nod from the general, and Rubiano turned back to the group. "The United States Congress thinks and feels the same way as you do. We—the Academy—might not be here next year because of a theory that prohibits time travel to a time that has already been set. To put it simply, we *can* go back into the past. But doing so is extremely dangerous. Some laws and rules must not be broken, and in this case, that law is the universal law of time. To go backward in time is more dangerous than anything imaginable. More dangerous than the virus itself. Have you heard of the grandfather clause?"

John's eyes widened, recalling his lighthearted joking around with Antonio on the plane back from Russia. He raised his hand, and stood when Rubiano pointed to him.

"As it applies to time travel, Professor, the grandfather clause means that if you travel back in time and cause your grandfather's death before he conceived your mother or your father, then how could you exist? And could you kill your grandfather if you were never born in the first place?"

Rubiano nodded at John, then turned to the audience. "Seems impossible, but can any of you answer that?"

After a moment of silence, one student raised his hand. "You're in another universe. There are two universes—a multiverse. One in which you were born, and one that you enter to kill your grandfather."

Rubiano shook his head. "Anyone else?"

Another student piped up. "Once you kill your grandfather, you remain alive, but when you travel back to your own time you don't exist . . . you just fade away."

"Another good try, but still wrong. Anyone else?"

No one spoke. Finally, he said, "You *can* actually go back in time and live a full life . . . as long as you don't kill your grandfather. Or become President. Or do anything that might change the future. A law called the Wayne Theory stipulates that time is like a living entity. That once time is set, time will actually *protect* itself from changes. To put it simply, something in nature will stop you from killing your grandfather. If you go back in time and ignore this law—for example, if you attempt to kill your grandfather—time will try to stop you. But if you're successful, you have just created a paradox in time that can only be resolved by another law—the laws of resetting."

One student asked, "What are the laws of resetting?"

"Let's keep the example of you killing your grandfather. If you do that, and therefore violate the laws of time, time will reset itself. Just like if you'd taken an electric clock, unplugged it, then plugged it back in. By resetting it, the clock would read zero-point-zero minutes and one second. That one second represents the rebirth of the universe. This is the law of resetting. The Big Bang. You would not only have killed your grandfather, but also destroyed the universe that you know and reset time to the beginning of the Big Bang."

He saw them still struggling to accept this, and turned their attention to a projector screen sitting on the stage. As he clicked through, various images came up. "We believe we have proof that this has happened before. These are photo representations of the universe today at 15 billion years, then at 1,000,000 years . . . and then, you see the universe depicted at negative 35 billion years. Students, we're located in the Milky Way, but in that universe, the Milky Way doesn't exist."

He turned back to them. "We've learned that the universe reset itself 15 billion years ago and formed the Milky Way that we now live in. What this means is that, 15 billion years ago, someone or something successfully tampered with a past timeline and caused the destruction of the universe."

A few students opened their mouths to speak, but Rubiano said, "I realize you have questions, but I want to keep on the subject, which is . . .we believe the universe protects itself with something called 'time eliminators,' or just 'eliminators.' We don't know what they are except in theory. But if you did go back in time and bump off your grandfather, or do anything else to change his history, chances are, you would see one of these entities."

Another cadet asked, "What exactly are time eliminators?"

Rubiano sighed. "In theory, they exist and don't exist. They are matter and antimatter. They are time and not of time. They have gravity and no gravity."

A cadet yelled out, "Hey, is this one of those Zen things?"

This brought a few chuckles, then another cadet called out, "Yeah, isn't there a theory that a time machine can't exist before the time it was created?"

"That's true and false," Rubiano said. He glanced at Mike Adams, then smiled at the first student. "And in an odd way, it *is* a bit, ah . . . Zen. Let's say the time machine was constructed of parts from Japan, Mexico, and many other countries. Say the metal that the Ascendia Corporation used in the time machine came from the car your grandfather was driving. And that suddenly, the time machine goes back to the same year your grandfather had his car.

"What will happen? I really don't know. In fact, no one working on this project could know. So Ascendia took precautions while building the time machine. They went to the Arctic Circle, where no one or thing existed for millions of years. There, they recovered all the materials to build the time machine and much of this facility. Materials that few people on this planet have ever seen or know about. So, to the extent we can be, we're protected from the potential problem you pointed out so well."

John held up his hand. Rubiano noticed and pointed to him.

"Thank you, Professor. Here's my question. What if the time machine goes back in time millions of years, and it bumps into the same material it was created from?"

"Put simply? We don't know. But we have no plans whatsoever to go back in Earth's past. The time machine has failsafe capabilities to prevent that from happening."

"Are you saying the time machine *can* go into the past, but you've programmed it not to?"

It was the kid in front of John who'd blurted it out—the kid who was scared before, almost scared enough to walk out of the hall and give up.

John returned to his seat, bemused. Rubiano, with an equally mirthful look, said, "I believe your name is Vincent Goff. Am I correct?"

"Uh, yeah, but how did you know—?"

"Your name came to my attention early during the selection process. We'll be speaking again, I'm sure. But for now, I'd like to address your question. *Have* we deliberately programmed the machine to avoid violating the law of time? Bingo. We don't want to risk causing a time-paradox that might cause the universe to reset. And so we've programmed the machine not to go backward in time past the universal constant time—the present.

"But, as with every rule, we're seeking a way to bend it when we need to. We have another form of time travel, called portal time travel. In portal time travel, one needs a solid object in the past to time travel to. A physical target to aim for, like a wall, or a tree, or even a tornado. But this type of travel has other limitations. A person can go backward in time only up to one month, and can only return to the future from which he or she started. And, it's limited only to Earth. Time-travel to other planets isn't possible, at least using portal time travel. In fact," he sighed, "portal time travel might be banned by Congress because of the theory of time eliminators . . . their theoretical danger. In fact, Congress will vote in a few weeks to keep portal time travel, or ban it. But thankfully, what Congress does or doesn't do won't affect this particular mission."

Without raising his hand, a cadet called out, "Professor, a moment ago you said 'the universal constant time.' What does that mean exactly?"

Rubiano shook his head as though chasing away a troublesome flying bug. "The universe has a constant time. Now—the present—is the universal constant time. Now, back to the mission. . . . A few days ago, we detected a future explosion on a planet called Peligroso, located in the Lejana Galaxy. The planet is about five billion light-years away. So we believe the explosion actually happened in their future.

"What's so unique about this explosion is that it wasn't a natural occurrence. Not like the exploding star called a supernova. Rather, we believe this explosion was somehow caused by an advanced society. We theorize that if they could make a bomb or other explosive large enough for us on Earth to detect it, they must be advanced in all the sciences. Most particularly, in medicine. We're basing our belief on evidence that the explosion was caused by a neutron-gene bomb—a genetic bomb. One that our scientists are just now beginning to theorize. If the population of Peligroso is that advanced in genetics, we believe they might be able to help us."

A stunning, coppery-complexioned woman stood. "Professor Rubiano, I've read the theories about the uses for neutron-gene bombs. None of those uses is for peaceful purposes. How advanced could this civilization be if they used this bomb? Perhaps they even used it on each other. It's . . . It just seems barbaric. Would we *really* want to depend on a civilization like that to save ours? Would they even be willing to?"

General Jones stood, and Rubiano relinquished the microphone to him.

"You're Charlene Vaughn? Is that correct?"

Charlene nodded, eyes wide that he knew her name.

"You've brought up a good question, Dr. Vaughn. This is only one reason why it's a dangerous mission. The machine could break or have problems on the way there, or on the way back. You might get there and find the civilization *is* hostile, and they will kill you before you can inform them you're there for a peaceful purpose. Or you might run into a planet that took five minutes to completely form, and our theory that it was a neutron-gene bomb was wrong. So many mishaps could happen. We're looking into everything . . . including our selection of the crew for the mission. Without them, we fail. Humanity fails."

Charlene's smile faded as Jones returned to his seat, and Vincent stood. "Sir, good speech, but you forgot something. Wouldn't one of your, ah, *time eliminators* appear and get us if we were to go to Peligroso in our past?"

"We're fairly confident the answer, in this case, is no," Rubiano said. "The bomb, and the planet's destruction, are five billion years in the future, so has not been set by time. We're going to the universal timeline of the planet—not the past or the future of the planet, but their time that is equal to our own.

"Light travels at 186,000 miles per second. What happened to them happened five billion years ago, so we know their future. But it's their *constant time* in which we're interested. We can go to a time that is in constant with our own, and no further. To do that, we'll arrive five billion years in their future, then reverse time, going to their present constant time, which is before they destroyed themselves. And so the time eliminators should not appear."

One cadet asked, "Are you saying we can travel to the planet, and once there, reverse time to before they destroyed themselves?"

Rubiano nodded. "You're exactly right."

Vincent asked, "You mentioned that the time machine's made of special materials. What's so special about them?"

Rubiano smiled at him. "You'll be learning all of this later on, so I'll keep this brief now. It's powered by a nuclear reactor using Uranium 238. And the hull is made of a material we call 'trilasteverium.' This metal lasts essentially forever, and it might even withstand the forces of traveling at the speed of light. I say 'might' because it's never been tested. Ironically, trilasteverium is made of the same material found on the comet that's been circling our solar system for billions of years. In short, if you are chosen for the mission, your journey will take billions of years, but to you only hours. And the trilasteverium will protect both you and the machine from harm.

"But more important, I think, is how the machine works. First, it stops time, so there will be no gravitational pull. As many of you know, you could jump 30 feet on the moon but only five feet on Earth because of the gravitational pull. But, with no gravitational pull, the time machine can escape Earth's gravity on its own propulsion. Once in orbit, the time machine can go at 500,000 miles per hour."

John said, "I thought the time machine could travel at the speed of light. At 500,000 miles per hour, it would take us over five billion years to get there and over five billion years to get back—"

"I think your plan is doomed," Vincent said, and all eyes turned to him.

"Our plan is not *doomed*," Rubiano said, his tone suddenly harsh. "Haven't you been listening? To finish what John was saying, at 500,000 miles per hour, and with the increase in time, the machine is going much faster. For example: light travels at 186,000 miles per second. If you continue at this speed for one year, you would have traveled one light-year. Yes, it takes five billion light-years to reach Planet Peligroso. But, even though the machine only travels at 500,000 miles per hour, the time machine *increases* time. So you're actually traveling thousands of times *faster* than 500,000 miles per hour. At that speed, you will reach your destination in ten to twelve hours.

"In fact, on your journey to Peligroso's galaxy, you'll be able to see entire galaxies make a complete revolution. You'll see stars being born, planets forming. And your estimated travel time to the Lejana Galaxy is twelve hours, ten minutes."

General Jones saw Vincent open his mouth again, and stood. Rubiano handed him the microphone, relieved.

"The science behind the journey is interesting, Mr. Goff. But again, you'll all learn much more to help you understand how the mission is possible. For now, it's only important for you to know what happens next. You will live in barracks and go through advanced basic training to prepare yourself for the mission. Five have left. The remaining 795 cadets will be divided into ten companies of about eighty each."

Jones nodded to another uniform-clad officer, who crossed the podium to stand next to him. The officer was a dark-complexioned, mustachioed African American of about 25. John noted that the man's stripes and symbols on his dark blue Navy uniform showed a rank of E-6 and his specialty as a mechanic. A similarly attired female Latino officer stepped beside him.

"This is Petty Officer Lynch," the general said. "He'll be the company commander for the first 80 male cadets. Chief Petty Officer Maria Javier will be in charge of the first 80 female cadets. The remaining cadets will be assigned to other company commanders. But—and listen well—each company will be a company of one. If you don't yet understand what this means now, you will very soon."

Petty Officer Lynch called the names of the first 80 cadets, asking then to bring their books and paperwork. Once he and Petty Officer Javier had gathered their groups, they led them out of the room.

John's name had been called, but General Jones asked him to stay. As soon as the other cadets cleared the room, he introduced John, saying, "This is Mr. Godunov," he said, "our top choice to go on the mission—"

"Ah, with all due respect, General, there was a mistake. My name is John Richards."

Jones nodded. "My apologies, and thank you for reminding me." He turned to Mike Adams. "It seems our computer came up with two names on the same person."

Adams nodded, then gave John a nod of greeting with the same searching smile he'd given Jones earlier.

"Regardless of his name," Jones continued, "this gentleman is prior military, served in Special Forces and is our number-one draftee."

Secretary Lanti measured John in his gaze, then they shook hands and gave each other a salute.

"Very impressive," Lanti said, "and welcome aboard. Hopefully, what you'll bring to the project will give it a hope in hell of succeeding."

John said, "Thank you sir." *I think.*

Lanti said, "By the way, Ivan— Forgive me, I meant John. Where did you serve in Special Forces?"

"It's, ah, confidential, but I think I can tell you, Mr. Secretary." He smiled, but his joke fell flat on Lanti. Rushing to explain, he said, "I served under the cover name of Ivan Godunov in a campaign known as the American Storms. My job was to identify corruption in our military, and to make sure all aspects of the Geneva Convention were upheld. I later took an assignment with the United Nations Special Forces."

Lanti nodded. "What part of the country are you from?"

"A town in Texas called Rockville. I own a martial arts school there."

Lanti's eyes widened at the town's name, and John noticed.

"Have you ever heard of Rockville, Mr. Secretary?"

"Yes . . . ah, no. I was thinking of another town. So many places I've visited, you see."

Lanti gave him a quick smile and a quicker chuckle. "Well, I suppose you'd better hurry and catch up with your company. I wish you the best at the Academy."

John saluted again and rushed off, wishing he understood why Lanti's reaction had seemed so odd.

19

With Petty Officer Lynch leading, the group headed to a building about three blocks away. In front of the building was an object that Vincent first thought was a sculpture, but soon learned was the company bell. That bell would call them to meals each day, or to meetings.

Once they arrived at the building, they were all assigned billet numbers beginning with the number 1-80.

"This number will be attached to everything at the Academy," Lynch barked at them. "This company is Company 001, nicknamed 'The Boneheads.'"

One student made the mistake of complaining, but a few terse words from Lynch taught all of them that protest wouldn't get them anywhere. At all.

Next, they walked, nearly jogging to keep up, to another building. Lynch ordered them to line up by billet number. It took the raw group a while to figure it all out, but soon, they were lined up and greeted by the Academy's tailors. Within three hours, the entire group had their uniforms. Next, they were taken over to get their toiletries, bedspreads, covers and pillows, and given sea bags to put everything in.

The next step was haircuts, and this was where one student decided that, Petty Officer Lynch or not, he was going to have his hair cut *his* way.

Vincent sat in the barber chair and gave the barber specific instructions. The barber chuckled, said, "Okay," then began cutting his hair. With one swipe of his clippers, Vincent Goff had a reverse Mohawk.

"Hey, what did you just do?" Vincent yelled. "Give me a mirror!"

Hiding a smile, the barber did as he was told this time.

Vincent saw his hair and turned on the barber. "Who the hell gave you your barber's license? I . . . I . . . My attorney will be getting in contact with you!"

Petty Officer Lynch overheard and stormed up to Vincent, saying, "Attorney? I'm your attorney, your judge and your jury, and you have just been sentenced to do 20 push-ups. Now. Outside!"

Sulking, Vincent complied, even when Lynch added, "Drop and begin. And after each push-up, you will say, 'I will not disrespect the barber, sir.' All the way to 20."

Tired and out of breath, Vincent stumbled back to his company. While he waited at the end of the line for the barber to finish the rest and return to him, he endured the whispers, jeers, chuckles and outright laughter from the rest of the company.

From the barbershop, they headed to the medical unit. The medical officer handed them medical records to fill out, saying, "As soon as you're finished, head to that door and wait."

Vincent cried at the sight of the needle. It took three medics to hold his arm down so they could take blood. When he came out of the lab, his tear-streaked face brought jeers and laughter from some of the other cadets.

The group was then lined up and were inoculated, then told to stand facing a wall, then pull their pants and underwear all the way down for a hernia check. The doctor started with the first cadet, but stopped when he got to Vincent, who still had his pants up. At the doctor's repeated instruction, Vincent said, "No. You're not seeing my private parts."

The doctor leaned close enough to whisper into Vincent's ear and said, "You have nothing I want, cadet."

"If that's the case, I can keep my pants up," he replied. "Otherwise, there *is* something you want. But you're not going to get it here, so I suggest you do an about-face and get out of mine."

With an, "I'll be right back," the doctor headed off and returned with Lynch . . . who got right into Vincent's face and told him in a cold voice, "If you don't pull your pants down, I'll rip them off and throw them in the nearest river."

Vincent cried this time too, and didn't stop crying during the exam.

Lynch barked, "You better exit those tears before I give you something to cry about."

Terrified now, he choked back his tears, then rejoined his company outside.

After they were taken to their barracks and assigned beds, it was supper-time—and their first lesson in marching as a unit. It wasn't a pretty sight, but they were able to head for their first meal as a company.

Outside the mess hall, Lynch barked, "Form a line to enter the mess hall, get your food, and take no more than ten minutes to eat."

Instead of digging in, Vincent got busy putting a napkin neatly over his shirt, then slowly and meticulously cutting up his food. Before he could get one bite, Lynch yelled, "Time's up! Fall out!"

Everyone rushed to put his or her tray up—except Vincent, who was taking his third bite.

Lynch stormed up to him. "You're not at the Regency Hotel, Cadet Goff. You take one bite of that food, I'll take a bite out of your ass. Now get outside and form a platoon!"

"But I'm hungry—"

"What you *are* is too slow. I said 'Fall out.' You can fall out yourself, or I'll do it for you."

Vincent put his fork down, took his tray to the window, and slouched all the way to the company waiting outside.

From there they were marched back to the barracks, where Lynch taught them how to make their beds, fold their shirts and polish their shoes, using the same tough-love manner. Before *Taps*, which was played at 10:00 pm, Lynch brought out a flag and explained, "Tomorrow, things will get more challenging."

His statement was greeted by groans. He ignored them. "We're in competition with other companies. The company that wins will be awarded something very special. Each person in that company will be advanced one rank when he graduates. The competition consists of our training. From swimming, running, academics, boating, marksmanship, obstacle course, hand-to-hand combat, we'll be graded by the observers. The observers have purple ropes around their shoulders outside their uniforms. Be careful around them and watch what you say. They have the power to judge a company, and to either reward or punish an entire company."

Lynch gave them a smile that was anything but friendly, and added. "They're the *inspectors*."

When he was satisfied that the group was thoroughly terrified, he said, "I'll need four group leaders from among you—a master at arms to maintain discipline in the company while I'm not here, a Recruit Company Petty Officer who is in charge of the company while I'm not here, an Athletic Petty Officer, and an Academic Petty Officer. These four positions are up for grabs. This means that whoever wants them will have to compete for them. I'll choose who I think is the best for each position. If you hold and maintain these positions throughout your training without having the position taken from you, you will receive advancement in rank once you finish.

"I'll take volunteers now."

John volunteered for the RCPO petty officer position.

A cadet named Feldman volunteered for the master at arms.

Vincent raised his hand for the academic petty officer but quickly dropped it when Lynch glared at him. Other recruits took the last two positions.

Lynch continued. "At the end, we'll have two major competitions. One is called 'Last One Standing,' the other is 'The Freedom Run'—which is just that: to pass this training you must pass the Freedom Run. To do that, you must be able to run 1.5 miles in eight minutes. But you will compete with other companies for the top running time. Now, reveille will be at 5:00 am. I suggest you rest, because tomorrow begins a new day."

That order, Vincent got the first time. By the 10:00 *Taps*, in fact, everyone was in their beds, exhausted.

But not all were sleeping. All night long, Vincent cried, occasionally saying, "I'm hungry," or "I want to go home."

John, in a nearby bunk, thought, *Kid, me too. But some things, you just gotta live with.* Before he finally drifted off, he thought of Bonita, and of his life before the yellow envelope, and wondered what the next day would bring.

20

At zero-five hundred, the barracks door flew open and a metal trashcan sailed through it, hitting first one metal bunk, then another, before coming to a jangling, crashing rest against the far end of the room. Petty Officer Lynch had changed into a demon from the dark.

"Get up, get your damn lazy asses out of bed," he yelled. "You have 20 minutes to shit, shower and shave, get dressed, do a height-line and form a platoon outside. Get up get up! Get up!"

Vincent looked at John wide-eyed. "He— He was almost nice yesterday. What's gotten into him?"

John smiled. "I know what he's up to, and I'm afraid you're still finding out. Just try to make things easy on yourself and go along, okay? You don't want to get a rep as a wimp. If you do, you'll be a target for him. And for most of the rest of the company, too."

Vincent hung his head, remembering the day before. Finally, he understood what his dad had tried to tell him about the world being a tough place.

Outside, it took only minutes for him to become the target John had warned him about. While Lynch was giving them their morning instructions, he did what he always did when he was nervous: he kept putting his hands in his pockets. Lynch warned him twice, but the third time he noticed, he said, "I'm not going to tell you again about putting your damn hands in your pockets."

Even later, he didn't know why he did it, but his response was to slide his hands right back into his pockets.

This time, Lynch lowered his face to his and growled, "Perhaps you're hard of hearing, Cadet. So I'll say it loud and slow: If I have to tell you not to put your hands in your pocket *one . . . more . . . time . . .* I'm going to tear them off your fucking body!"

Vincent took his hands out of his pockets and started crying. John saw, and winced, but could do absolutely nothing to bail the kid out. Not that he should.

Each of us has to sink or swim on our own, he thought. But, remembering his own training days, he knew that each of them would come far in the next several weeks—or get a quick ride home.

Throughout the day, Lynch taught the company the basics of marching and working as one. But throughout the entire day, Vincent proved to be the problem cadet.

Again, *Taps* was at 10:00 p.m. Again, Vincent cried all night.

The next morning at 5:00 a.m., they were again awakened by someone throwing a metal trashcan in the barracks. But this morning, the voice informed them they had only ten minutes to get dressed and get outside for roll call, followed by, "The last one still in here will be doing push-ups."

Vincent had somehow managed to sleep through both the trashcan *and* the yelling.

John tried to help him because they were bunkmates. "Hey, wake up," he said as he rushed to pull on his boots.

Two minutes later, Vincent was still asleep. John tried again.

"Go away and leave me alone," Vincent said as he turned around and covered his head with the blanket.

John sighed, said, "As you wish," and headed outside.

When Lynch counted, he counted 79 terrified, shivering cadets.

He counted again. Finally, he did a roll call and got to the G's. Then he headed back into the barracks.

Two minutes later, Vincent was outside, hastily dressed, doing push-ups for the group.

After breakfast, they were escorted to the dental clinic for x-rays and exams.

While in line, John caught Lynch's eye. "Look, PO Lynch, I'm former military, so I understand exactly what you're doing and support it. But . . . Cadet Goff might just be a problem no one can fix."

Lynch looked around. Finding no one within hearing range, he turned back to John. "Cadet Richards, I can't say much, but I can say this. It was no accident that you two are bunkmates. There is something extremely special about him. I don't know what it is. I was just told by my captain that the success of the mission depends on him. We knew he would have trouble with this part of the training. That's why we set it up so you could help . . . if you will."

"What makes Vince Goff so special? He sleeps in, can't follow simple directions, he can't march, make his bed or even fold a shirt."

"I truly don't believe he *can't* do these things," Lynch replied. "According to our background info on him, he's been exposed to martial arts at a very low level—hobby level, you might say. Which means he *is* capable of learning. When he wants to. But . . . only the generals know what makes him special to this mission. My job is to turn him into a TTA graduate and ready for this mission. Again, we're hoping you'll be willing to help."

John's grin was somber. "Is that an order, sir?"

With a return grin, Lynch said, "If that's what it takes, it can be. Your choice."

"Speaking of mission, can you tell me more about it?"

Lynch shrugged. "You know as much as I do. As for Goff, can I count on you to help him?"

"The only question I still have is why. Why should I help him?"

With a sigh, Lynch said, "Because the higher-ups are selecting ten to go on this mission, and he's already been selected. And the captain, whoever he turns out to be, doesn't need anyone on this mission who falls apart as easily as Goff does."

"Already been selected?" John said. "I'll ask again . . . what makes him so special?"

"He's said to be extremely intelligent, that's all I know. I don't know how intelligent he is, but the generals and admirals do . . . and they personally asked me to convince you to help him if you objected. I'm asking now."

John thought about the times, in Special Ops training and after, when some handpicked recruit had almost gotten him or one of his buddies killed. He had a life now, a good one. Why should he risk everything he had, including his life, for a spoiled, lazy, snot-nosed child who'd done nothing but rebel and whine since he set foot at the Academy?

Yet he knew that someone like Lynch would have never asked unless the situation was desperate. "He needs to be a doctor or maybe a teacher, not a time traveler," he finally said. "And you know as well as I do that he has to help himself. I can't give you a decision yet. But I promise I'll talk to him. We'll see."

Lynch nodded. "Fair enough. But I'm counting on you to make the right decision. We're all depending on it."

His mind heavy, John returned to the barracks and began preparing for tomorrow

That night, after the third time Vincent burst into tears, John asked him, in frustration, why he joined. He replied, "I didn't come to them. They came to me. But . . . now, it's . . ."

The anger left his face, and he tried again.

"At the observatory, I thought I was doing important things. That I would make a discovery that would change the world. I did. I'm the one who discovered Planet Peligroso. But . . . when I almost left the other day, I remembered that whatever General Jones called us for, it had to be something really important. Something that might change the world. And I was right. If the world ends in three years, like General Jones said, we're all goners. But maybe something I can do, or something else I discover, will help stop that from happening. I guess you could say I want to serve my country."

He wants the same thing I want, John thought in wonder. *To serve his country. But how can he possibly learn how to do that in time? And how can he learn enough to keep from doing something stupid that kills the rest of the crew?*

At that moment, John resolved to do everything he could to make Vincent a man.

╼═ ❀ ═╾

The next time he saw PO Lynch, he gave him an unqualified yes. That same day, Lynch informed the group, "Tomorrow we start our remaining seven weeks of training. You'll be exposed to everything from swimming, to small arms, to enduring a gas chamber, to marching and martial arts. In a couple of days, you'll take your swimming test."

As soon as Lynch said the last words, John heard Vincent gasp. He glanced at him and saw his eyes welling up. "What's wrong?" he whispered, but Vincent refused to tell him.

In class the next morning, Professor Rubiano was interrupted by Vincent, who had figured out an extremely hard quantum equation and made a small mistake, then corrected the mistake and changed a small portion of the equation. Even with the change, nobody understood it, including Rubiano, who in anger and frustration said, "Do you want to teach this class?"

John held his breath, expecting to see Vincent's smartass side. Instead, Vincent quietly said yes. Soon, he was teaching the class and Rubiano was in his seat, occasionally raising his hand to ask a question. John, in awed admiration, saw what Lynch had implied: Vincent Goff was gifted beyond anyone else he'd ever met.

Vincent continued to teach the class until it ended. Rubiano stopped him before he left and said, "Cadet Goff, someone like you comes around far too rarely. The last was Einstein, and Leonardo DaVinci before him. I'm excited to have met you."

Charlene Vaughn, watching, muttered, "DaVinci's got nothing on this kid. Nothing!"

John had to agree.

╼═ ❀ ═╾

Unfortunately, John was so soundly asleep, he wasn't able to prevent what happened that night. Three other cadets, jealous over Vincent's wowing of the professor, decided to give him a blanket party—a surprise abduction accomplished by throwing a blanket over the victim so the victim couldn't see or tell who was doing it, then beating the person up.

That night when everyone was asleep, the cadet-guard on duty awoke his two friends, and they grabbed a blanket. Next, the guard woke Vincent, telling him he had to stand night-watch duty next.

Vincent, half-asleep, said, "I'm not on the schedule."

"Yes, you are, Cadet, they changed the schedule."

Grumbling, Vincent put on his shoes and walked downstairs to check the duty schedule. As he was peering at it, two of the three threw a blanket over him, then carried him outside behind the barracks and began beating him.

The next morning, John saw his black eye. "You hit your head on your bed-rail or something?"

Vincent shook his head. "I don't know who did it, but somebody grabbed me and wrapped me in a blanket, and carried me outside. Then did this." He pointed to his black eye and then showed a couple of other bruises to John. "I recognized their voices, but I don't want revenge." He smiled. "Revenge will come in its own good time."

John nodded, angry with the cadets, but also pleased that, for the first time, Vincent wasn't crying over something bad that happened to him.

Feldman, whose bunk was on the other side of Vincent's, took one look, then rushed to get some ice to stop the swelling. From that point on, Vincent had at least two friends.

Friends that, unfortunately, couldn't help him when it came time for the swimming test.

The company gathered outside to march to the test.

"Ah, I don't know if I've ever mentioned this before," Vincent whispered to John, "but I can't swim. And hey, why do we have to learn how to swim anyway?"

"Swimming is easy," John said. "I can't believe you never learned."

"I . . . I'm terrified of water. Always have been. My dad used to rag me about it, too."

"Well, if you can't swim, don't worry too much," John whispered back. "This is your quick and dirty intro."

The lead swimming instructor shouted, "Everyone who can swim, swim across the length of the pool. If you can do that, you've passed your test."

John and most of the others dove into the water and did the test. Vincent stood there, shivering in his suit.

Then the instructor shouted, "All that can't swim are to jump into the water off this 15-foot platform into 20 feet of water. Below are two swimming instructors waiting to help."

A few jumped into the water, then others. Until one terrified cadet was left. A cadet so scared, he wouldn't even climb up the ladder until forcefully told to climb it by the instructors.

When he reached the top, he screamed, "I can't swim! I'll drown!"

Lynch turned to the company and said, "Do an about-face."

Everyone did, some more reluctantly than others.

One of the instructors climbed up the ladder and stood at the opposite end of the platform. "If you don't jump in the water now, I'll throw you in!"

Vincent stood there, trembling, as the instructor in the water below kept yelling, "Jump in! I'm here!"

The first instructor took a step toward Vincent, which seemed to make up his mind. He jumped . . . and landed right on top of the instructor who'd been waiting in the water. The instructor was rendered unconscious from the blow, and was now caught in the screaming Vincent's flailing legs.

John heard the commotion, whirled around, dove in and began swimming toward both of them, getting there just as the second instructor did. Together, they hauled the gasping, flailing Vincent's head above water. As soon as they did, the instructor shoved him away to make enough space to grab the drowning and still-unconscious instructor. When he shoved Vincent, Vincent began swimming. In fact, he swam as if his life literally depended on it.

John and the instructor pulled the third man out of the water and soon had him on the side of the pool, coughing but alive and apparently unharmed.

John overheard Lynch muttering, "Well, he passed. But what a hell of a way to do it. Is the kid ever going to do *anything* the easy way?"

In spite of the near-tragedy, John couldn't help laughing. And when he saw that Vincent, the kid who couldn't swim, was still swimming toward the edge of the pool, his laughter turned to bellows. Soon, the entire company was laughing, and Feldman was slapping the gasping Vincent on the back and saying, "Good job! See, you really *do* know how to swim!"

Vincent looked at Feldman, and the amazement on his face was enough to change the laughter to encouraging hoots. From most of the cadets, at least.

After that day, Vincent seemed to, little by little, gain fewer enemies. This wasn't to say that he made any real friends, or was any less defiant. One day, Lynch caught him making fun of another cadet who was sentenced to push-ups, and ordered him to drop and do 40 himself. Angry because the cadet in question was one of the cadets involved in giving him the blanket party, he turned his anger on Lynch.

"I quit," he said. "I quit, I quit, I quit!"

Lynch replied, "You don't quit us, we quit you."

"I beg to differ. According to the pre-employment documents, my service is contingent on successfully passing training. If either one of us deems that this training and employment is not a match, then neither is legally bound by the contract. That's clearly stated on Page eight, Section Two in the pre-employment agreement."

He edged closer to Lynch and threw his shoulders back. "Furthermore, just in case you're slow and didn't understand *me*, maybe because *your* IQ's below 100, then I'll make it clearer and reiterate. I quit!"

He took his hat off, walked over to the company bell, put his hat over the bell and rang it twice. As he walked away, the commander said, "You're not in the Navy SEALs!"

He kept walking until two cadets grabbed him and dragged him back. By then his anger had abated, and he counted off the 40 push-ups Lynch had assigned, then returned to the formation.

In spite of Vincent's attempt at fitting in, things only got worse from there. The company headed for the track next. As they marched, the other companies were making fun of Company 001 because they weren't marching in formation; Vincent had everyone off step. Lynch ordered the entire company to run four punishment-laps around the track. As usual, Vincent was the last one to finish. Lynch forced the entire company to wait for him, winding up late for dinner.

John's heart went out to him, but he was determined to not help him unless he really needed help. That came that night, when Feldman got wind of a second blanket party being planned. As before, the cadets kidnapped Vincent and took him off. But once outside the barracks, they discovered that Vincent and John had switched bunks. This time, even three-on-one, the cadets were the ones who took the beating.

They tried again the next day. Noticing John on guard duty, they grabbed him, covered him in a blanket and proceeded to take him outside. But this time, Vincent and Feldman joined the fray. This beating, fueled by Vincent's anger, was worse than before.

Now these cadets were terrified of Vincent, not just from the beating he'd given them, but because John, Vincent and Feldman as a team were formidable opponents. John allowed himself one small hope: that none of the three harassing cadets were chosen for the mission. Even if John were chosen, too, it would be difficult enough for Vincent to watch his back while on such a dangerous journey.

21

Secretary of Defense Lanti arrived at the Academy to attend the Last One Standing competition—a display of what the cadets had learned in their hand-to-hand martial arts training.

"All companies are to be in the auditorium fifteen minutes before the Last One Standing," General Jones told him. "So when the competition begins, every cadet will be here except for those standing watch." Jones smiled and added, "I think you'll be impressed by what we've been able to accomplish in such a short time here."

He looked past Lanti. "I had told Mike Adams you were attending. Thought he'd be here to greet you."

"Oh, I saw him by the men's room on the way in. He said he'd be here in just a bit."

"Excellent." Jones chuckled. "I hope he makes it before the last cadets arrive. There's quite a crush at the last minute."

+⊱—— ⚜ ——⊰+

"Come on, come *on*!"

Vincent checked his watch for the tenth time in as many minutes. It figured. Besides the academics, martial arts was the one thing he was good at. So he knew he'd do well in the competition. But he had to stay on watch until Cadet Vaughn relieved him. And if his stupid replacement didn't show, he'd miss the demonstration or be late, and either way, Lynch wouldn't let him compete.

"Sorry, I'm so sorry!"

Vincent whirled around to see Charlene Vaughn, her brown bangs flying, running toward him.

"*Really* sorry!" she said, gasping for breath. "I know you've got to get to the auditorium."

Vincent gave her a tight smile. Any other cadet, he'd have yelled at. But not her. Charlene was one of the few from other companies who'd even speak to him.

Who didn't take one look and dismiss him as a geek. Who actually admired him for his intelligence, because she was a brilliant and passionate researcher too.

"I'm just glad you showed up," he said. "I'll let you know how it went."

She smiled. "Great! Now scoot!"

As he ran, he checked his watch again. The forced laps had helped him, just like John said they would. If he could keep running at this pace, he would make it in time.

Just as he entered the auditorium, still running at top speed, his loosened shoelace came untied. His only warning of the fall was a slight tugging before the shoe flew off.

Groaning, he reached up, grabbed the first protruding thing his hand hit and pulled himself upright.

The alarm was so loud, he was pretty sure he'd be deaf.

But he wasn't. He was able to hear someone yell, "Everyone out of the building! It's a fire alarm!"

Then he looked up and saw that, in his hurry, he'd grabbed the fire alarm to pull himself up with.

He didn't have time to yell out that no, there wasn't a fire. No one would have heard him anyway—everyone in the building was streaming past him through the entrance. Most were quiet as they ran, but some were screamers and criers.

Like I used to be, he thought in wonder.

Once everyone was assembled outside the auditorium doors, he saw Petty Officer Lynch striding toward him.

"PO Lynch, I'm glad you're here," he said. "Long story short, I accidentally tripped the fire alarm."

"What?" Lynch said. Then, without allowing Vincent to say another word, he yelled out, "Company 001, report!"

Moments later, Vincent was surrounded by all the company commanders and students. And the first words out of Lynch's mouth were, "This is my most screwed-up recruit. And now, he's decided to start playing pranks. Cadet Goff, you're going to be doing push-ups until we're *all* hot and thirsty."

With a sigh, Vincent went down into push-up position.

Then the auditorium blew up.

Those farthest from the entrance could only watch as those closer, including Lynch and John, who'd just arrived, were lifted from their feet by the powerful blast. Everyone left standing went to the ground . . . except Vincent, who was already there.

In the melee that followed, Lynch and the other company commanders worked quickly to calm the cadets and treat the few minor injuries. In the process, Lynch apologized profusely to General Jones and Secretary of Defense Lanti.

"But I assure you, sirs," Lynch added, "this incident will be resolved quickly and the Academy's training won't be interrupted. We'll just switch our group training sessions to the outdoors."

"I expected nothing less from you, PO Lynch," General Jones said, then turned to Lanti and Adams. "Well, Mr. Secretary, when I said you were in for a surprise, I had no idea it would be this."

Lanti gave a weak laugh and slapped Jones on the shoulder. "Well, these things happen. All's well that ends well, eh?"

John, standing nearby, wondered why the Secretary of Defense was otherwise so calm about the destruction of the Academy's auditorium. But, being only a cadet, he decided to say nothing. For now.

<hr />

The bomb had been secreted under one of the bleachers. The device was found to be an old, very specialized design known only to the military. The tech staff analyzed each attendee's likelihood of being the one who planted the bomb. Jones was shocked that, of all those there that day, only one had the specific expertise to make that type of vintage explosive device: Secretary of Defense Lanti. Because the bomb came near to destroying part of the Academy's physical structure, he decided to share what he'd learned with Mike Adams.

"I don't know about you, General," Adams said. "But I've worked too hard, and so have you, to see the Academy harmed. I think Lanti has his own plan. It's what he talks about every time I see him—to prevent the Academy from becoming the sixth branch of his department. And what better way than to stage something like this? Something to convince Congress to either stop the mission, or privatize the Academy to avoid liability."

Jones peered at Adams. "With the fate of Earth's entire population at stake, he'd have to be psychotic—"

"Yes, but think of what pride can do to someone. Even someone with an ego much smaller than Lanti's. Look, I'm not saying it's Lanti. Just that he's the most likely, and he has a motive."

Jones smiled. "The same could be said about you, you know."

Adams shrugged. "Sure. I'm ex-military, and I have explosives experience too. But would I really have blown up something that I built from the ground up? That's just not good business, General."

Jones sighed. "You're right. I'll talk to the President. I have to inform him. But there just isn't enough evidence to arrest Lanti."

After conferring with the President, Jones ordered the investigation dropped, and then buried.

22

Antonio was at his office at home, trying to balance the school's books for the month. One reason he struggled was because the previous month's ledger was still back at the school, locked in the safe. Until the curfew imposed by the mayor a couple of weeks before, the school's office was where he usually worked on the books at night. "Well, there's only one way to fix that," he muttered. He stretched, yawned deeply, and decided to take a break.

He found Bonita in the kitchen, her textbooks and papers spread before her. The sight brought him a sigh. It had been nearly three weeks since John's last communiqué. And it had been so cryptic, it was all he and Natasha could do to console Bonita afterward. He felt sorry for her. But, short of his business partner showing up, he could do little to ease her worry.

"Have you seen Natasha?" he said. "I have to go back to the school and get some papers out of the safe."

She looked up at him. "I . . . I've been meaning to ask you . . . have you heard anything else? It's been a week now. And that strange message he left for me. All he said was not to worry, and he missed me."

Antonio shrugged. "I can only guess it had something to do with his job with Special Forces. He's terminally secretive about that. I'm sure he thinks about you all the time, no matter where he is or what he's doing. But I kind of wish he'd give us another phone call or something. Just to let us know he's fine." *Or alive.*

Bonita fixed her eyes on the paper she was drafting. "I guess if he cared about me . . . I'm worried about him."

On impulse, Antonio decided to try something he'd been thinking of for a while. Something that might dissuade her from obsessing over John. Something to allow her to get on with her life if John didn't return right away.

Adopting a sarcastic tone, he said, "Yeah, some friend and co-owner he turned out to be. Just left us all hanging." He forced a chuckle. "Heck, for all we know, he's eloping with that girl he met on a date."

"What girl?"

Seeing her anguish, he almost decided to give up the ruse, to tell her it was a joke. But, he had to at least try. "Oh, he met some girl from a dating service. Right before we came to Russia to pick you and Natasha up. He didn't talk much about her, which isn't like him. I wonder about that sometimes. That maybe he only wanted me to *think* he'd been called back into service. That maybe he just left Kahn and me to run the business while he ran off with some woman."

While Antonio spoke, Natasha entered the kitchen and overheard his last words. "I don't know, sweetheart. That just sounds so . . . unkind. Wouldn't it be wise to call the police? And maybe put a missing person report on him?"

Antonio shook his head. "The first thing the police would ask us is if we talked to him before he went missing, and what were his last words. I'd tell them he said he'd be gone for eight to nine weeks, and he can't discuss anything. They'd probably tell me he's not missing because he informed us he'd be gone. My take? We just wait and hope he'll return soon."

He sighed, and this one was genuine. "But if he pulls this again, I'll sell Gary Collins my half of the karate school and start my own business someplace else."

"Who is Gary Collins?" Natasha asked.

"Remember, honey? I told you about him. He's the one who owns that company next door. Wants to buy the school so he can build a larger parking lot." Another sigh, then he added, "Yeah, if John doesn't come back when he said he would, or even call us, Gary Collins might get what he wants."

Natasha smiled and slapped him lightly on the shoulder. "Don't say that. You and John have been friends since you were children. You told me so yourself. A matter like this should only test your friendship to make it stronger, not to destroy it."

"She is right," Bonita said, looking away.

Anthony rubbed his shoulder just as thunder rumbled outside. "Wow. I'd better get to the school before it starts raining."

"But can you go there this late?" Natasha asked. "Didn't the mayor order a curfew? Because of the gang problems?"

"Yes, but that doesn't apply to me. I have a business to run."

Worry crossed his wife's face. "I don't know, sweetheart. Curfew or not, you told me the neighborhood is dangerous at night."

He turned around and took her in his arms. "I'm not concerned about a bunch of punks going around causing trouble. Not only do I know ten Japanese words," he grinned, "I also know Smith and Wesson."

"Huh?" This came from both women.

"Just before John left, he insisted I start keeping a gun in the safe," he said. "A little one. A revolver. And besides, some rules are made to be broken. And the mayor's in no position to tell *me* what to do. Besides, it wouldn't hurt to check in once in a while, make sure Kahn remembered to lock up. That kind of thing."

His eyes brightened. "Here's an idea. Instead of staying here worrying, come with me." He glanced at Bonita, then at what she was working on. "You've probably been at the books for hours, like always. You could use a break." *And maybe it'll get your mind off John.*

Minutes later, they gathered their rain jackets, piled into his SUV and headed for the school.

+⫶⟹ ❈ ⟸⫶+

He noticed that something was wrong the instant he turned the front doorknob. "I'm sure I locked the front door behind me yesterday. Now it's unlocked."

"Does anyone else have a key?" Natasha asked.

"Only John. Kahn only has keys to the side and back doors." He thought a moment. "Let's head downstairs and check the basement. I have to go down there anyway, the safe's down there." *And the gun*, he thought, wincing.

In the basement, he turned on all the lights and looked around. "Well, everything looks fine down here."

He opened the safe and reached in to retrieve the ledger.

A thumping noise came from upstairs. "Probably just a tree branch hitting a window," he said. They stayed quiet for a moment, listening, and the noise came again. "Stay here, I'll check it out," he told them.

Take the gun!" Natasha said.

With another wince, he complied with her request and headed up the stairs.

No one was upstairs, so he walked outside and looked around. Seeing nothing, he headed back inside to continue his search. In his hurry, he forgot to lock the front door.

+⫶⟹ ❈ ⟸⫶+

When Natasha and Bonita heard the six shots, one after another, they screamed, then huddled together in fear. Moments later, unable to bear not knowing another second, they headed upstairs.

When they were about halfway up the stairs, they heard a new noise.

"What is that?" Natasha whispered.

"Someone's . . . crying," Bonita replied, and they quickened their pace.

They found Antonio just outside the open office door, sitting next to a body already surrounded by a pool of blood. His gun was on the floor next to the body and his shoulders were heaving. The women raced to his side.

"It's Kahn!" Antonio sobbed. "He must have come in the back door. I didn't know, I didn't know!"

Natasha, terrified, yelled, "Let's call the police and ambulance."

She reached for the phone, but after a moment, looked at them with panicked eyes. "No dial tone. It's not working."

He pulled himself from the floor and checked the phone, leaving his gun next to Kahn's body.

He listened, then said to Bonita, "She's right."

−101−

"Maybe the electrical storms knocked the phones off," Bonita said.

He shook his head. "Not possible. The phone lines aren't connected by the same lines—"

They all turned to the front door, which had just been flung open. The Mal-A-Dies gang flooded into the room, followed by the hulking Gary Collins.

Collins took in the scene, then said, "Hum. I was heading over here anyway, but you've just made things easier for me. Seems as though you just shot your janitor, who was breaking into your school to rob it."

"What are you talking about?" Antonio sputtered. "He didn't break in—"

"But don't you see? You shot him dead. I heard the shots and rushed right over, thinking to help you. But when I get here, I find out that you and these pretty women got into a fight with him. And during the fight, he managed to stab all three of you before you shot him. Everyone dies, and no witness. The police will love it. Easy wrap-up, you see."

He smiled at Antonio and waved to the gang members. "Little change of plans, boys. You'll need your weapons."

Some of them drew knives from their belts.

"I hope you don't take this the wrong way," Collins said. "This isn't personal, this is just business. You all die tonight, and I get my payback tomorrow."

Collins glanced at Antonio's revolver, then turned to the gang leader. "I heard six shots. He's out of bullets. Go ahead, do them all. And then burn this place to the ground. Save me the cost of demolishing this junk heap."

"NO!"

Before Antonio could stop her, Bonita began running down the hallway toward the basement. A gunshot rang out, and a millisecond later, she fell, bleeding from her back, and was still.

"You idiot!" Collins yelled. "Don't shoot anyone, stab them. The evidence has to match the story we'll tell the police."

While Collins was distracted, Antonio tried to make a run for the front door, but was captured by the gang members and stabbed to death. Natasha was soon cornered and met the same fate.

+⊱—— ⚜ ——⊰+

After their first slip-up, the Mal-A-Dies did as instructed. By the time the last one rushed out the door, flames were shooting from the front window. By the time the fire department arrived, it was too late to save the building.

A few days later, Gary Collins applied to buy the property from the city. It only took slight grease on the wheels to have the property condemned; since the owners didn't immediately lay claim to it after the fire, the city considered it abandoned property. Thanks to the total destruction of the existing structure, Collins was able to go from abandoned, empty lot to parking lot within two weeks.

While he stood and watched the parking lot striper applying lines to the fresh asphalt, he pulled his cell phone out and made a call. The voice on the other end was pleased at the news, as he expected. Before he ended the call, Collins smiled and said, "Sometimes it's nice to have a fox like you in the henhouse. Makes it easier to take care of business."

"Yes," the voice replied. "But this time, it was more than just business . . . it was personal."

Collins laughed, then said goodbye. As soon as the police and fire department left, he had a lot to do.

23

John, Feldman and Vincent continued their training. The past weeks had been brutal at times, but John found himself gaining more admiration each day for Vincent, especially since the young genius was willing to help him and the others with the tougher parts of their academic courses. One day, after a particularly grueling run, Lynch allowed them a ten-minute rest before going to the next exercise. They flopped down under the nearest shade tree and fought to regain their breath.

"Well, I *had* kind of worried about you guys," John said as soon as he was able. "But here we are—nearly finished with basic and ready for the Last One Standing."

"I still can't believe that you're nervous about it," Vincent said, pulling himself to a sitting position and wiping the sweat still pouring from his brow. "I mean, from what you told me about your military service, *nothing* should bother you."

John turned onto his side, groaning with the effort. "Like I said, I've been through challenges in a mock wilderness setting, but I've never done anything that prepared me for space travel."

They'd been told that the competition would take place in a specially built chamber that had little gravity. Thanks to the low gravitational pull, the cadets could perform incredible feats of gymnastics and martial arts to show their skills in hiding and using the element of surprise. A five-man team would be chosen from each company. Each team would wear different colors from all the others.

"I can kind of understand why we have to wear camouflage makeup," Feldman said, wiping sweat from his face with a towel. "It's a psychological thing. But that life-light we'll have to wear on a belt—it just sounds kind of creepy."

"Not creepy," John said. "Practical. Remember, we're getting ready for a dangerous mission. The life-light will remind us just how serious our training really is. When we start, everyone's light will be shining. That means the cadet's active. Alive. If our opponent hits our light, that's a lethal blow, and the light goes off. When the entire team's lights are out . . . well, that means that team is out. At least we'll be able to choose our weapons."

Vincent leaned against the tree. "Yeah, made of plastic."

"High-impact plastic that can still kill a man," John reminded him. "I figure most of us will choose batons. That's what I'm going to pick. Best for hitting an opponent's life-light."

Vincent and Feldman listened with care, and nodded, knowing that when it came to hand-to-hand combat, Cadet John Richards knew what he was talking about.

⊹⟫⟫⟫ ❦❧ ⟪⟪⟪⊹

From Company 001, John was elected captain. John's first choice for his crew was Feldman; his second was Maria Ross, a cadet Vincent admired for her level head and ability to overcome, with ease, every physical challenge the Academy threw at them. To tease him, John waited until the last call to choose Vincent. Vincent didn't care. He'd figured John was just doing that to rib him. Still, he was secretly ecstatic at hearing his name finally called. Until then, he'd thought John was only helping him survive the Academy. Now, John had chosen him for its most important competition.

He checked the heat detectors on his wrists. They'd been issued the devices to know where the opposing team was located. Then, he looked at John who, like the rest of the team, was dressed in navy blue with a white belt.

As soon as he heard General Jones ring the bell and call, "Let the competition begin," he vowed to do his best.

One by one, each team lost one of their teammates. Soon, only two groups were left: Company 001 and Company 008. Feldman, Maria and one other had been eliminated, so only John and Vincent were left from their team. Their problem was, the other team still had four live members.

Vincent checked his heat detector, noted the other team marching straight their way, and devised a plan. As the group neared them, they connected two batons together and buried the connecting wire under the ground. Then they hid in the bushes on either side, grasping their batons.

As soon as the other team got close enough, they each pulled their baton toward themselves, which raised the wire and tripped the other team, causing all four to land on their life-light buttons.

⊹⟫⟫⟫ ❦❧ ⟪⟪⟪⊹

Their winning team was awarded points, but still not enough to be the #1 team. But now, it was time for the Freedom Run. If they won the Freedom Run, they would be able to advance in rank. The time to beat was 7:20 minutes.

Vincent had progressed, but was still their slowest runner. John would run with him, and Feldman would keep track of the time and set the pace for the rest of the company.

Things went great until Vincent fell halfway during the race, forcing him to catch up with half a lap and 30 seconds to go. He pushed himself harder than he ever had, chanting to himself, *I can't fail, I can't fail!*

He finished the race at the exact time of 7:19 minutes, and fell to the ground in exhaustion. John dropped down beside him, followed by each member of the company as they finished. After a short rest, he found himself being picked up and carried on their shoulders all the way back to camp as they all shouted in victory.

⁎⟞⟝ ✿✿ ⟞⟝⁎

"Hey, you okay?"

John looked up at Vincent, who was polishing his new boots. "Am I okay?" he said. "Funny . . . usually it's *me* asking *you* that question."

Vincent grinned at him. "Fair enough. But I've gotta say, you've been pretty quiet today."

It was the next day, and they were settling into their new dorm. Every cadet had been issued new uniforms, but the top-ten cadets in each company were assigned new and better living quarters on the opposite side of the base. The next day, those cadets would start a one-week class in Time Clauses 101, the course promised them at the beginning of their training. In spite of repeated questions, all they'd been able to find out was the class would cover their Time Travelers Academy Manual, but much more in-depth.

Seeing their high spirits about winning the race, Lynch had chewed them all out that morning about their grooming. John well knew that it was to keep their egos in check; but finally, Vincent had learned not to take Lynch's attitude adjustment sessions personally.

Vincent slapped at his boot tip with the rag to give it a high shine, just like John had taught him, and then returned to polishing. "So, you never answered my question. What's going on in the great and wonderful Cadet Richards's head right now?"

"Oh, I'm just thinking about home," John admitted. "Thinking about the leave we'll get in 30 days."

Vincent kept polishing, but eyed him. "What, you got a girlfriend back home?"

"Yeah. Is it that obvious?"

"Not really. Just the most likely reason someone would be homesick, I guess. But hey, I'm sure she's waiting for you, just waiting to hear how you're doing. Like I hope my mom and dad are."

John looked away from him and said, "I hope so. After all this, I . . . don't know. When I got drafted, we were still working out where we were." He chuckled. "I'd even bought her a ring. Was too chicken to give it to her. Now, I wish I had."

Vincent gave the boot a final buff, then stowed his rag in his kit. "Well, don't worry. In 30 days, you'll get your chance."

"I hope so," John said just as the bell rang for chow.

"During this training," Professor Rubiano said, "you'll learn all the laws of time travel, the mechanical needs of the time machine, the dangers of time travel, and how the time machine works. This is the last and final class. It's one week long, and on a pass-fail basis. Your manual will be your guide, but since you've already read it, we'll be heading for unknown territory now, you might say. You've already been through all the scientific classes, math, chemistry, and so on. In this class, you will put everything together."

John glanced at Vincent and muttered, "About time."

Vincent stifled a chuckle and kept his eyes on Rubiano.

"As you learned in your orientation," Rubiano said, "the time machine simply increases time while going at a fast speed. It can't travel at the speed of light, *but* it can reach other galaxies by going at a fast speed *and* increasing time. Once it reaches its destination, you'll be able to use the machine to reverse time to that time matching the constant of universal time. Earth's time.

"We will cover the following time clauses: the grandfather clause, the twin clause, Williams' theory of relativity, chaos theory, time-equilibrium range, and . . . the time eliminators theory."

At the last mention, everyone perked up. Finally, they might learn more about them—and mostly, how to prevent them from showing up on their mission.

"First, the laws of the universe. Most important to your survival, all laws must be obeyed. The universe is a living, dynamic entity. Its existence is beyond human comprehension. Any life has a birth, a beginning. The universe's birth came in the Big Bang. Since the universe's first birth, it has been destroyed once that we know of."

Feldman held up his hand. "I remember your saying that on our first day. What possibly has the power to destroy the entire universe?"

Rubiano grinned. "I'm glad you asked. You. You have that power. And here's how you do it. You go backward in time and cause a paradox so severe, the universe will collapse. At that point it will explode in a Big Bang, basically restarting time again. But," his face lost its grin, "the universe, like any living thing, has defenses. The universe protects itself with entities called time eliminators."

"What are they?" Vincent asked. "I mean, I've been dying to know since the first time I head the term. You mentioned they were theoretical. So what basis is there for believing they're real?"

"It's more than just a term, and if you don't know about them, you literally could die . . . as well as destroy everything in your current universe," Rubiano said. "Time eliminators protect the universe from harm, specifically from dramatic changes in the universal constant time. As you've already learned, it's comparatively easy to go into the future. It's also possible to go into the past. But going into a time that has already been set—the past—will cause time eliminators to appear and stop you. At least, based on everything we know.

"Part of the reason they might appear is because of the grandfather clause: the theory that says that if you go back in time and take some action, like killing your grandfather, you would have changed everything in history from that point. In fact, with your grandfather dead, you would never even have been born. So, if you ever go back in time, you have to be careful. Anything you do will cause a change. Simply eating food, buying a certain pair of shoes . . . anything you do might cause a disruption in the time that has already been set."

One student asked, "Eating food? Buying shoes? But . . . those are such minor things."

"Chaos theory basically states that causes can come from seemingly minor effects. Like a bird that flaps its wings, if that bird isn't there, then that ripple in the air from its wings wouldn't be there, either. That ripple might lead to a tornado or storm. If that bird was in the past, it could change the future by something as simple as its wings flapping.

"Using the grandfather scenario as an example, what if you ate the same food your grandfather was supposed to eat? And since you ate his meal, he decides to eat something else, something that gives him food poisoning. He becomes sick, and decides to rest and sleep instead of conceiving your father that day. Guess what? You were never born!"

"Then what happens to me if I was never born?" asked the student.

Rubiano smiled. "I don't think you'd ever finish your meal, because you weren't meant to exist at that point. If someone or something causes you not to be born, or even if you caused yourself not to be born, something would stop you before you took your first bite of the food."

"Why?" asked the student. "What will stop me from finishing my meal?"

"Time eliminators."

The class was silent, considering the implications. Rubiano broke the silence.

"Imagine yourself in a world that happened in the past. And that the meal you ate was connected to the birth of your father. By eating something your grandfather was supposed to eat, you caused a paradox in time. This paradox triggered the time eliminator. So the meal you ate was a time bomb of sorts. In fact, we'll be learning a great deal about time bombs, starting today. How to spot them and try to avoid them, for instance."

Feldman asked, "Sir, you're saying that time travel in the past is possible. But if someone *were* to go into the past, these so-called time bombs could be anything from a meal to a car or even a simple phone call. So how can we possibly know which action could be a time bomb?"

"Good question. First, let me add, the farther you go backward in time, the more time bombs you'll encounter. But, to your question: We *can* detect these time bombs, thanks to a law called the Wayne Theory: Once a time is set, it can't be changed, because time will protect itself from change."

He paused, passed his gaze over each cadet. "Even though we've never seen a time eliminator—and I pray that none of us ever does—we know what the effects of doing so would be. Even if you don't believe they exist, I cannot warn you enough: If you are ever called back in time, you must do everything in your power to avoid triggering, or calling out, a time eliminator. They will take whatever action they must to protect the timeline . . . even if it means destroying you."

For the first time, the class began to understand the risks of the mission before them. Some of the cadets looked down at their desks; others looked away from the professor.

"Now, on to answering Feldman's excellent question." Rubiano picked up an object from the table.

"As an example, let's use the meal you ordered that you shouldn't have—the one your grandfather was going to eat, but didn't. When you were at the counter ordering the meal, the time-equilibrium range, or TER, jumped from 30 points to 70. How do you know that, and what do those numbers mean?" He held up the watch. "Because this detects that range. The higher the range, the more in danger the wearer of disrupting the timeline and alerting the time eliminators."

Necks craned, but only befuddled looks were shared by the students.

"I don't get it," Vincent muttered. "Something that high-powered should look high tech, but it looks just like an ordinary wristwatch."

John shrugged. "Easier to hide that way."

Vincent's eyes widened. "Oh, I get it. Dick Tracy stuff."

John grinned at him.

"Now, back to that infamous meal," Rubiano said. "While the meal is being prepared, this indicator jumps to 75. Once you sit down to eat it, it jumps to 77. When your fingers move toward the meal, the reading, called a TER, reaches past 80. What happens when it reaches past 90 on its way to 100?"

Vincent answered, "Time eliminators appear at 100?"

"Yes, but that's just an assigned number based on the Williams theory. The theory proposes that there is a point when the universe reaches its peak and resets itself. We have given that peak the number 100 for ease of measurement. Once this number is reached, time will reset itself and the entire universe will collapse at the point of the disturbance. The wearer's goal, then, is to always be aware of the watch, and if the reading begins rising, to immediately identify why so they can prevent it from rising.

"And that's why the time machine's reverse-time feature—the one that enables it to go past the universal timeline into the past—has been turned off. Those of you selected for this mission won't need it. Your only worry would be if you traveled twice in the future to the same timeline, and then tried to change what has already happened. For example, if you went into the future on Planet Peligroso and one of you died, no one could try to save you by going back before the tragedy occurred and trying to stop the tragedy. What has happened has happened, and can't be changed."

At that moment, an image jumped into John's mind. *The two men. That day at the jewelry store. One kept looking at his watch, and they both jumped out of the way of that couple, like they were scared of bumping into them. They had to go back in time to find me, and that's why they acted so odd. They were afraid of alerting the time eliminators. . . .*

He looked at the watch in awe. *So that's why they took so long to serve me with the draft papers. Too much risk. Until I was in that airport bathroom, I always had other people around me!*

He shook his head to clear the thought and turned his attention back to the class in time to hear Vincent say, "So if *any* past event can cause the time eliminators to appear, what if the light of a galaxy from one billion years ago hits Earth?

Rubiano nodded. "If you receive light waves one billion years old, chances are the planet no longer exists, because those light waves traveled one billion years at the speed of light. The light is only an illusion, so there is no disruption in a timeline."

Feldman asked, "Are you saying that if I went back in time and simply threw a rock into the Pacific Ocean, I might have caused a tsunami?"

"Exactly. Something that simple could change the world you know as your present. In fact, that tsunami might have other detrimental effects."

"Speaking of theories, though, here is the theory of how we believe time eliminators work. As you know, everything is made of atoms: protons, electrons and neutrons. When the time eliminators attack, they first separate all protons, electrons and neutrons, absorbing each, starting with the electrons. So, once the time eliminators attack, your body shoots out electrical sparks. Then all your protons, then neutrons are absorbed. And then? Well, you're gone out of existence."

He shrugged. "But, likely, none of us in this room has to worry about that . . . as long as we don't detonate any of the time bombs and create a severe paradox. Time travel is possible into the future, and no doubt, someday, anyone can travel to the future if they wish. But travel to the past must be outlawed because of this danger."

Except when the government needs to do it, John thought, yet thought it best not to challenge the professor about that—yet. But now, he finally understood just how risky this mission really was. If they succeeded, they could perhaps find a cure for the plague that threatened to decimate Earth's population. If they failed, humanity would disappear. But if they made one mistake that alerted and drew to them the time eliminators, they would destroy the current timeline of the universe, including Earth.

⊹⊱═══ ❀❀ ═══⊰⊹

At the end of the week, they took their exams. The next day, the results were in. The Academy was ready to pick the ten who would go to Planet Peligroso.

Vincent was a given. Chosen for his knowledge of physics and quantum mechanics, he'd already been training on repairing the time machine if it malfunctioned. Because time was so short, Mike Adams was personally tutoring him.

John wasn't a given, or didn't consider himself to be. But he was chosen to be in charge of the mission.

He was relieved to hear Feldman's name called. Sure, Feldman was a clown and a joker. But he was Vincent's best friend next to John, and would serve well as the mission's geography and security specialist. Maria Ross would also be part of the crew, and he was grateful. Her calm nature would be vital, as would be that of Juan Perez, the son of Mexican immigrants, who had proven himself as a team player.

James Wong was chosen as the crew's expert in mathematics, as well as its main pilot and navigator. He, along with Mission Specialist Suzie Cho, would also plot courses on their journey to avoid unforeseeable objects in space, like asteroids and black holes.

Sam Sizemore and Abdul Mohammad would serve as security speciaists. John didn't know about Sizemore, but knew Abdul was very religious, and very patriotic to America. They would serve the mission well.

John was less certain of Fred Willis. Not that Willis gave him any specific reason for worry. It was just that he didn't know Willis as well as the other crew-members. But, as the science officer and co-charge of the mission, he was certain he'd soon get to know Willis well enough to bet his life on him.

"Humanity is depending on the ten of you," General Jones said when he finished reading the names. "From this day forward, you will be called our planet's first galaxtronauts. You will now go through seven more days of training on the time machine. And . . . I regret disappointing the others . . . the class graduation will be postponed until the crew comes back. But . . ." he smiled, "considering that the mission involves time travel, we won't even have time to miss the crew before they're back."

His words brought chuckles, but then each cadet seemed to simultaneously fill in the missing words: not *when* the crew returned, but *if* they returned. A more somber group was dismissed and began mingling, speculating about the what-happens-next for both themselves and the mission crew.

It isn't fair.

Charlene Vaughn had rarely said or thought those three words in her life. She wasn't a whiner, and didn't respect people who were, but . . . it really, truly wasn't fair. She'd listened eagerly as the names were read, but felt sadder with each one called that wasn't hers. And even though her team didn't have the highest scores in the competition, she felt more qualified than some of the other names called.

While he was talking to Mike Adams, General Jones spotted her and summoned her aside. Then, she learned that the Academy had other plans for her talent—to stay and work in the facility's research lab.

"You won't be by yourself here," Jones assured her. "And you'll have much more freedom than before. The other 784 students will also be working at the Academy. You're the most important of them, though. It's just that . . . I very much hope the mission is successful. But there are so many variables. If the team doesn't make it, we need the research for a cure to continue."

"Look, I know it's not my area," Adams said. "But I think you'll be the perfect person to lead the research."

Charlene allowed herself a small sigh, then accepted the post as graciously as she could and arranged to have her possessions moved from Washington to a nearby apartment. Including the Pomeranian. And her first call was to Dr. Davies, who congratulated her on her new job and offered his full support. "We'll miss you here," he said, "but you're most needed right where you're at."

The ten galaxtronauts traveled by military Jeep back to the barracks to gather their clothes and personal belongings, then were taken to some newly built barracks on the opposite side of the base for more intense training. The new living quarters were like small apartments, housing one person to each room. Even though Vincent had long since stopped crying himself to sleep, John was happy to have his own pad again. Until that first night, when all he could think about was Bonita, wondering if she was angry at the time that had passed, and promising himself to make it up to her as soon as he could. If successful, in less than thirty days, he'd see her in person. And now, he was certain that he could give her the ring in good conscience.

After all, he thought, turning over to find a more comfortable spot on the new bed, *a guy who's saved the world needs to settle down on it as soon as possible.*

24

The seven days of training were solely about the time machine—how to lift off, navigate it, land it and what to do if something broke down.

"Which," Adams told them, "I pray never happens."

Finally, they were taken by Jeep to see the machine they'd been learning about on paper. Adams begged off, saying he had paperwork to catch up.

As they reached the building housing the time machine, they could see a helicopter bringing it in from the open dome. About the size of a large SUV, it was surprisingly nondescript to John, being constructed of the drab gray trilasteverium and with only small portholes for windows.

He glanced at Vincent, whose expression was very different, as though eager and energized at the sight.

While they viewed it, General Jones said, "And oh, by the way, the Ascendia Corporation fixed it."

"What was wrong with it?" John said. "Was it broken?"

"*Fixed* meaning we changed its programming so it can never go backward in time past the universal timeline."

John nodded. "Yes, Professor Rubiano mentioned that in class."

"Regrettable," Jones admitted. "One of the main purposes of the Academy was to be able to go back in time to a disaster or emergency that had just occurred—to either warn about the upcoming disaster or stop it ourselves. But," he sighed, "when it was theorized how the universe would stop us if we do, the plan was scrapped. Congress just recently banned it. Until this plague crisis happened, we were one step from losing our funding and being disbanded. Either that, or being placed under the control of a private corporation. . . . That's another reason this mission is so important. If successful, it will not only save the Earth, but the Time Travelers Academy, too."

John gave a low whistle. "I had no idea the very program was at stake, General. But believe me, if there's a way, it will be done. I'll see to it."

Jones looked at him fondly. "I suspected I'd made the right choice of person to lead the mission. Now, I'm sure of it."

He returned his gaze to the machine. "Knowing what you all know now, perhaps you can understand why I turned down a promotion from the President so I could stay here and oversee the Academy's success."

"What was the position you turned down, sir?" John asked, then grinned. "You're a four-star general, there's not much higher than that."

Jones returned his smile. "A few years ago, the former President asked me to accept his nomination for Secretary of Defense. But when I turned him down, I explained my goals for the Academy. He agreed with me. In fact, he wanted to see this Academy become the sixth branch of the military service and be renamed the United States Department of Time Travel. The current President offered the same promotion, but I declined it."

He turned his head toward the sentry guarding the entrance to the hangar. "Step outside. Close the door behind you."

Once the door closed, Jones turned back to the crew. "There's another reason why I want this Academy to succeed. Why it *must* succeed. It's something I swore I'd never tell anyone. But I need to tell you, so you'll know just how important your mission is.

"I was the first person to test the time machine," he said. "I volunteered to go on a brief journey three years into the future. Once there, I saw . . . something I couldn't believe at the time. I saw what we're experiencing now."

"You saw the plague happen, General?" Feldman asked.

Jones nodded, his eyes showing uncharacteristic unease. "To try to stop the spread of the disease, all uninfected persons in the world were forced to relocate to isolated islands. Then the order was given to launch nuclear weapons at the rest of the planet . . . not on our adversaries, but on ourselves. To decontaminate Earth. That was our only hope: to give the small number of remaining people on Earth a chance to survive. I managed to come back to this time just before the bombs were detonated."

He looked at each of them in turn. "We can't afford to fail. I have no idea what happened, but considering the fallout from a nuclear weapon, likely, there were no survivors. And you're the only living souls I've ever told about this."

⊱ ✾ ⊰

That night, a long black limousine eased through traffic toward the Pentagon. A lone man sat in the back. When his cell phone rang, he answered.

"Sir, we've cut and rewired some of the navigational aids," the caller said. "Not many. They'll get off the ground. They just won't be able to get back." He chuckled. "Unless they can figure out which wires we crossed. With only a week of training, that's not likely."

"Very good. Let's see if they can get back without eyes and a map."

The man ended the call and looked up at the lights of the capitol speeding by.

25

Because of security precautions and the need to keep the mission secret, there would be little fanfare for this, the time machine's first official mission. With Mike Adams, General Jones, and Secretary Lanti standing by, the support crew raced around, doing their final checks. As new head of the Academy's research team. Charlene was there too. Her eyes held longing, but also resolution. Adams noticed, leaned toward her and whispered, "Don't worry, Dr. Vaughn. Remember what the general said. The TTA's next mission, you'll be part of the crew."

"*If* there's a next mission," she whispered back. "*If* this mission can help stop the plague."

He studied her face, which had turned stony, and shifted his eyes back to the launching pad.

Because it wasn't yet known how the machine would handle takeoff holding a full crew, it had been moved from its hanger to the landing pad next to it. Should something go wrong, the multimillion-dollar hangar would be preserved.

One by one, each of the ten galaxtronauts eased through the machine's open door and took their seats. Then the support crew sealed the outside door and stepped back. General Jones wished them good luck. John nodded through the front porthole and started up the time machine.

Time slowed to a stop. Through the craft's windows, the crew saw everyone outside as frozen in place. For them, time was moving normally. But John knew that those outside saw him and the other crewmembers moving and talking at blinding speed.

With the help of the other crewmembers, he rotated the time machine's bow upward, toward the sky. The engines turned on and the time machine took flight.

As soon as they escaped Earth's gravity, he aligned the time machine with Peligroso's coordinates. Their speed increased to 500,000 miles per hour yet they also increased time; they were now going hundreds of thousands of times their current speed. He was surprised at how few vibrations the craft made, and relieved that everything on the craft was behaving exactly as their training told them it should.

They would reach Peligroso in ten to twelve hours. On their journey, they could see Earth turning rapidly and all the planets moving rapidly around the sun. As a precaution, they wouldn't try to reach their maximum speed until they escaped the solar system. Still, the sights fascinated them. They saw stars being born and supernovas, they saw planets form, galaxies making complete revolutions.

"Kinda like being Christopher Columbus, isn't it?" Vincent said at one point.

"Yeah. The first to travel to a distant, unknown land, not knowing what we'll see once we get there."

"Isn't it amazing?" Feldman added. "Christopher Columbus and his crew thought the Earth was flat. Now, we're the first to travel to another galaxy." His comment brought smiles and nods from Suzie Cho and Maria Ross, who were monitoring the consoles assigned to them.

James Wong was currently piloting the craft. John jokingly asked him, "So, what do we do again if the machine breaks? We're all alone here. And who would we have to depend on to repair it?"

"Yeah," Wong replied. "Where's a nerd when you really need one?"

This brought grins all around as they looked at Vincent, who was doing perhaps his hundredth review of the time machine's manual. He looked at them with a geek smile. Since the day he'd taken over the instructor's class, Vincent's nickname had become "Mr. Nerd," or just "Nerd" for short. He didn't like it, yet when someone he liked called him that, he tolerated it. But not without retribution.

Feldman pointed his finger at him and said, imitating a recorded warning message, "Here is my Nerd alert . . . Nerd, Nerd, Nerd."

Vincent came back with, "This is my *fake gold* alert," and pointed at Feldman's front teeth, which were all gold with the initials E.L.F inscribed on them. Then he said, "You should have gotten a second opinion from another dentist. Or maybe you should have called a nerd for advice before you did something that *dumb*."

But it was all in fun, John knew. Each of them depended on each other for their lives, and if it came down to it, they would give their lives for the others if need be.

Thirty minutes into their flight, they passed the edge of the Milky Way and into deep space. They heard a loud boom as they passed out of the Milky Way, and looked out their window to see the galaxy making full-revolution turns. Soon, it turned to a pinpoint in the distance, and then disappeared all together.

"Well, there goes our home," Maria whispered. "But we'll be back."

Within ten hours, they reached the edge of the Lejana Galaxy. Moments after, Vincent told them, "Okay, we've got Peligroso in our sights, folks."

One hour later, they saw a massive cloud of dust and gas about 10,000 times the length of the solar system. This was unexpected, and potentially dangerous. Now, John had to decide whether to go around the massive nebula of dust and gas, or through it.

"Wong, come over here," he said, and explained what he needed.

Moments later, Wong looked up from his workspace and said, "It'll take about five minutes to get through, so I vote we just plow through it."

John nodded. "Through it we'll do it, then."

Six minutes into the nebula cloud, an alarm sounded. Wong scanned the readings he had now while Vincent did a visual out the window.

"I don't understand it," Wong said. "Everything on the screen looks fine."

"Then you should look out the window," Vincent said. "I don't know what the heck's going on, but nothing's matching your screen readings. Nothing!"

A quick decision was made, and Vincent and several other crewmembers stood at separate portholes and the front window, talking John through steering a series of sharp turns to avoid the many new planets forming—planets the auto-pilot wasn't picking up and Wong wasn't seeing on the screen. John tried to steer away from and around all the newly formed planets, but as soon as they avoided one, another one was formed and became a deadly obstacle in their path.

They had nearly reached the edge of the cloud when a small planet made of pure gold was formed. One of its asteroids hit the time machine, causing them to flip off course.

Thankfully, things were happening so fast there was no time for panic, as though they had made a silent agreement that panic could come later, when they finally had a clear approach to the planet.

Once they regained control of the craft, Vincent, Feldman and Wong did a quick check of all their navigational devices. To their dismay, during their brief loss of time control, millions of years had passed.

After a self-diagnosis of the time machine, it was determined that a sensor was damaged under the hull.

"Vincent, you make the repairs," John said. "Wong, please help him."

The repairs required exiting the craft, but they'd been trained for such an emergency. Vincent and Wong suited up and ventured out. The others, inside, listened in and watched through the portholes.

As they worked, small meteorites of pure gold passed the men.

"Wow," Maria, the second-in-command, said as she watched them. "Those must have been the ones that flew away from that planet we almost hit. Any one of them could be worth tens of millions of dollars back home."

Wong apparently had the same idea. While Vincent located, then repaired the sabotaged wires, Wong reached out and tried to grab one of the small objects. Distracted by his side-mission, he ended up venturing about 100 feet away from the craft, disregarding John's warnings by saying, "Hey man, you know I'm not going anywhere without you. I just want a little souvenir to take home. Might even open up a little auction house and pick up some cash."

As he spoke, he reached and grabbed three of the objects and inserted them into one of his suit's many pockets.

But John had just seen something Wong and Vincent hadn't. As soon as Vincent reconnected the wires, he was able to determine they were near a giant star that would soon ignite in a massive explosion, giving them only minutes before they had to be far away.

At John's admonition, Vincent quickly gathered up his tools and headed for the ship's hatch. But a larger asteroid pulled Won further away from the ship into a ring of millions of the small gold, and then platinum rocks. He was now 250 feet away, and moving farther away each second.

"You have to get back to the ship, and now!" John shouted into the transmitter.

"Just a few more, come on!"

"No, we have an emergency here—"

A bright light emanated from the cloud, indicating that shockwaves and heat from the star's explosion were imminent. Wong didn't even flinch, just kept saying, "I'm rich, I'm rich!"

"Wong, this is your last chance. Either come back this instant, or you're on your own."

Wong looked at him, but his eyes no longer held any reason. "You go on," he said. "I'm fine. Just pick me up on the way back." He held up one of the platinum rocks and grinned madly. "Got my fare right here."

Reluctantly, John made the hardest decision of his life. "Vincent, Suzie, get us out of here."

None of the crewmembers spoke, but none protested. They all knew what was at stake.

━◆━ ◆◆ ━◆━

The crew managed to navigate their way out, but Vincent, looking at his instruments said, "We still have problems."

John whipped his head around to look at him.

"This star is so large and unstable, it'll go supernova any moment."

John considered what would happen. If the explosion didn't kill then, the shockwaves would. "Increase the time-speed," he said. "We have to get away from it."

The strategy worked, but it threw them off-course. They were now one billion years farther into the future than they had expected or needed to go. They arrived at Peligroso's coordinates, but the planet wasn't there. All the crew saw was empty space.

Vincent said, eyes wide, "It's been engulfed in a black hole. And we're headed right into it."

There was no other choice. John said, "Reverse time until the planet appears."

Over the next several minutes, they saw planet after planet emerging from the black hole. Finally, Vincent shouted, "That's it! That's Planet Peligroso."

John nodded. "Good. Now, keep going back until it's far enough from the black hole that we don't have to worry about falling into it. Aim for our approximate time coordinates while you're at it."

Vincent gave him a sideways grin. "You know, just because you're the boss, you don't have to be so . . . so *bossy*."

"Yes, I do," John said, allowing a small smile to emerge.

Once Vincent accomplished the order, they slowed time and prepared to land. John's heart was still breaking over Wong's death, but that the mission had survived past the star's explosion helped offset his grief. The mission had to be their priority now.

26

Their landing was without incident, but they were shocked to find a barren planet with no sign of life. "It's like a desert," Maria called out from where she and Muhammad were checking the planet's readings.

"Come over here, John," Muhammad said.

When John did, he pointed at the screen. "See that? Some kind of dense underground structures."

"Likely, an ancient city at some point in the planet's past," Suzie speculated. "But . . ."

"What?" John asked her. *What else could possibly go wrong?*

"If my calculations are right, we're not at the right time," she said. "We're about one million years into the planet's future. *After* the bomb destroyed it."

John thought a moment, then said, "We're still going to explore it. Maybe it'll give us some idea about the civilization that once existed here. What've we got to lose? If we confirm what you just said, we'll just get back on and go back a million years. That's what the time machine's for, anyway."

He held up the time sensor, firmly strapped to his wrist. "As long as we're careful, the sensor will tell us if we're in trouble."

"Want me to stay behind and watch the place?" Feldman said, although his face said something completely different.

John shook his head. "No need. We'll just secure the machine and leave it. I'd feel better if we all stayed together."

They locked the time machine's doors and parked it against a nearby hill. Then John heard Vincent gasp.

He looked in the direction Vincent pointed, and saw something that looked just like the satellite towers back home, if buried with sand almost to their tops.

"They must have used VOR to communicate with each other," Vincent whispered in awe.

John looked at him. "What's that?"

"VOR? Stands for very high-frequency omni-directional range. Like . . . Like satellite television works. VOR's used by air traffic controllers to guide planes in, and for transponder communication. No reason it couldn't work here."

Willis, the science officer, spoke up. "Before we left, I did a rough assessment of the history of life on the planet. Just speculation based on Peligroso's inhabitants being organic life-forms like us."

"So what did you find?" John asked.

"Based on my projections, the bomb that destroyed this planet evaporated all water on the surface and mutated all the animal life. The planet once had a plenty of water, but the bomb caused all hydrogen and oxygen atoms to repel each other. The plants and animals that survived? Their defense was to go underground. Their source of water is the blood of other animals."

Suzie winced. "Like vampires? Eeewwwww."

John chuckled. "Maybe so, but I don't doubt what he said. I recall reading that the storms on Planet Peligroso would be electrical in nature, and would be attracted to liquid, and blood's a liquid. Let's move on."

Using motion sensors, they determined that something was moving underground. They moved in the direction the sensors indicated, watchful for any openings that an unfriendly presence might use for a surprise attack. They soon encountered a cave with what appeared to be ruins of a primitive living-space. In the cave, they encountered something familiar—a symbol identical to the Time Travelers Academy logo on their suits.

"How can that be?" Willis asked. "We've never even *been* here."

"Forget about that," Vincent said. "Just forget it."

Alarmed at how shaky Vincent's voice sounded, John immediately looked at him.

"That . . . That looks like tombstones," he stuttered.

He followed Vincent's pointing finger, and a closer inspection revealed that Vincent was right. Gruesomely so. It was impossible to make out the names on each of the five stones. They could only tell that one name contained a "V," another the letter "G."

Feldman did a Carbon 14 dating on the cave. "Well, at least my dating equipment came through the trip without being sabotaged," he said. "It's showing about one million years ago from the time we expected to land."

John's face was grim. "So it looks like we *have* been here before. Five memorials and nine of us now. Looks like only *four* of us are going to survive to go home."

Muhammad dropped to his knees and started praying. After a moment, he looked up. "I'm praying for all of us," he said. Then, more reluctantly, "mostly that I be one of the four who makes it back home."

Suzie looked at memorial that showed the letter G. "The letters are so old. That could be a Z, or an E, or—"

"Attention!" John barked. "Listen to me, and listen to me clearly. The only thing we're sure of is that we have to get back on the ship and go farther back in time. Something awaits us there, and Earth is depending on us. We're at an advantage because we already know this future. But . . . this future hasn't been set. We have to be careful when we go back in time on *this* planet that *this* future isn't the one that awaits us. Because if someone dies, we can't go back to the same timeline in the future to stop it or change it. What I mean is, maybe this is a warning we left ourselves.

"And remember your training. What we see here isn't real, or the last answer. The future can change. All we know is that there's danger. We also know that if we make the right moves, we'll all make it back home alive."

"But how can we *know* that?" Vincent said. "And what could we possibly do to prevent," he waved a hand toward the tombstones, "*this* from happening?"

"Remember, what you're looking at is this planet's future, and its future hasn't been set yet," John said. "We'll establish a rule that we all stick together. No one will separate from another. And no one will be left behind."

"Sir, what if the decisions you're making now were what caused us all to die in the first place?" Vincent asked.

John leveled his gaze at him. "You're the genius, you tell me."

"Okay, I will. No matter what we do to prevent this, our efforts might have actually caused it to happen."

"But what if we do nothing?" John countered. "That might also cause the five memorials. But we're at an advantage . . . time that hasn't been set can change the future, and at least we already know ours."

A long moment later, Vincent nodded. "You're right. I just wish we knew how it was all going to turn out."

John reached out and patted his friend's shoulder. "You and me both. But the only way to find out is to keep going, no matter what."

He looked around the cave entrance, deemed it safe, and said, "Okay, while we're here, let's look around a bit more."

Deeper in the cave, they found more evidence of their future existence, and soon, Willis felt they had enough to plot a timeline to go one million years back. But as they headed deeper in the cave, Vincent said, "What's that noise?"

Before any of them could respond, a humanoid being that looked eerily like a giant Hercules leaped out from a hidden passage, and proceeded to try to make some of the crew his dinner. But thanks to his great size, he was slow, and the two crewmembers were able, if barely, to evade him.

"Run back to the time machine!" John yelled, and they all raced back toward the cave's entrance, then kept running in the direction of the time machine.

"Hey, if that's the future of this planet," Vincent gasped as he ran, "I don't want it."

"Just be glad we were forewarned," John replied, breathing heavily. "And be glad you're still in shape from the Freedom Run."

The future Vincent didn't want came upon them anyway. Before they could get back to the time machine, they saw what looked like a thundercloud generating red lightning in the distance. But this thundercloud was almost on the ground. Within seconds, they were buffeted by gale-force winds.

The flashes came closer, and John gave the order to run back to the cave "Faster," he screamed against the howling wind and crackling flashes of light.

Then, he saw an open crevice in the nearby rocks. "Over here," he yelled, and they all headed for it.

Except Fred Willis. As soon as they hid themselves, the wind died down a bit and the dust cleared enough for them to see Fred Willis, running about twenty yards ahead of them, too far to hear John's command. Before any of them had time to react, lightning struck Willis and they watched, in shock, as he began shrinking, collapsing into himself like a paper bag having the air sucked out of it. Under his suit, a red fog began emanating from the screaming man's nose, mouth and ears.

"Willis!" Feldman screamed. "Run!"

But he couldn't, it seemed. While they watched, his face continued collapsing, as though every bit of fluid was being pulled from it. Soon, they saw what was left of him, including his suit, turn to dust that was swept up as a blood-red fog into the storm.

Moments later, the wind and lightning abated as though it had never been.

Fearful that what had happened to Willis would happen to them if they tried to make it to the time machine, John decided they were safer back in the cave for the time being. "Just until we can make sure that the storm won't return," he said. "Or . . . until we can figure something out."

In agreement, they headed back to the cave entrance, and soon had a plan to repel the creature in the cave. Figuring it was sensitive to ultrasound, at Maria's suggestion, they put their communication devices on the highest pitch. After a few hours with no reappearance, they decided to make another run for it.

"You know something?" Vincent said. "We started with ten, and now, with Wong and Willis . . . dead, now we're only eight."

"Cut that out," John said. "There's no sense in worrying about the future, especially since it hasn't been set yet. Now, let's go. And remember, everyone stay together. No running ahead."

When they were a few hundred feet away from the cave, they heard a roaring noise and turned around to see a large tornado. Now they couldn't run back to the cave, but could only run forward.

As though by silent agreement that they wouldn't let anything else hinder them from their mission, they kept running toward the time machine trying to escape the massive twister.

The tornado grew strong and closer to them, yet somehow they all managed to make it to the time machine, then stop time and begin searching for the right timeline on Peligroso.

27

They were successful this time. But when they stumbled out of the machine, a group of men dressed in military uniforms took them captive.

The translation difficulties John had feared wouldn't be a problem. Surprisingly, the language on Peligroso was a quite understandable form of English. Unfortunately, the leader of the group, who identified himself as a captain, didn't want to hear John's explanation of why they were there. The captain left two of his men behind to guard the time machine. The rest hustled John and his crew toward a strange-looking building. Soon, they were in front of a long table. Behind the table were seated dour-faced older men and women the captain had identified as the city council.

The man in the middle asked John, "Explain your presence here."

"We're galaxtronauts," John said. "We come from a planet very similar to yours. A planet called Earth in the Milky Way galaxy. Our purpose is to . . . ah, to exchange technology." He had thought about it on the trip there, and decided that it was best to reveal as little as possible about their desperation to find a cure for the disease that threatened Earth. After the rough treatment by their captors, and seeing the distrust on these people's faces, he decided to continue the ruse.

But then, the stern look left the chief city councilman's face. "Your intent is only to exchange technology? So you have no wicked intentions toward us?"

"Ah, that's right," John said.

"Very well." He pointed to the guards standing on either side of the group. "Release them and get them comfortable chairs. I have many questions. And," he smiled at John, "I hope we can give you the answers you seek."

None of the crew had expected it to be so easy, but all John had to do was explain their dilemma—that because of meteorites that had come from Mars, two otherwise manageable Earth diseases had combined to become one that threatened to kill everyone on Earth within three of their years.

"I know just the person who can help you," the councilmember said. "And she is sitting right at this table."

He pointed, and a tall, blonde-haired woman stood. "My name is Auyda," she said, adjusting the robe she wore made of soft-green fabric. "I will be happy to help you, if we have the knowledge to do so. Based on what you have said here, I believe we can. But in exchange, we need your help. Your knowledge.

"Our nation is engaged in a war for our independence from our mother nation. Our reasons are many, and I will tell you those later. But, we are a small colony, and our mother nation does not wish us to have our freedom. Our world, until now, has been peaceful. And our small nation has no weapons. But we have heard that, on other planets in the past, they have many powerful weapons. Some called bombs. Others called guns. Others are also called nuclear bombs. These stories have filtered down to us through history, as well as the theory that there is a planet called Earth."

She smiled at them. "And now, our theory about a planet called Earth is proved as fact. So, in exchange for knowledge of how to save your Earth, we ask for any knowledge you can give us to gain our freedom from those who wish to take our freedom away."

Bombs? Guns? Nuclear bombs? They've got to be kidding.

But the earnest looks on all their faces told John they weren't. Unfortunately, the crew was under strict rules not to give technology to any civilization they could use to make a weapon. Even so, after hearing that she might be able to help them with a cure for the plague, he chose his words with care.

"Our civilization is peaceful," he said. "And we're not permitted to exchange weapons of destruction. But we're able to trade medical or scientific technology."

He glanced at Vincent, who glanced back and nodded, understanding what John wanted him to do. Vincent's expertise was in time travel, not medical science. Unfortunately, with Willis's death, they no longer had a science officer. But Vincent had already proved that he could talk his way out of just about anything.

"How about stem cell research?" he said, and quickly explained what that was. "Have you developed that?"

Auyda shook her head, and hers was one of several befuddled looks around the council table. "But if it can cure diseases, perhaps we can use that to negotiate with the mother nation for our freedom."

"Exactly," Vincent said. "You'll have knowledge they don't. Lifesaving knowledge. They'll be willing to listen to you if you have something they don't. Better than a weapon." He chuckled. "Because nobody gets killed."

⁜ ❧ ⁜

In her laboratory, which was a dream-lab by any scientist's standards, Auyda asked many questions of her guests from Earth. As it turned out, besides being beautiful enough to grace any fashion magazine back on Earth, Auyda was the head scientist at the colony's main government hospital, which had a staff of hundreds.

After viewing the lab, she took them to a large room that turned out to be their dining facility. But, except for the usual-looking tables and chairs scattered about, the room looked like the inside of a huge, glass-walled beehive.

Feldman looked at the honeycombs viewable through the glass and bees buzzing between them. "Wow. If it wasn't for those glass walls, I'd be really nervous right now."

Auyda smiled. "Our population has adapted to nourish ourselves with what I believe you would call honey. However, we haven't forgotten the old ways of preparing food. If you'd like something—"

"Ah, much appreciated, but no thank you," John said, smiling back at her. "That's another one of our orders."

Auyda nodded, said, "As you wish," and pointed to a nearby table surrounded by chairs.

Once they settled, she explained the situation on their planet. "Our nation is looked at as a runaway colony. We are considered renegades and traitors to the motherland. Soon after our declaration of independence from the mother nation, they declared war against us."

John glanced around at the calm surroundings. "So, should we be on our guard right now?"

"There is little danger to you," she said. "So far, the mother nation has mostly used threats, plus economic sanctions. Also isolation. We were all banished to this place, which is actually an island surrounded by water. But lately, the mother nation has become more aggressive. We're constantly being invaded from across the water. When the wind changes directions, we know they will come in their military balloons and attack us, throwing various poisons that pollute our water supplies."

"Balloons?" John said, surprised.

She nodded. "We have heard that other planets in history have something called planes that fly through the air very fast. Perhaps you have them on Earth. But our society has never been able to learn what they are or how to make them. But," her face fell, "I am glad for that. Perhaps with planes, everyone in our colony might already be dead. Our only safety is the water that separates us, because this gives us time to prepare for their attacks. We get most of our warnings through satellite transmissions. Mostly, we hide in the caves until the threat passes, and then decontaminate the water. It takes time and our precious resources to do this, but we have managed so far."

"Ah, yes, we saw things that looked like satellite towers," John said. "Can you believe that, on Earth, people use those to receive entertainment?"

Her smile became even sadder. "Perhaps someday, that will be our satellites' only purpose. I dream of that day." She looked away, then back to him. "But for now, we must help you with your mission. Because your plague might also be different than what we've seen, we need a copy of it to be sure."

John nodded. "That won't be a problem at all. We've brought samples of it. But . . . and you don't have to answer this if you don't choose to . . . what made your colony break away from your mother nation?"

"In our culture, fighters fight to the death in an arena, using ancient fighting techniques that I believe you on Earth might call martial arts. The practice began to protect the king, and grew to be a requirement for our compulsory military service. At the age of eighteen, a man must prove himself worthy at the skill. In the arena, he will either survive, or die. The mother nation was taking our best and brightest men, only to have them die in this dueling chamber." She looked down. "One of those men was my brother."

"Oh, I'm so sorry for your loss—"

"It's all right, it happened long ago." Then she looked up at him. "But we—the colonists—decided we couldn't let this continue. There were some of us who believed that . . . I suppose you might call it peace . . . that peace, as a force, was far more powerful than violence." She sighed. "We have been at war for the past four years."

"Our society is somewhat the same," John explained. "We have a draft, and at the age of eighteen, a young man must register his name. But it's not to take him off in a dueling chamber to fight to the death. It's just to have a list of contact information . . . in case of a national emergency."

She smiled. "That makes so much more sense to me. To have young warriors *ready* to defend our country or planet, but not require them to risk death until there is a real need. Our mother country could learn much from Earth."

"I hope we can learn much from your planet, too," John said. *Especially how to keep Earth from becoming as deserted as I saw your planet a million years from now.*

+⊱══ ❀❀ ══⊰+

He was escorted back to the time machine. There, he retrieved the safety-storage vial containing a sample of the plague organism. He gave this to Auyda, who charged her research team to find a way to cure the virus without destroying the Earth-human DNA.

In about an hour, the lead scientist came back with the results.

Auyda said to John, "You are very fortunate, as are we. He said that your plague organism is almost identical to one our planet was able to conquer—eradicate—thousands of years ago. We did this through a substance I believe you call a vaccine. Later, we developed a cure that would work even after someone contracted the plague. And we long ago had cures for both the bubonic plague and the avian flu."

"Wow," Maria said. "One cure for the flu? How do you get around the viruses mutating? That's been our biggest challenge on Earth—we figure out the virus, but it mutates."

Auyda thought a moment. "It will take a long time to describe our method for that, and based on what you have told me, I don't think your science is advanced enough to duplicate our method."

Maria sighed. "So, maybe someday, huh?"

Auyda gave her an understanding smile. "Yes, someday. But at least we can help your population with this plague."

Now it was Auyda's turn to sigh. "Unfortunately, we are not 100% sure that this particular cure will work. We adapted it from our cure, based on what we found in the plague organism. The cure works by breaking the bond between the two organisms. It also acts as a vaccine. If a person doesn't yet have the avian plague, they will be prevented from developing the disease.

"But, remember, even when the ML-20's bonding ability is deactivated, the organisms it joined are still active. So, the vial also contains cures for the bubonic plague bacteria and the avian flu virus. You will be able to duplicate the cure in mass quantities. We will give you instructions for that. But, there is a problem."

John forced himself to say, "What is the problem?"

"The problem is, there is no proof that it works on Earth-humans."

"So how do we prove it?" John said. "There has to be a way."

"There is," she replied. "The cure has to incubate inside the human host to be effective. According to my assistant, if we had someone here that was from Earth and infected by the plague, we could know that the cure is close enough to be effective."

He shook his head. "We don't have anyone infected. If we had, they'd be dead or dying by now. My orders are that, if we find a cure, to just bring it back home to Earth and let the scientists worry about it."

"There is one other way," she said. "Not to test the plague organism, but a test for the bonding organism itself. A simple test will determine if you have it. It's not as certain as incubation inside a human host who has the conjoined plague organism. Yet it should yield enough data to prove the cure works."

"A test?"

"Yes, a test of your blood." She smiled. "Actually, that's unusual. We have many medical sensors to identify diseases. We rarely need actual blood for testing. However, sometimes a blood sample is needed. So we are prepared . . . if you and your crew are willing."

That made sense to John, so he was the first to hold out his arm for the needle—which, he noticed with relief, they'd learned how to make painless on Peligroso.

His statement that none of the crew had the plague was true. But Vincent, Mohammad and he had somehow acquired the benign ML-20 organism. The other crewmembers were negative.

Auyda handed each of them vials containing the cure. "As you know, the ML-20 is harmless by itself. The harm comes when it causes two destructive organisms to join. If our theory is true, this should break the binary effect—ML-20's ability to seal the conjoined disease organisms. Then, our normal methods can eradicate the individual diseases. You don't have the diseases, of course. But hopefully, by your taking the cure, we can at least determine if ML-20's bonding effect is neutralized."

"At this point we'll take anything," he said. "Because all we have now is hope."

He gave the vial back to Auyda, but she shook her head. "All one needs to do is to take it. Swallow all of the liquid in the vial."

John looked at the vial, astounded. "On Earth, many of the vaccines and cures *we* have require a needle. Can't even get a simple flu vaccine without getting stuck."

She laughed. "I suppose progress is actually a good thing, then. My only regret is that I won't be able to know if it worked against your plague."

"Yes, and I'm very sorry about that, too," John said. "But . . ." He reached inside his suit and retrieved his satellite phone. "This is our Earth technology. It's called a sat phone. If it works with your satellites, you can also send us messages called e-mails. You're the first civilization we've ever encountered, and we'd like to keep in touch. If we can."

He demonstrated how to send messages. And thankfully, their written language matched as well as their spoken language. He was able to read the sample message she typed into the phone.

Entranced, she said, "Oh, you Earth people have so many things I have never seen. Perhaps someday—"

"I was just thinking that myself," he said. "Unfortunately, travel to the past is prohibited by my planet. But, maybe someday, that will be possible."

"I very much hope so, John Richards."

28

The early test worked, at least on the organisms in the test tubes. No matter how many other organisms Auyda and her team tried, including the bubonic plague and avian flu, the ML-20's bonding ability was deactivated by the cure.

"This brings me to a quandary," Audya said, peering at the test results. "Vincent, Muhammad and your ML-20 levels are still present your bloodstreams."

John shrugged. "From what you said, it's benign by itself."

"Yes, but as long as you still have it, you are at risk of developing the plague." She looked up at him. "I think you three should take the cure now, before you return to Earth. But . . . right now, we don't really know how it will affect you here on Peligroso. And it's like all vaccines. . . . It might even cause you to develop full-blown plague."

John thought a moment, then shook his head. "No. The plague moves too fast to take the chance. Until we get the cure back to Earth, we can't take any risks that might cause us to fail. We'll take the cure once we complete the mission. I'll ask Vincent and Muhammad, but they'll feel the same way."

Now, her gaze held admiration. "I respect your willingness to accept that risk."

Her esteem turned to surprise when he laughed and said, "Believe me, after what we went through just to get here, the TTA team's proven they're willing to handle risk."

As they returned home, they received one e-mail after another from Auyda. Each message was instantly sent, but it took her five years to send all fifteen messages they eventually received. But, because of their speed, the crew received the messages seconds apart.

The first one made them euphoric when Auyda wrote how much they already missed their visitors, and that she and her people wished them well in their quest to return safely home. *I hope the cure works,* she wrote. *And Vincent, thank you so much for the technology on stem cells. We are working with it now to find ways to cure many diseases we have no cure for yet.*

This message made Vincent beam as only a nineteen-year-old kid can.

But after that, the messages grew increasingly disturbing. The fifth one described how two of their scientists had developed a bomb from the stem cell technology, but that spies stole the technology and gave it to the mother nation.

The seventh e-mail brought muttered oaths from all the crewmembers gathered around the computer screen.

> *Bad news. We have done further research, and believe the vial we gave you will not cure your plague. Your Earth atmosphere might only cause the plague organism to hibernate, only to awaken years later, still communicable. More when our research can confirm this.*

She also described a strange bomb dropped from a balloon by the mother nation's military. "It exploded and made people sick. In six months, the people affected by the bomb grew extra limbs and mutated. We think this was just a test bomb, that perhaps they are planning something more powerful. I fear they used the stem cell technology they stole from us in a terrible way."

Auyda's eleventh e-mail helped, telling them that they had discovered a true cure for the plague, one they were certain would work. *However,* she wrote, *the cure must be incubated for five lunas, which is equivalent to 5,000 years.*

"Whew," Maria said, reading this, "I don't think we've got time for that."

The twelfth e-mail was a discouraging update on the status of their ongoing war for independence.

> *Our worst fears are confirmed. The stem cell research, combined with our own technology, has enabled the mother nation to develop weapons to be used against us. They overtook a nearby city years ago, and are holding it.*

They couldn't figure out the thirteenth e-mail. The message itself said only: *Cure.* But this message contained an attachment.

"Maybe it's a coded message," Vincent said, hopeful. He quickly downloaded it and displayed it on the screen.

It was only a map of what appeared to be a city on Peligroso.

By then, Vincent was a desperate man. He grabbed John's shoulder in a way eerily reminiscent of the way the doomed Wong had grasped at the gold and platinum meteorites. "Maybe that's a map to where they hid the sure cure, John," he said, his eyes wild. All we have to do is go back there—"

John gently pulled Vincent's hand from his shoulder. "You know that's not possible. But we'll . . . we'll think of something. As soon as we're back home."

The fourteenth e-mail seemed to dash any hope of ever returning to the planet. *We are being invaded,* Auyda wrote. *Everyone is taking to balloons to* escape. *Some are staying to fight. I'm one of them. I'm staying with my fiancée to help with the war. I owe this to my brother.*

The fifteenth was her last one.

> *I hear the soldiers right above my head where I am hiding. I have nowhere else to go, and nothing more to fight with. I will be slated for extermination. I don't know where my fiancée is. His name was Kayo. But if you can make your time machine come back 5,000 years from now, you can use what I have attached to try to cure your planet. Goodbye, my friends.*

Her last e-mail came with another attachment. But it was the same as before, just a map of a city on the planet.

Then, John noticed something else on this map. What appeared to be a message was hand-scrawled across the bottom. He peered at it, trying to make out that part of the grainy image, then whispered, "Incubated cure. I think that's what it says."

"We have to go back!" Vincent shouted. "It's her last message to us!"

John sighed heavily and looked at the locked cabinet holding the vial. "I have orders to bring back whatever might cure the avian plague. If this is a cure, I have to get it back home to our scientists. Millions of people will die from any delays. We have to go home."

Minutes later, they saw the planet engulfed in a bloodred-colored electrical storm.

"It's the genetic bomb," Vincent yelled. "This is their future. They eventually destroyed themselves, remember?"

"John, come here."

He turned to Maria Ross, who said, "It's the cloud again."

He looked at Mohammad, who had taken over as navigator after Wong's death. "Go around it. I don't want to risk flying through it again."

Mohammad headed on an uncharted path, avoiding the cloud. John was relieved to find that going around the cloud only put them an hour behind. Soon, they were lined up on a direct course to Earth. Within 12 hours, they were home and back in their current time, watching as the Academy's helicopter crew moved the time machine from the launching pad back to its storage hangar.

⊹⟩⟩⟩⟩ ❋ ⟨⟨⟨⟨⊹

Over the next three days, John and the entire crew was examined and debriefed. John had smiled at the way General Jones looked when he handed him the vial, saying, "You better test this to see if it works. Until or unless Vincent, Muhammad or I get sick, we have no way of knowing."

Jones had held the vial reverently, and in a hushed voice said, "You have no idea what this means to us. And to you."

Three days later, John was fed up. Before leaving, he'd been promised a short leave to see his family and attend to his business. Then he would return for the Academy's graduation, which had been delayed by the urgency of the mission and its aftermath.

When he was told that all leave requests were cancelled, he asked for, then demanded a meeting with General Jones. When he entered the general's office, he noticed that Mike Adams, Rubiano and the other school leaders were there, but he didn't even bother saying hello.

He leaned forward on the desk. "A few days ago, you told me you had no idea what the success of our mission meant. Well, what this means to *me* is that I survived. And do you know what that means? That means that it's over for me. I've just been thoroughly debriefed, examined head-to-toe, *and* I delivered what you sent me to find. And now, it's time for me to go home."

Jones looked at him, confused. "But you *are* home."

John shook his head. "I have a girlfriend, and friends, and a mother who must be going out of her mind with worry by now. I have a business that I haven't been able to run for almost two months—"

"John, I understand how very stressful this has been for you, but you simply can't leave in the middle of a top-secret mission."

"I lost two crewmembers. I wasn't able to save them. Wong and Willis should be remembered as heroes. And . . . I don't care what your so-called expert engineers say about chances of natural failure. I'm convinced that someone tried to sabotage the time machine's navigational controls. All I know is that I'm never going to get into it again and risk being killed."

He leaned farther forward. "General, I understand what 'top secret' means. I won't say anything to anyone, ever. But . . . that doesn't mean I'm willing to spend the rest of my life away from the life I had before. You'll probably find hundreds of people, just as qualified as I am. But not me. This is over for me, and I'm going home!"

Adams flew up from his chair. The other generals, who'd been listening, surrounded him as if they had something to say. John didn't want to hear it. He pushed past them on his way out the door.

He wanted so much to just make a run for his car, which was back at the airport in Texas. But he couldn't. Even if he could, his car keys were back in his room at the barracks. His keys, and something far more important. He headed there, not surprised to find two guards outside his barracks. But, like the sentries he met on the way to the parking lot, they only glared at him as he passed them.

But why do they have to stop me here? he thought bitterly. *If they want to get me, they'll just send those men again, or others just like 'em.*

At that instant, he knew that even if he tried to reclaim his past life, he would never be truly free.

Back in the barracks, he turned his clock radio on to play music. If they had bugged his room, he figured the music would obscure what he was about to do. Using his cell phone, he called Antonio's home number, then the karate school, but got no answer. Not even a recorded message greeted him. That had never happened before.

He next tried his mom's number, but there was no answer, or even a recorded message. That had never happened before either. Never.

And then, he remembered. General Jones holding the vial, looking at it as though it was some miracle. And then, the general saying. *You have no idea what this means to us. And to you.*

"What the hell did he mean by that?" he muttered, not wanting to think about the answer.

He turned around and went back to the school, stormed past the guards and right back into Jones's office, and yelled at the startled general, "What have you done to my life?"

Jones stood slowly. "It's not what we did, but what you need to do. I tried to tell you, but you ran out of here before I could. I have bad news, John. The cure didn't work. We just used it as a test, but it failed."

John didn't remember lowering himself in the chair, just the next frame, where he was sitting in it, looking up at Jones.

"I read the report and the e-mails," Jones said. "You have to go back to Peligroso on a second mission. You have to find the incubated cure you mentioned in your report. It might not work, but . . . it's the only hope we have left."

"I'm not going anywhere—"

"John, you don't understand. It's our only hope . . . and it's your mother's only hope."

"She went to visit your business partner, and was coughing then," Jones said. "Thankfully, we were able to use a top-secret method we've developed to stop her from dying."

Adams stood with them at an observation window. Beyond it, John's mother lay. Except for being very still, hooked up to tubes and unmoving, one wouldn't know she had been cryogenically preserved. But the thought that they had frozen his mother without his consent angered him.

"You can leave," Jones said gently. "No one will stop you. But you won't only be turning your back on us, but also her."

"Tell me how it happened," John said numbly. "How you found out."

"We were contacted by the US Department of Nuclear, Biological and Chemical Deterrence. All family members of cadets are listed with them, with instructions to keep us informed of anything significant that happens to them. They told us she had contracted the avian plague, and we requested that she be brought here. We wanted her to be one of the first to be cured of the avian plague. It would have been fitting; she's the mother of the person who led the mission to find a cure.

"But," he sighed heavily, "the cure doesn't work. That's why you have to go back. From the message from Peligroso, they must have been able to accelerate the incubation process for the cure. Charlene Vaughn—you remember her, she was one of the cadets—has told us that they can take the incubated cure, duplicate its new DNA pattern, and mass-produce it. You have to go back to Peligroso, retrieve that vial and bring it back here. At any cost."

The general patted him on the back and left him alone.

⊹⊱━━ ❀❀ ━━⊰⊹

Two thousand miles away, the President looked at Secretary Lanti across his desk. "Try as I might, Lanti, I still can't understand why you called the TTA mission a failure. They accomplished something barely dreamed of only a hundred years ago."

"And what *did* it accomplish?" Lanti asked. "Trillions spent, and we're not one bit closer to stopping the plague than we were before. We're getting increasing reports from every country in the world. Iran and South Korea are accusing us of having a cure for it, and they're stirring up other nations against us. Even Canada and the UK are beginning to believe them!"

He shook his head and fixed desperate eyes on the President. "We gave the Academy a chance to prove its worth, but it failed. Miserably. This program is hopeless, and shouldn't be part of my department. We should reassign it to Mike Adams and his company and let him bother with it. Or maybe to the Department of Education, and use the funds Congress allocated to develop my nuclear program against terrorists and—"

"Does anyone have anything else to say?" the President said, his voice already weary. "General?"

Over the President's open speakerphone, General Jones's voice boomed out. "Mr. President, as I've already mentioned, the scientist that traded us this technology said she has another one prepared. One she seemed confident would work."

Lanti opened his mouth, but the President's look closed it.

"General, I'm sure you know what we all face," he said into the speaker. "To date, one million people have died from the avian plague. Do whatever it takes to obtain that second vial. I'll *personally* okay it."

"Mr. President, we'll try again. Thank you, sir."

Jones heard a click, ending the call, and looked at the man across his desk. "John, if we can get it together, I've scheduled the next mission to begin forty-eight hours from now. You're the leader, and therefore have the option to pick and replace your lost crewmembers. I do have a recommendation, but . . ." He glanced away, then back to John. "I'll admit, it's not one that I'm terribly excited about. But I believe I need to send one of my best administrative staff on this mission."

He punched his speakerphone and said, "If Dr. Vaughn has arrived, please send her in."

Moments later, Charlene entered. But soon, she was fighting for the right to follow her dream.

Look, Captain Richards—"

"It's John," John said. "Just John."

She nodded and continued. "When the general told me you lost your last science specialist, I knew I'd be perfect as the replacement. I'm fully trained, and I'm the one who found out about the ML-20 in the first place." She gave him her most charming smile. "If it hadn't been for my discovery, you'd still be scratching your heads. And you'll need someone to test the cure there. I know what to do, top to bottom, with no additional training. Once I determine if the cure will break the bond between the two other organisms, we're home free."

"Dr. Vaughn, that was a good speech," Jones said. "But to remind you of my original objections, we need your talents here. You might come up with the cure here. This way we have two alternatives instead of just one. Our ace in the hole, as it were. I just don't think we can afford to lose you here."

John took another glance at Charlene's earnest face, recalling her outstanding performance in the training. He stood up, moved his chair backward as he did, and looked directly at Jones

"General Jones, sir, you just gave me the authority to choose my replacements. Just like you, I want the best, and I'm requesting Dr. Vaughn to be my science specialist on the next mission. And Vincent Goff to serve as the navigator."

Jones didn't immediately respond, just sat there in his chair staring at John. Finally, he said, "In truth, both are excellent choices. But Dr. Vaughn, there isn't enough time to send you through the one-week additional training on the time machine. Just pray you don't get into a position where you have to pilot or repair the machine. You will leave at oh-eight-hundred in two days. You are dismissed."

+⋟— ❁❀ —⟨+

Outside the general's office, John asked Charlene, "Do you know what you're getting into?"

"Yes," Charlene said, "and I've been waiting for a long time."

John thought a moment, then said, "This mission is extremely dangerous. Did you see my report?"

He saw her brow furrow. "About the tombstones?"

"Yes."

She smiled. "You also said—and correctly, I believe—that whatever led to those memorials being constructed happened very far in the future. And that there were no identifiable names left on them. Sure, there's a chance one of them's mine. But there's also the chance that my name was never on them." She shrugged. "If you and the rest of the crew are willing to risk it, so am I."

John couldn't help returning her smile. "Very well, then, Cadet."

"Cadet? Not anymore. I'm the science specialist!"

—⟨⟩— ❋❋ —⟨⟩—

Two days of hurried preparations later, General Jones wished them all good luck. "And remember, after the tampering incident, we had alarms installed. You each have the code, so no one touches them except for authorized personnel."

As before, John ordered Vincent to stop time and proceed to Planet Peligroso, to retrieve the vial Auyda had hidden 5,000 years before.

29

As they had planned, they arrived at the planet 5,000 years after their last visit. It was also night, however. "We'll stop here, get some rest and begin our search in the morning at the first sign of light," John said.

The next morning, they looked out the portholes to find only a desolate landscape.

"It looks as though that last war really finished off the planet, didn't it?" John said.

Vincent hung his head. "If I had known that the mother country would use stem cell technology to make genetic bombs—"

"I know. But did any of us imagine they'd do something like that with such a peaceful technology?" He turned his head toward the control console. "Science Officer Vaughn, what's the air out there like?"

Charlene looked up. "A little dry, but breathable. At least they didn't ruin the air. Or maybe it's had time to regenerate since the war. The oxygen reading's a little high, but better too much than not enough, I always say. Once we're outside, I'll check the water in that lake over there. Plus find out if any of the plants are edible. Or at least that I can guarantee they're safe for us to eat if we're stuck here for a while."

They struck out on both hopes. "Well, I guess 5,000 years makes a big difference," Charlene said, packing her testing instruments away. "This water isn't drinkable. And . . . even odder, its hydrogen and oxygen atoms are being separated. In a few hundred thousand years, there won't be any water on this planet at all."

"So what's the verdict?" John asked.

"No matter what, do *not* drink the water. And I wouldn't even trust it if we recycle our own. We'll just have to make do with the bottled water we brought. I saw a few trees, too, but none of them have any sort of fruit on them. And based on the water tests, even if we found food, I wouldn't trust it. So I guess we're stuck with the MREs we brought." She looked up at the others and gave them a reassuring smile. "But with a bit of luck, maybe we won't be here too long."

They moved the time machine between an open cave entrance and the massive rocks surrounding the entrance, ate some of the food they'd brought, then headed for bed. Vincent volunteered to stand first watch. It had been determined that it was safe enough for them to go outside the ship, as long as they stayed close. This was important; even though the planet appeared to have no life, there might be. The only way to know for certain was to do visual checks to supplement what their onboard monitors told them.

After a while, hunger and sleepiness overtook Vincent. On one of his rounds, he encountered some vegetation growing out from under one of the boulders.

"Hey, that's interesting," he muttered. "Charlene said there wasn't any fruit here. But those are berries on that bush."

Without thinking, he plucked one of the berries and put to his tongue, intending just to taste it. It tasted fine, so he slipped the berry into his mouth and bit down.

The next thing he knew, he was sitting in a place he didn't recognize, gazing at the stars, amazed at how beautiful the planet was. A handful of the berries was in his hand. He ate them one by one, sitting for a while, until he saw a shooting star. He made a wish for the cure for the disease, and that they all make it back safely back to Earth.

The morning came, and he headed back to camp to wake the others.

"I thought you were going to wake me up after three hours," John said, rubbing his eyes.

He shrugged. "No need. I feel great. Actually, better than great."

"So you don't want to get any sleep before we head out?"

"Nah. Feel like I could run a marathon. Let's boogie."

With narrowed eyes, John asked, "See anything . . . unusual last night?"

"Just a shooting star. I saw it while I was eating some berries I found. Charlene was wrong. The food on this planet's fine. Pretty good, actually."

John tensed. "I gave you a direct order not to eat anything on this planet. Do you have a problem with following rules?"

Charlene and the others heard John yell at Vincent. "Wait," Charlene said. "I want to examine him."

"We don't have time," John said.

She walked over to John, put her hands on her hips, and pulled herself up to her full height. "I would like to examine him first."

"Look, he's just wired up from staying up all night."

"No, *you* just wait a minute. I'm here as a team member, and I'm here for the safety and health of the crewmembers. Now would you let me do my job?"

John sighed. "Sorry. You're exactly right. Go ahead."

While she was examining Vincent and analyzing his blood, the other crew-members went outside and began looking at the map. When Charlene called to John, he looked up from the map.

"Not here. Come over here."

"Something's wrong," Charlene said when they were alone. "His blood . . . his retinas . . . his reactions . . . they're all off. It's like he's changing. Problem is, I'm not sure what's causing it. It might be because he acquired the ML-20. Or maybe it's because the planet's so near a black hole now. Or maybe the berries he ate. Or some combination of those factors, or ones we not aware of yet. But something's happened. His molecular structure is different now."

John considered her words for a moment. "Is he okay to go forward with the mission?"

"I . . . I think so. He's not acting any different. A little more energetic, but that's all."

He stood. "That's all I need to know. Now let's find that vial."

Vincent came up to him and overheard. "Why don't we just use the time machine to take us around?"

John replied, "Because we don't want to bump into something and not have a way home. Besides, it's not really designed for on-planet travel. Just interplanetary and time travel. And . . . remember, we don't yet know what we'll encounter here. If anything happens to that craft, we'll be stuck billions of light-years from Earth."

That's when Charlene and John both noticed that Vincent seemed to be having trouble breathing.

"I sure am getting tired," he said. "This is worse than the Academy."

Feldman heard him and called out, "Stop complaining, nerd."

"You stop complaining, Goldie," Vincent shot back. "By the way, this so-called *nerd* is the only one who knows how to get us back home. You call me *nerd* again and you'll be walking back to Earth. According to my calculations, you'll have a very long walk."

Vincent's breathing soon improved. John debated leaving him with the craft, but decided against it. In light of him eating the berries, combined with Charlene's concerns, he wanted to keep an eye on him. So, with Vincent and Feldman occasionally scowling at each other, they walked until they came to a river.

But it was what they saw across the river that stopped them. The giant snake, lying on an island in the middle of the lake sunning itself, had a mouth big enough to swallow a person whole.

John rechecked the coordinates on the map and looked at the others. "Sorry, folks, but to get to where we need to go, we've got to cross that island."

He looked downriver and saw a series of rocks that seemed to form a natural bridge. "If I'm right, we can go down there and run across."

The entire crew ran across. Vincent was last, and fell into the water. John raced back to rescue him, calling out, "You guys stay here!"

Vincent, gasping, screamed, "Help me, somebody please, I can't swim, I can't swim, help!"

John jumped into the lake after him, his only thought to save his crewmember and friend. When John reached him, Vincent pulled him under the water in his panic.

Dead silence came from the river. To the crew above, the seconds seemed like hours.

Suddenly they heard a cough coming from the opposite side of the river. Both John and Vincent had emerged, coughing and sputtering. The crew got there in time to hear John saying, "I'm beginning to wonder if you're an asset or a liability. This is the second time I had to save your life."

Vincent, coughing, replied, "Getting 100% on my swimming test wasn't important to the generals. But I guess I should have tried harder. Thanks for saving my life again." He grinned. "I guess we're even now."

John grinned. "Hey, you're more of an asset then a liability. If the time machine breaks down, you're the only one here who can fix it. That's what's important . . . not that you swim a lick, but that you're with us."

Leaving the snake behind, they continued their journey. The next major landform they encountered was a mountain. The black hole near the planet had pulled this mighty landmass upward in just a few years. Bizarrely, the river they'd just crossed ran uphill and right over the top of the mountain.

"Unfortunately, the map says this is the only way to get to the other side," John said. "At least it's not too steep an incline."

A visual check revealed no other options. They began climbing the side of the mountain.

The ground tremors started small, but became stronger the higher they climbed. They knew it was another effect of being so close to the black hole, since the planet was being pulled out of its orbit and closer to the black hole that one day would engulf it. But it was annoying at first, then outright nerve-racking to have the ground shaking under their feet.

At one point, Vincent stumbled and reached out to steady himself on the mountain's face, as he'd done several times before. But this time, his hand hit a rock ledge, which broke in half.

He looked at what he'd done and said, "Hey, guys, I don't know what's going on, but I've never been able to break a rock like that!"

Even though none of the crew had eaten any of the berries, they soon felt themselves changing too. They became stronger and faster on their climb, just the opposite of what they expected. At one point, Suzie said, "It's weird, but I feel . . . lighter somehow." To illustrate, she bent her knees, then jumped gently. She rose ten feet in the air before she returned to the ground.

Vincent told the others, "Something strange is going on, folks. Maybe it's got something to do with the black hole or the planet's atmosphere, but . . . we're changing."

John didn't hear the last part of the sentence. "Yeah, some thing strange *is* going on. The tremors are weird, and—"

Before Vincent could say anything else, the next round of tremors shook him off the path. He grabbed the ledge below them and held himself up by one arm. John rushed to try to pull him up, but another, stronger tremor hit. This one knocked John down and caused the ledge Vincent was holding to break away. He fell hundreds of feet below into the ocean, hundreds of huge, loosened boulders following him.

John peered down the several-hundred-foot drop to the crashing waves below, but couldn't see his friend. His heart breaking, he said, "There's . . . no way anyone could survive a fall like that."

With the tremors so strong, there was no time for grief. They had to get off the mountain before another of them fell. They had a brief moment of prayer. "Vincent will never be forgotten," John told them. "And if we make it back to Earth, I'll ask that he be remembered as a hero. Yet we must not focus on loss and grief. There are billions of people back home depending on us. We've come too far to give up or turn back now. Let's move forward."

Discouraged, they continued down the rocky path. But they were able to move faster down the mountain to get to the opposite side. Putting their sorrow behind them as best they could, they continued their journey to find the vial.

30

The map given to them by Auyda was vital. They had downloaded it into a hand-held computer. As they walked, they discovered that her planet's technology was even further along than they thought. The map had a form of GPS embedded into it; when they got closer or farther from the vial, the computer beeped. A louder beep indicated when they were getting closer, a softer beep showed they were moving away from the vial's location.

"It must work from the satellite towers," Suzie said. "Vincent . . . Vincent would have loved knowing about this, wouldn't he?"

With a grim nod, John pointed the computer in the direction of the coordinates. The beep got louder. They kept running, and soon crossed over a hill and saw the ancient city detailed on the map.

Feeling success getting closer, Charlene began running toward it. Suzie followed, then Feldman. They ran, and kept running, their excitement about reaching the city great.

After their euphoria settled, John told the crew, "We got to the hard part, now let's get that vial."

Their homing device brought them closer, but they often stopped to see the remarkably well preserved city. Even though partially obscured by the sand blown into it in the years since the planet's destructive war, the buildings stood, as if as testament to the city's great, if lost history. They were watchful but found no signs of life, only a city of mystery.

"What happened to all the people?" Charlene whispered. "Surely some of them made it out alive."

She was holding the homing device as they approached the spot the vial should have been. But when they reached the place indicated inside the ruins, there was no vial, or any spot where Auyda might have hidden one.

John consoled the disappointed group, then allowed his frustration to show. "It has to be here," he said. "It just has to."

Charlene looked around. "You know, unless I miss my guess, I think this was a laboratory at one time. Hummm."

They tested the chairs still in the room and found them sturdy enough to sit. John chose the chair at the end of the long lab table. As he lowered himself into it, they heard a noise.

"Look!" Maria said, and pointed. To their left, a panel was sliding open. The homing device beeped louder.

"What the hell is that?" Charlene said.

"I . . . it just came open," Suzie said in wonder. "There wasn't even a door there, just a wall!"

A cautious inspection showed only stairs leading downward, but the beeping was even louder now. John turned to the group. "I won't ask you to risk any more than you have, but we have to find out what's down there."

"Nonsense," Charlene said. "We're going with you, and that's final."

One by one, John leading, they headed through the opening and down the hidden stairs. Muhammad was the last one through. As he passed the opening, the door slid closed behind them.

"Uh, oh," Suzie said. "I guess our only way out now is at the end of this staircase."

John sighed. "Yeah, I think you're right. But . . . whoever set this up probably planned it that way. And if they planned a way to get in, surely they planned a way to get out."

All they saw at the bottom of the staircase was pitch-black—until they got there, and a bank of overhead lights came on.

"They must operate on some kind of sensor," John said, looking around. "Or perhaps someone was expecting us."

Charlene grinned. "Well then, we'd better get a move on, with bells on."

This brought chuckles all around, and lightened their apprehension a bit as they went down the corridor revealed by the lighting.

Unfortunately, the corridor only led to a y-shaped split. Now, they had to decide which way to go.

"We'll have to separate," John said. "This will be our center point, where we'll all meet again." *I hope.*

He put his sat phone on the ground. "Okay everyone, power up your phones."

They did, and were gratified to find that each phone's individual GPS unit functioned fine when tuned to this position.

Then, John remembered something he hoped no one else would: that on their first trip to the planet, there were five memorials with the Time Travelers Academy symbol over the memorial. Inside the memorial, a sat phone had been placed. He looked down and realized his sat phone's markings were identical to the one placed in the dead crewmembers' memorial.

"Switch phones with me," he said to Charlene. Perhaps if he made such a small change, he could change enough of their timeline to save the lives of five of his crew.

Charlene did as instructed, using her sat phone as the marker beacon. Then she said, "What's going on? You look as if you've seen a ghost."

"I wouldn't say a ghost, but the future."

"Is there something I should know? . . . Something we should know?"

He sighed heavily. "Yes, there is." He called the others to him, then swept a hand over the scene. "I doubt this looks familiar to the new crewmembers, but it should to the rest of you."

Muhammad's eyes widened, and he immediately began praying. The others began an excited babbling, and John turned back to Charlene.

"This spot . . . it looks identical to the memorial I told you about before we left. Right down to the markings on my sat phone. This might be the memorial to five of us standing here right now."

She nodded and held out the sat phone he'd just given her. "And you think that switching phones might change what happened."

He nodded.

"But maybe those memorials aren't to us," she said. "Perhaps they're of a new crew, on a new mission, who arrived here after we did."

Then, she shrugged. "I don't know too much about time-paradox, but I *do* know if a future hasn't been set, it can be changed."

"Charlene, there was something else. Something I wasn't certain about, so I didn't put it into my report. About the five memorials. There was more on them than I reported. I couldn't make out four of them, but I made out the fifth one. That person's name was 'Cadet,' followed by the letters V and G The first letter of the name started with a V and the fourth letter was a G. Put it all together, and it's your last name: Vaughn."

Charlene shook her head. "V.G. could also mean Vincent Goff, not me."

John said, "It was only one name, not two. The clues point right to your name.

I hate to tell you what I'm thinking." He pointed to the sat phone. "But I'll do everything in my power to keep it from happening. And that's one thing."

He turned to the others. "Charlene, I want you with the two security officers. Feldman and I'll go into this tunnel, you all go into the one straight ahead. The last two will go into the tunnel behind us. Watch everything, even the walls. Maybe the vial's hidden behind a panel, like the entrance to this place was. Remember to keep your phones on, and at the first sight of the vial or . . . anything else, hit the emergency-locator button on your phones. Let's get started."

They headed in the directions John indicated, leaving a homing device as their meeting point.

About 20 minutes had passed when John heard a loud scream through his sat phone. When he recognized the voice, his gut clenched.

"Charlene! Answer me! Answer! Are you okay? Security, what's going on?"

Feldman said, "Sir, we lost her. She wandered off. Said she saw something she wanted to check out. I ordered her to say with us, but as soon as we turned our backs, she must have . . . We'd just found six caves. We thought we could find her without causing a panic."

"Find her now!" John growled.

John raced toward her coordinates. Within two minutes they reached her, huddled against the cave wall.

"What happened?" John asked her.

She pointed at a large glass frame, partly obscured by a smoky dust on the outside. The rest of the crew slowly walked up to it and glanced in. There were seven glass cells sitting in the room. What they saw inside them sent chills up John's spine.

"What, what is it?" Suzie said.

John shook his head. "I don't know, but what I do know is that I don't want to wake them up."

In each chamber was what appeared to be creatures that looked like some sort of mutated monster—recognizable as animals very much like those on Earth, but grafted with parts that looked eerily human. All of them appeared to be alive, but sleeping . . . for now.

"I saw it on the map, but I didn't believe it," John said.

Feldman turned to him. "What did you see?"

"It was . . . something that I could only see when I zoomed in. Something Auyda called the six mutants of death. Told us to watch out for them. But . . . the rest of what she wrote in that section made so little sense, I thought she might just be delirious."

Now, he picked up the homing device, zoomed in on Auyda's last words, and began reading while he went from one of the creatures to another.

"This must be the first one," he said. "It looks like a dragonfly." He gave a sour chuckle. "A ten-foot-tall dragonfly. But it's actually half-human. Auyda said it can fly, but not at great heights. It moves so rapidly, it's tough to strike it. And its wings are sharp as swords. But its belly is soft. She said if we encounter one, to strike for the belly. . . ." He read further, and his face fell. "If we have time."

The second creature looked like a cobra, if a cobra had human hands and was eight feet long. "Its defenses are the four other snakes protruding from it," John read, and pointed. "Each of those heads is venomous. Its weakness is its head. If blinded, it's vulnerable."

The third creature, in a cell much larger than the others, reminded John of a grizzly bear. "Its defense is its size and strength," he said, reading the notes. "Its claws too. Auyda said that once it grabs you, it never lets go. Its weakness is the soles of its feet. Very sensitive."

John gave a grim chuckle. "Hey, maybe it's ticklish."

No one joined his attempt at humor. They were busy staring at the 12-inch claws protruding from each of the creature's beefy appendages.

John walked to the fourth cell, where an ugly creature that looked like a giant leech rested. "Look," he said. "It's got two mouths, and what looks like tentacles sticking out of them." He peered at the map, but found nothing about it. With a sigh, he said, "We can only assume its fighting powers are blood-sucking. That it defeats its enemy by sucking their blood."

The fifth one was clearly half-human, half-shark. "She called it a boca," John read from the map. "It can eat you in a single bite. And its saliva is acid. More than 100 times stronger than stomach acid. You'd be dissolved in that one bite."

Feldman asked, "Why does it have two very short legs and two long legs? It looks like it could lay flat on the ground if it wanted to."

John said, "That's another defense, I think. Just imagine walking over leaves and sticks. Its body's camouflaged to look like leaves, dirt and sticks. But once you step on it . . ."

He didn't have to finish the sentence. Their imaginations were filling in the rest, in gruesome detail.

The sixth mutant appeared to be a giant wasp, if with three tails. Each tail held a stinger and separate wings. The stingers were about 18 inches long. "Just being stabbed by one of the stingers is fatal," John read. "Its venom causes complete paralysis of the nervous system."

"So why are they in these containers?" Charlene said. "They all seem to be in a state of cryonic sleep. Or perhaps this is their normal state? I mean, why would she have described the mutants in such detail when she had so little time left?"

"I'm not sure," John said. "Maybe she wanted to warn us of any dangers we might encounter." He sighed. "But as long as they're in there, I don't think we have to worry about them. Just keep an eye out in case they have any buddies."

"Hey, look."

John looked in the direction of Charlene's pointing finger. About ten feet away from the glass cases was another opening.

He looked at her and grinned. "Ready for a little more exploring?"

She chuckled. "Yes. But this time, I think I'll let you go first."

31

The entrance led to another underground compartment. Here, the homing device's bleeps turn into near-screeches.

"Ground zero seems to have been reached," John said. As he spoke, he noticed a computer console screen. The crewmembers walked over to it, but Charlene stayed back, studying some symbols on one of the room's walls.

Feldman said, "It looks like some sort of control panel."

"Yes," John said, "and it looks like the guy who thought up the Rubik's Cube designed it."

The computer console did, in fact, resemble a multicolored puzzle, with a 1-to-16 combination for solving it. Feldman studied the glowing screen above it. "Hey look, this shows where the mutants are. So maybe it was some sort of monitoring station. Or maybe where they studied them."

"I think you're right," John answered, then looked at the bleeping homing device in his hand. "But the way this thing's acting, the vial's got to be somewhere near here. How do we know what that panel controls? Pushing one of those buttons could lead us to the vial. But, it could just as easily open the chambers holding the creatures."

He thought a moment, then studied Auyda's map. "There must be something we're overlooking. I don't want to make a mistake. The way those creatures look, I'm sure they're not going to give us hugs and kisses once they wake up. Maybe have us for dinner, though."

His joke brought groans from the entire crew.

He peered at the map a while longer, noticed a marking he hadn't seen before. He looked in its actual direction and saw a door. "Come with me," he told Feldman, and they left the others looking at the control panel.

The door had a handle on it. "Well, been nice knowing you if this doesn't work out," John said, and pulled down on the handle.

The door opened to what appeared to be some sort of storage cabinet. At that instant, the homing device not only increased the volume of its beeping, but began to flash red.

Some investigation showed them that the door was like the door to a dumb-waiter. They could see elevator-like tracks leading down the front of it where the storage cabinet had risen, probably when John pulled on the handle.

"But why?" he muttered. "And how the devil are we going to get that cabinet open?"

They all peered at it, but no ideas came to them. Finally, John said, "Well, I don't see any way to unlock or force the cabinet open, so I guess it's back to the console. But . . ."

They stood waiting.

"Okay, here's what I've got in mind. I just keep thinking that the vial's got to be inside that cabinet. I think the monsters were put here to protect the vial. Remember, Auyda left the vial here for us. So maybe these monsters aren't meant for us, but for someone who might inadvertently awaken them by trying to take the vial." He took a deep breath. "No matter what the intent, she didn't leave directions on how to get to the vial. That, we'll have to figure out ourselves.

"What I'm going to do is push one of those buttons. If nothing happens, I'll keep pushing buttons, in different number combinations, until something does. If the cabinet opens, we'll grab the vial and leave. If the chambers holding the creatures open, we'll stay here and fight. Main point, if the vial's in there, we can't leave without it. But I'm not going to ask any of you to stay in here unless you understand that we might be fighting to the death if I hit the wrong combination."

The crew looked at each other, then back at John. "I'm in," Feldman said. "There's no way I'm going back to Earth without what we came for." He reached in his suit and unsheathed his knife from his belt. "And if we have to fight ten-foot-tall monsters to do it, I'll give them the fight of their lives."

One by one, each crewmember withdrew and held up their weapons, and pledged themselves to help the others deal with whatever happened.

John walked to the control panel and studied it. Three of the buttons were bigger than the others. Ironically, one was white, one was red, and the third was blue, the same colors as the American flag.

"Here goes nothing," he said, then pushed the red button.

Nothing happened.

Punching the white and blue buttons had the same result. Then, he decided to begin punching them faster, in random sequence. "I wish my business partner were here," he said at one point. "Antonio's an accountant. He's not too hot at martial arts, but he's a whiz at math games. Bet he could figure this out in no time."

There was no laughter, and he hadn't expected any. He was only talking to steady the crew's nerves.

After expending his options by punching different colors one at a time, he decided to try multiple punches of the same color. He hit red, red, and red. Then red, red and blue. Nothing either time. Then red, blue and red. Still nothing. Then blue, red and red.

Feldman's eyes widened. "Hey, maybe it's just like you told Auyda—that the American flag is the Good Old Red, White and Blue—"

Just as he said the words, John hit the red, blue and white keys. The glass screens holding the monsters moved slowly downward, and the creatures began moving. Smoke from the chamber came began hissing out, then they heard a faint roar from one of the cells.

Feldman saw and screamed, "Hit red, white and blue again!"

John did. And finally, the cabinet opened. As John had suspected, the vial was sitting inside it.

Feldman grabbed the vial, saying, "Let's get out of here before they completely wake up."

But it was too late. The creature called the boca snaked out one of its appendages and grabbed Charlene. The other crewmembers, knives at the ready, jumped back when it emerged from its glass cage and raced toward the cabinet.

As soon as Feldman had grabbed the vial, the cabinet began descending the tracks. The boca squeezed itself into the opening it left and was pulling her after it. The other crewmembers grabbed her as she screamed, "It's tearing my arm off!"

John pulled his knife and stabbed the creature's exposed arm. It let go, and they all ran. As he ran, John glanced at the map. "This way!" he shouted. "There's an exit up this staircase!"

Using the map, they climbed higher and higher. As they did, Charlene rubbed her shoulder where the beast had tried to pull her arm out of its socket. They heard roaring, grunts and screeches from behind them, faint at first, but then growing closer.

"They're chasing us," Suzie yelled.

"I kind of figured that," John called back to her. "Just keep climbing and try not to think about it. Remember, they've been asleep for a long time. Maybe it'll take them a while to get up to speed."

Once more, the added strength and agility given them by the planet saved them. In moments, they stood on a platform and were breathing free air while looking over Peligroso's landscape.

Suzie looked down and said, "It's just like we're standing on one of the pyramids of Egypt."

It was true. The platform where they stood was one of several, and below them were seemingly endless flights of stairs to the ground, just like the famous Egyptian pyramids. But John knew they couldn't stay here long. They were hundreds of feet from the ground, and judging from the sounds he heard through the opening they'd just come through, the mutants were still after them.

"Maybe the creatures can't come outside," he said. "Anyway, let's go."

They began their climb to the ground on their way back to the time machine and. eventually, Earth.

Five minutes into their descent, they heard a roar, like an angry lion's, from below them.

"I don't know about you guys," Muhammad said, "but that doesn't sound very good."

With his enhanced sight, John saw that all six monsters had somehow made it outside to ground level, and were now climbing the pyramid to get to them.

"Turn around," he yelled. "Now!"

At the top, Suzie said, "We have to go back inside the pyramid. It's our only option."

"Not a good idea," John replied. "If we go back inside, they might trap us in there. We have to make our stand here."

Once again, they took out their knives and waited for the first monster to arrive at the top.

As Charlene took out her knife, she looked around. "Hey, guys, look."

She was pointing at what appeared to be a trapdoor in the platform on which they stood.

Soon, they had removed a dusty floorboard, revealing a square subfloor with a recessed lever beside it. Saying, "Here goes nothing," she reached down and pulled the lever up.

The subfloor began rising from the ground. To their amazement, the huge compartment revealed what appeared to be a deflated balloon.

"That's right," John said, remembering. "Auyda said they didn't have planes, so they traveled everywhere by balloon. The balloons were powered by solar cells in some way."

Charlene looked at him. "You know how to work this thing?"

He shrugged. "No, but if I can learn to fly a time machine in a week, a solar-powered balloon should be no problem."

They heard a roar behind them, and he added, "And hey, do we have a choice?"

They unfolded the balloon and turned a switch on what they hoped was the solar-powered engine: what appeared to be intake and exhaust hoses snaked out of it. Immediately, they heard air being sucked into the intake nozzle. They pointed the nozzle into the balloon, which filled with helium and began to rise.

"This is good," Suzie said.

"What's that?" John asked.

"There's a gauge here. If I'm figuring right, it'll tell us how many pounds it can carry based on the amount of helium in the balloon."

They had to shout over the roaring and other noises made by the creatures growing closer. Too close.

John glanced at the balloon's base, which appeared to be a collapsible gondola. "What's the worst that will happen if you all get in before the balloon's full?" he asked.

Suzie shrugged. "It just won't take off until it's light enough."

"Then go ahead and climb in," John said. "Our welcoming committee's almost here to finish their greetings."

Suzie called to the others and they all climbed into the gondola. A few moments more, the balloon attempted to rise. But with the extra weight, it wouldn't leave the ground.

And then, the creatures reached the platform.

John and Feldman leaped from the gondola and pulled their knives out, ready to try to hold the creatures off. At that instant, the balloon began lifting behind them.

"Come on!" Suzie yelled.

John looked back, but decided the risk was too great. Feldman's additional weight probably wouldn't, but adding the weight of *two* full-grown men might make the balloon sink again. If that happened, the flying creature could reach them and rip a hole in the balloon with one set of claws. No, for the rest to have a chance, he had to stay.

"Go on!" he shouted at Suzie, then turned toward Feldman. "Goodbye my friend."

Feldman said, "Where are you going?"

"Nowhere. I'm staying, and you're getting back on that balloon."

"No can do."

"That wasn't a request, or a reply . . . that was an order."

Feldman had just enough time to climb into the balloon before it was too high for him to do so. It slowly rose, minus one crewmember, and John breathed a relieved sigh.

He looked around, saw a platform about six feet higher than the one on which he stood, and leapt onto it. The mutants were less than 20 feet away now.

Then, he looked up to see a rope being thrown over the side of the gondola, right over his head. Seconds later, Suzie's face followed the rope. "We got the balloon filled," she shouted. "The indicators say it can hold one more person!"

John looked down at the creatures and smiled at them. "Six against one. I like those odds. Wish I could stay. But duty calls."

He grabbed the rope and allowed the balloon's momentum to pull him off the pyramid and away from the six mutants, who screeched and howled in rage.

✢══ ✤✥ ══✢

"Dang, that was beautiful, wish I'd been there. But then again, if I'd been there, they might not have been able to get off the ground."

The same way he'd watched the confrontation at the top of the pyramid, Vincent used his enhanced eyesight to follow the balloon's progress for a while, then continued on his journey to catch up with the crew. John had been right;

under ordinary circumstances, falling off a mountain into a rock-filled ocean would have killed him. But after eating the berries and thanks to the ML-20 still in his bloodstream, Vincent Goff was no longer a normal human. Since rising from the crashing waves, spitting and gasping but definitely alive, he'd been amazed to find what he was capable of in his new form. Once, when he'd tried an experimental karate chop against a huge boulder, the boulder was crushed into a pile of rubble. He liked the feeling of power that gave him.

The only problem he had was his sense of time. Or, perhaps his euphoria over surviving the fall had made his mind wander a while. He had no idea how long he sat on the cliff, in wonder, letting the waves crash over him.

Whatever the reason, even though he'd walked many miles and had many more to go, he felt charged, energized. He hoped the way he felt now would never, ever end.

—— ❧❧ ——

"John, I wouldn't celebrate just yet," Charlene said, pulling the binoculars away from her eyes. "I just saw those six . . . *things* following us. That means they can track us. And we're going the wrong direction. The time machine's to the west, but we're going east."

"That's not the worst of it," Suzie said from behind them. "The sun will set soon, and we'll have to put this thing down."

"Wait a minute," John said, befuddled. "I thought the balloon floated because of helium."

"You're partly right," Suzie replied. "But apparently, the people on Peligroso set it up to require solar power to keep making just enough helium, continuously, to keep the balloon in the air. In other words, without the sun, our goose is cooked."

John followed her gaze to the darkening sky above them.

32

An hour later, with the sun long-set, they were creeping along on the last few cubic centimeters of helium. Finally, with a low, gasping sound, the balloon gently lowered them into an open field.

Charlene checked her heat sensor. "John, there are seven sources of heat heading this way. Don't know about the one traveling alone, but I'm guessing the group of six are the mutants. About one hour away, at the rate I saw them moving before."

John grimaced. He hated losing the balloon, but it was so large, it made them a sitting target for the creatures. "Any likely hiding spots?"

She grabbed her GPS device and peered at it. "I'm detecting a city two miles east."

He couldn't help a grin. "You know, for a science officer, you've turned into a pretty good navigator."

She returned his smile, but her smile quickly faded. He knew that, like him, she didn't want to waste time getting away from the balloon and minimizing the chances that those mutants would find them.

"Let's go that way and double-time it," he said.

They began a fast pace toward the unknown city, made faster by their increased speed and strength. After about a five-minute run, they neared a forest, which seemed strange in such a desolate and ruined landscape.

As if by mutual agreement, they slowed their pace.

With bellows and shouts, a group of about fifteen armed soldiers emerged from the trees and overtook them.

They tried to fight back, but their knives were no match for the guns the soldiers later identified as pulse guns.

The lead soldier was kind enough to identify their group as Selohsians to John before taking away all their electronic devices and knives and, John was dismayed to see, the vial containing the cure. The Selohsian leader tossed the vial into the air and caught it, as though he were playing with a baseball.

"Hey, be careful with that!" John shouted.

The man smiled at him and said in understandable English, "If it's that important to you, then you will obey every one of our orders."

John cursed himself for giving the man yet one more way to control him and the crew.

They were all blindfolded, then marched to what John guessed was the nearby city. He could feel them walking downward for a while after that, and from the dank, damp smells around them, figured they were being taken underground. Their blindfolds were removed, and all of them were put together in one cell, a dark and cold place, but at least with wooden chairs to sit on. Solid rock lined both sides of the cell, and metal bars in front of the cell were sure to keep them from escaping.

"We mean you no harm," John told the guard. "If you let us go we'll leave peacefully, and cause you no trouble."

Their response was to hit him in the stomach and administer several sharp kicks. "If you keep opening your mouth," one guard said, "You will not make it to the dueling chamber, because I'll kill you now. On our planet, you have to fight for your survival and earn the right to live."

The guards left, and they heard the sound of a door opening and closing shut. John listened for a few moments, then turned to the group. "We have to get the hell out of here. If he means the same thing by 'dueling chamber' that Auyda described, we're in big trouble." *And this might be the fulfillment of the memorial we saw.*

To their questions, he told them the planet's version of a draft—that at the age of eighteen, each man had to fight to the death to prove himself.

"Whew, now I can see why Auyda and her group rebelled against that," Feldman said.

John checked to make sure they were still alone, then grouped the crew together as if they were in a football huddle and he was the quarterback devising the next play in the game.

"Charlene, you know about rocks. See what kind of rock this is and tell me its weakness or weak spots."

"Well, most of my rock-gazing experience is with meteorites, but I'll give it my best shot."

She went to the wall and began examining it, and he walked over to the bars, grabbing and tugging on them. "These bars are old. Probably thousands of years old, if this place was around when Auyda's colony was exterminated. Maybe we can break or bend them."

They all grabbed a bar and tried to bend it, but even as ancient as they were, the metal in them held tight.

John looked down and noticed that the bars were embedded into what looked like ground that was softer than the rock walls. "Maybe we can dig our way out," he said.

He looked at Feldman and Muhammad. "Take off your shoes. There's metal in the soles."

They complied, and started digging while he continued to look for other avenues of escape.

A strong, deep voice said, "You're wasting your time. There is no escape."

John peered through the bars and saw what he hadn't before. In the darkness across the chamber, there was another cell.

"Who are you?" he said. "And why did you say there's no escape?"

"My name is Guerrero," the voice said. "That means The Great Warrior. For what that is worth." The chuckle that followed held such bitterness, John almost didn't want to speak again. But he had to—if this person was from Peligroso, maybe he could give them some ideas for getting out of here.

"If you're so great, why are you content to stay here and die?" he called out. "Why don't you escape?"

Guerrero replied, "They feed me here, give me clothes. Even though it's a cell, it's a place to stay. I've earned my freedom through the many battles I fought and won in the dueling chamber, but . . . I no longer look at this as a jail cell, I look at it as my home."

John sighed. "My friend, if you don't want to leave, that's fine. But help *us* get out of here."

A long moment passed, then Guerrero said, "I am not your friend. I have no friends and trust no one. I learned not to make friends, because I might meet them in the dueling chamber and be forced to kill them. I can't kill my friends, so I don't make any."

Charlene whispered into John's ear, "I found something that might interest you about these rocks."

He walked with her to the back of the cell, where he didn't think Guerrero couldn't hear them.

"We're in a volcano," she said. "And a volcano has elements like sulfur, coal, flint. If we could find enough of those elements and combine them, we could make gunpowder and blow our way out of here. Or maybe make a weapon of some kind."

John was tempted, but he remembered the ethics he had agreed to. "This society doesn't know gunpowder yet . . . and we're not going to give them the technology, even if it means it'll save us."

He sighed and looked away. "In a way, we're responsible for the way this society has turned out. On our first trip to the planet we traded technology—stem cell research for a cure for the avian plague organism. The technology we traded was stolen and used for creating a genetic bomb. We're the cause of this world as it is now. I . . . I just can't risk it."

"Then how are we going to escape!" Charlene said, suddenly angry. "I don't want to die on this planet five billion light-years from Earth that's moving right into a black hole."

He turned away. "I'm the captain. I'll find a way, or die trying. But I can't risk corrupting this society any further than it's already been corrupted."

There was the sound of a door opening. Moments later, three soldiers appeared with weapons that looked like crude bayonets, but the knives were attached to poles rather than rifles. They opened the locked cell, and one of them said, "You," indicating Mohammad, "come with us."

When he didn't move, they grabbed him and dragged him out of the cell, then slammed the door and locked it behind them.

John grabbed the bars and shouted at them, but it was like talking to pillars of stone. "Guerrero," he yelled, "where are they taking him?"

"To the dueling chambers. Your Mr. Mohammad must fight other prisoners to the death. Whoever wins lives to fight another day. Whoever loses, dies in the arena."

"But that's so wrong!" Charlene called out.

"It's their way of justice," Guerrero replied matter-of-factly. "They don't have to keep prisoners crowded in the cell that way. This eliminates overcrowding and repeat offenders. It is also considered a less barbaric way of dealing with crime and punishment, because the government hasn't sentenced anyone to death. Instead, that is the choice of the prisoner."

"Not barbaric?" John said, his voice rising. "Not barbaric? That's the epitome of barbarianism. You've been brainwashed because it's been so long since you knew freedom. They've fooled you into believing this is the way life is supposed to be. But it's wrong. I come from a civilization where this kind of stuff is wrong!"

Only silence came from the dark cell.

Soon, the sound of the door opening and closing came again. Again, three soldiers came to their cell and opened it.

It was John's turn this time. As he was taken to the stairs leading up, he heard "I'm your friend," from Guerrero.

"Some friend," he muttered.

⊹⟩⟩⟩⟩⟩⟩◈ ✺✺ ◈⟨⟨⟨⟨⟨⟨⊹

"We are taking you to meet the imperial king," one of them said while they hustled him along. They paused only long enough to shove an overcoat hastily over his head and force his arms through the armholes. Then, his hands tied behind his back, he was walked onto a red carpet that seemed endless, passing through another room.

In this second room, lines of soldiers stood on either side of the red carpet. Their hands rested on their long swords, the tips embedded into the ground. They stood with blank stares as John passed.

The imperial king sat atop a throne in the distance. John walked until they were only ten feet apart, and the soldiers ordered John to kneel, then forced him to kneel.

"You may rise now," the king said in a sonorous voice. John stood with the help of the soldiers, but wobbled in their rough grasping.

"What brings you to our world again?" the king asked. "We have heard of you from the ancient ones. As if one attempt to destroy us wasn't enough, you come back to try to finish the job?" He held up the vial in his hand. "Could it possibly be that you have tried to bring us even more harm in this tiny bottle?"

Out of breath, John said, "I tried to tell your soldiers . . . We're on a peaceful scientific mission. To find a cure for a plague on our world. The cure is in that vial. If you'll just give us the vial and let us go, we'll leave and cause you no harm."

"We can't let you leave," the king replied. "I have questioned your Abdul Mohammad. You brought a great harm to us, and this is punishable by death. I have ordered you brought here for your sentencing. As the leader of your group, you will be held responsible for the actions of your people. However, your crew-members will also suffer your fate."

John said, "We've done nothing to warrant this treatment. I demand that you give me a cause or justification for our arrest and our sentencing—"

The imperial king stood, walked to John and grabbed his hair, forcing John to look at him. "Don't exercise your tongue to me with your lies." Then he forcefully threw John to the floor and kicked him in the stomach.

Leaving John writhing in pain, the king walked back to his throne, saying, "If you don't know why you are here, I will tell you. Many years we were at war. We won and established a united world, free of breakaway colonies demanding their independence. But a secret society arose. Remnants of the breakaway colonies used a technology to develop mutant fighters—a technology that the legends say was brought by you on your last trip here. These fighters nearly destroyed all of us. They disappeared, and we could never locate them."

He glared at John. "And now, you have brought us more trouble. A few days ago, a platoon of our soldiers was attacked by the mutants. Before almost all of our soldiers were killed, the mutants said they were looking for you and your crew. They know we have you here, and have agreed to leave us alone if we ensure your deaths. We could simply give you over to them, but in exchange for their peace, I'm sentencing you all to death in the dueling chamber."

The king shifted his gaze to the guards. "Sentencing has been imposed. Take him back to the cell."

Even knowing it was futile, John struggled to get free, but to no avail. As he was being taken away, he shouted, "Where is my crewmember, Mohammad, where is he?"

The king said, "He already met his fate in the dueling chamber, the same fate you all will in a few hours." Then looking at the guards, he shouted, "Prepare all of them for the dueling chamber!"

This time, John memorized the path they took back to the cell. The knowledge might be worthless, but if there was any way he could get back to the king and retrieve that vial, he had to remember the way to the throne room.

A quick glance at the floor where he walked showed a glint of metal. He recognized it as a wire and formulated a quick plan. He started an argument with the guards and began to struggle with them. Startled, they released him, and he ran and fell to the ground, over the wire, grasping it in his hand.

⊹⟫⟪ ❀❀ ⟫⟪⊹

The crewmembers in the cell heard the door slowly open, and then the sounds of footsteps. The two guards escorted John into the room. Or perhaps more accurately, Charlene thought, they were carrying him, since John was hog-tied.

Without looking at them, the guards opened the cell and threw him into it, saying, "You all have two hours to prepare."

Then, they walked over to the cell across from theirs, unlocked it and took Guerrero. Charlene watched to see him, having never seen him before in the darkened chamber. She noted that he was older than they were, and as she had imagined, his eyes held only a dull spark of life.

While the crew untied John, Feldman asked, "Where did they take you?"

John shook his hands free of the bindings and wiped a hand across his sweating face. "They took me to meet the king. *Not* a friendly person. He had one view. *His* view. He passed judgment on us for freeing the six mutants of death, and for bringing the stem cell technology. We . . . We've all been sentenced to death. We need to get the hell out of here."

He noticed that some food had been given to the crew, but it didn't appear they had eaten any of it. John's hunger overcame his orders not to eat the food. After eating, he was strong enough to stand. "I need a status report," he said. "Have any of you found a way to escape?"

Feldman shook his head. "This cave is impenetrable."

He pulled out the wire he'd shoved into his pants and gave it to Feldman, saying, "You're the lock expert, try picking the lock."

While Feldman worked on the lock, John told the crew, "There are ten guards outside that door. We have to take them. Once we accomplish that, we'll head to the imperial palace and take back the vial. The throne room's guarded by hundreds of sword-toting soldiers. If we manage to escape, we have our work cut out for us."

Charlene grabbed his arm. "You mean to tell me that after we leave here we're not heading straight for the exit door of this place? We've already lost some of the crew. We're not going to prove anything to anyone in a final act of heroism. Remember, five memorials. So far, there are two. Who'll be the next three we lose?"

With a heavy sigh, John said, "Very good speech. Outstanding. But you're not in charge of this mission. We started with ten. There are five memorials. That means at least five will survive to make it back home with the vial. Whether that

−160−

includes me or you or Suzie over there, I don't know. But someone's getting that vial back."

"You don't know that," she spouted back. "This planet's history hasn't been set, remember? We all could die today—"

Screams came from outside the chamber door, followed by unfamiliar noises.

"What's that?" Suzie said, terrified.

John listened. "I don't know. Might be the mutants. Maybe they found us. Or maybe they're coming to get us for the duel. . . ."

His words trailed off and the crew stood in tense silence, listening.

The door to the chamber crashed open. Whether it was the mutants of death or some as-yet-unknown attackers, they could now see the guards being thrown like toy dolls past the open door. One guard raced inside the chamber and looked around, eyes wild.

And then, John saw what was doing the throwing.

"Vincent? *Vincent?*"

Vincent raced into the chamber, grabbed the guard and threw him thirty feet across the chamber. Then he turned to John. "Who did you expect? Katie the cleaning lady? Stand back."

They did, and with two hands, he bent the bars, smiling as he did. "They just don't make jails like they used to, huh?"

"We thought you were dead," John said, astounded, and slid through the opening Vincent had created. "How did you survive the fall off the mountain? No one could have survived a fall that high. Not to mention those boulders that fell on you—"

"Hey, hey, slow down," Vincent said. "Usually, it's *me* who gets too excited. But, to answer your question, I don't know what happened. I felt it start after I ate those berries. Before I could tell anyone about it, I passed out and fell off the mountain. When I came to, I saw you guys on the pyramid. I followed your balloon, then tracked your footsteps and saw you being taken here.

"But, for whatever reason, it's like . . . like I've adapted to this planet. No, better than that." He pointed to the bars he'd just bent to free them. "Doing that? Didn't even break a sweat. And . . . it's like my mind is completely clear now. It's like I know things, and I don't even know how I know them. Like . . . I know that this planet has changed all of us. That we all have a hidden strength. And that eating those berries just helped bring mine out."

John reached out and patted his arm. "Whatever the reason, I'm glad you're back with us. We need you and your, ah, your newly found strength. We have a mission to complete."

Vincent looked around the cell and counted to himself. "Mohammad. Where's Mohammad?"

John said, "He was forced to fight in what this civilization calls the dueling chamber. He . . . lost his battle. There was a guy named Guerrero down here with us. They took him a little while ago. We're all scheduled to do the same in the next hour. But before that happens, we have to make it to the throne room. I'm sure they're keeping our equipment somewhere in there or near there. And the king had the vial, too. But it's surrounded by hundreds of guards. With swords."

Vincent shrugged. "If we make it, save the imperial king dude for me, and let's get the hell out of here."

They all stepped out of the jail chamber and began walking down the hall. While they walked, Vincent pulled two short-handled knives from the sheath on his belt. "I grabbed these from the guards. Figured they might come in handy."

John hefted the knife in his hand. "Thanks. You don't know how much I've been missing this."

He instructed the others to take the knives from the unconscious guards. Feeling that their chances had just gotten better, they moved forward.

But then, he stumbled to his knees, grabbing onto Vincent's shirt.

"What's wrong, man?"

"I . . . feel kind of queasy," he said. "No, actually, I feel terrible. It must have been the food I ate."

The nausea receded, and when his strength returned, he stood.

Vincent looked at him with concern. "If you ate the planet's food, you might be changing too."

John shook his head. "I . . . don't know. I just felt sick all of a sudden. Could've been anything."

After a moment, he stood. "Let's do this." He then led them over the bodies of the fallen guards and down the hall.

Their first test came before John was ready. Before any of them were ready. When they headed up the stairs on the first leg of their journey to the throne room, they were confronted by more weapon-brandishing guards. Vincent called over his shoulder to the rest of the crew, "Okay, now's the time. Show me what you got!"

With Vincent, Feldman and John in the lead, they all started fighting knife-style. Vincent defeated over half the guards, yet John again fell to the ground. Only Vincent's quick thrust at the soldier ready to finish him off kept him from being killed.

After the melee ended, Vincent looked around. Sam Sizemore and Juan Perez lay in pools of their own blood.

Charlene opened her mouth, but John said quickly, "Don't say it."

"If I don't, will it change anything?"

"Maybe not, but there's no sense worrying about something we can't do anything about. Let's go."

He led the remaining crew around the bodies, and they marched on.

Losing two more of the crew didn't stop John's determination, but it did make him more cautious. When they reached what appeared to be a side door, he said to the remaining crew, "Find a way out of this city and return to the balloon. If Vincent and I haven't made it back to the balloon within two hours, take off without us, find the time machine and return to Earth."

"But John," Suzie said, "we shouldn't leave without you and Vince—"

"That's an order!"

They saluted John and left. John nodded at Vincent, and they continued on through the mazelike palace.

As they neared the final corridor to the throne room, they discovered there were no guards waiting for them. But then wall panels on either side of them flew open and hundreds of guards appeared. The entrance at the other end of the corridor slid closed, creating an open chamber where they were in the center of a circle of guards, outnumbered and out-armed.

The lead guard, the one who had taunted John before, spoke up. "Welcome to the dueling chamber, John Richards."

Surrounded, John and Vincent faced in opposite directions, backing each other, then pulled out their knives.

"I hope you've been practicing," John whispered to Vincent.

The imperial king appeared from one of the open wall panels.

"You're very punctual," he said. "You couldn't have timed your destruction better. I was going to send troops to come get you out of your cell, but instead you come here to it. Welcome to the dueling chamber." Then he looked at the lead guard. "Kill those two first, then find the rest and kill them too."

The encircling guards raised their weapons and ran toward Vincent and John.

The soldiers seemed to be no match for Vincent. With one kick, he sent each of them flying through the air. When they rose and ran toward him again, with one punch, he knocked each soldier hundreds of feet away, where they lay unconscious. In the process, his enhanced quickness allowed him to dodge every move of their swords.

Meanwhile, John was enduring a lightning-quick lesson in his own enhanced power, which hadn't reached its peak, but was enabling him to hold off much longer than he expected. Eventually, though, the soldiers overwhelmed him. Just as he could no longer fend off their blows and knife slashes, Vincent appeared.

After a fierce battle, they finished off all the soldiers in the chamber. Some of the guards and the imperial king had disappeared, though. So their next move was to administer one karate kick each to the throne room's door. That was all it took to break down the massive double-door.

John looked around, surprised that his vision had enhanced along with his strength and speed. But his new eyes didn't reveal the vial, or any likely location. "We'll have to search for it," he said.

"You know, before I ate those berries, I'd be saying, 'I'm tired of all that searching we've been doing,'" Vincent said with a grin. "But now, whatever we have to do, we'll do—"

At first, they couldn't tell where the noise was coming from. Both of them went still, listening to the growing buzzing, trying to identify it.

After a second, Vincent looked down. "I . . . it sounds like bees buzzing. And it's coming from the floor."

It took them a while to find the corridor leading downstairs, one that John hoped would take them directly to the source of the strange buzzing. As Vincent had implied, not only were his physical strength and senses enhanced, his intuition seemed almost supernaturally strong. He couldn't shake the thought that when they found the vial, they'd find their other belongings, too—including their sat phones and the handheld computer they had used as a homing device.

At the end of the down staircase, they entered a large cavern.

"It's like some sort of giant warehouse," Vincent muttered in awe. The buzzing here was so loud, he put his hands over his ears. "Or a torture chamber, maybe."

In a room next to the storage area, they found the source of the noises. Rather, they walked into the middle of it. With one step through the door, they'd walked inside a corridor comprised of a giant beehive. To their sides and above them, millions of bees worked diligently among what appeared to be miles of honeycombs. But each of these bees was over a foot long.

"Amazing!" Vincent whispered.

"And a little dangerous," John replied. "I think we'll be okay, though—at least until they notice us. And look," he pointed to a table about twenty feet into the corridor. "I think that's what we came for."

As they walked further into the corridor, the noise of millions of bees grew even louder. John's earlier safety concerns faded when they discovered that, even if the bees wanted to attack them, they couldn't, thanks to a thin mesh of wires holding them against the corridor's walls and ceiling.

Still, the men edged warily toward the table.

The storage chest wasn't locked, and John eased it open it, gratified to see not only the vial, but also all their equipment.

Their celebration was cut short by a dark figure that entered through the same door they had. "It's the king," John whispered to Vincent. "Oh, goody."

The imperial king stopped about eight feet away, his face full of anger, and reached out and hit a button on a nearby wall panel. Slowly, the wire barrier separating the bees began to open, "Because you gave the colonists the stem cell research," he called to them, "our bees' venom is one thousand times more potent than the original bees on this planet. I hope you like honey!"

With that, he opened up his robes, revealing three more sets of arms. Eight large knives came out of his pockets and leaped into the hand at the end of each arm. Swinging all eight knives in attack formation, he began walking toward John and Vincent as the metal screens holding the bees back began retracting.

Keeping his eyes on the king, John told Vincent, "If we've adapted to a planet that's sitting next to a black hole, then, just like a black hole, I bet we can bend light now."

Vincent nodded, then gazed at one of the overhead light fixtures. Instantly, the light shifted from its downward direction, concentrated itself, and shot straight into the king's eyes. With the king blinded, John ran to him and gave him a powerful kick. The force of the kick propelled the king into the giant beehive, awakening the bees.

The bees, easily evading the slicing knives from the king's multiple arms, attacked him with their venomous stingers. Some of the bees flew toward Vincent and John, who had already grabbed the vial and their equipment and were running to the door at the end of the corridor.

To keep the bees from pursuing them, they slammed the door shut, then kept running until they were outside the imperial palace seconds later.

With their enhanced speed, they quickly caught up with the rest of the crew, who had already reached the balloon. As before, the device used the sun's power to change oxygen molecules to helium, and the balloon lifted. The colorful craft took off into the clear sky. As they rose into the air, they saw the city getting smaller. Higher and higher the balloon carried the crew, and the blowing wind carried them over uncrossable mountains to the time machine.

As they headed in the craft's direction, Charlene said, "I'm not crazy about this planet's politics, but it's a beautiful sight from the sky, isn't it?"

"Yeah," John replied. "But like Dorothy said, there still no place like home."

As they relaxed in triumph and exhaustion, their thoughts and conversations centered on returning to Earth with the cure for the deadly disease.

About the time Charlene told John, "We're nearing the time machine," the wind started changing direction. "Land on that mountain over there," John said, then turned to Vincent with a grin. "Recognize it?"

"Oh, yeah. That's the mountain I fell from. Where I first learned that I was like Superman. Only without the tights."

John laughed aloud. "Yep. One and the same. Only this time, none of us is going to fall into the ocean. We're just parking there so we can use it for extra lift. Just in case we need this balloon again. Don't want any more slow starts like we had on top of that pyramid."

"You got that right," Vincent said. "But with a little luck, the time machine's still in the cave where we hid it, still fine." He looked around. "If it is, we won't ever need to think about this balloon, or this planet, ever again."

The balloon made a soft landing, and the crew gathered their equipment and headed down the mountain. They were on guard against any possible tremors this time, but except for a few slight vibrations from the unstable mountain, nothing happened.

Taking the same route they did before, they would cross the river soon. "Be sure to look out for those giant snakes we met with before," John instructed them. "We don't want any nasty surprises this time."

Vincent laughed and made a dogpaddling motion with his free arm. "Don't worry, boss. Not only am I a better swimmer now, but I've had some great practice with diving too."

But as they approached the river, what they found shocked them. The gigantic snake that once terrorized them was now a giant skeleton. Not even its skin was left.

"What could have caused this?" John asked. "You think there are piranha fish in the river?"

Suzie and Charlene looked around, nervous, and Feldman said, "I don't think it's anything in the water, John. The snake's not even in the water. It's like someone took it *from* the water and stripped all its flesh off."

"I don't know what did this," John said, "but I'm not going to stick around to find out. Let's get to the time machine and get the hell off this planet." He paused a moment, then added, "If everybody's rested up, let's double-time it."

The crew began trotting at a faster pace toward the time machine.

Finally, the cave-in where they'd hidden the time machine was in sight. They went inside it and pushed the craft out, then Vincent, Feldman and Suzie ran it through its internal and external checks.

"It's right as rain and steady as a rock," Vincent said as he settled into the copilot's seat beside John. "Let's fire this baby up and head home."

"Not yet."

Vincent turned his head toward him, noticed him looking at the screen that showed the rear of the machine. "What's up?"

"We've got company."

"Huh?" Vincent peered into the viewer.

"It's . . . someone you never got a chance to meet."

⇥— ❦ —⇤

"I took your advice and escaped," Guerrero said after John stepped out of the time machine and shook his hand. "I told them that I refused to fight, and took my earned freedom." His tired-looking face broke into a smile. "Until you reminded me that freedom is possible, I never even thought about doing it. And I never had anyone think about my well-being before. After I escaped, I saw your balloon. So I found a balloon someone had hidden inside the palace and followed you here. I had to tell you goodbye, my friend."

They walked until they were about twenty feet away from the time machine, and John said, "It makes me sad to leave you on a planet that doesn't value each person's freedom. If I thought it was possible, I'd take you with us. But, we have no idea how the time-travel, or Earth's climate, would affect you."

Guerrero waved a hand. "Not necessary. I have no fear of anyone here. It was simple to break free of my captors once I used the power of my voice to declare my freedom. And . . . I've heard of a few of us left on the planet who are also searching, but lost. I will find them. When I do, I will tell them the message you taught me. In time, perhaps things will be different on Peligroso."

John's heart was too full to allow him to speak, so he nodded.

"I know I'll never see you again, but I wish you the best in your pursuit of life, liberty and happin—" He stopped speaking and turned his head.

In their rush of triumph over escaping the imperial king, they had forgotten about their other enemies on the planet. The mutants had found them.

In a flash, the one called the boca had covered Guerrero. Its acid left nothing but a skeleton.

There was no time for John to mourn. A huge boulder, thrown by the mutant bear, sailed over his head toward the time machine. As it crashed into their only way home, John saw the other four mutants approaching.

"Stop time!" John screamed toward the machine, running toward it.

A second later, Vincent stuck his head out and shouted, "I can't, the rock did something—"

"Prepare to fight then" John yelled, and whipped his knife from his sheath.

All six mutants of death attacked the crew. John and Vincent held them off with well-placed kicks and knife-thrusts, but it was clear that the mutants' greater size, quickness and strength would eventually give them a deadly advantage.

John yelled over his shoulder, "Push the machine back into the cave!" Then he called over to Vincent, "Any ideas?"

Vincent fended off one of the creatures with a karate chop to its neck, then yelled back, "Yes, but it's dangerous."

John whipped his knife at one of the creatures, who dropped back only a little. "Any more than this?"

Without replying, Vincent began spinning. John couldn't watch; he was busy with all six creatures now. But after a second, even the creatures stopped their frontal assault and stood, in amazement, at what was happening.

Vincent's spinning had increased until he could no longer be seen in the small triangular cloud his motions created. As John watched, the creatures edged closer to the spinning tornado. One creature reached out a hand.

John jumped away, but the creatures weren't that quick-minded—one by one, the cosmic tornado Vincent had created sucked all of them in.

The cosmic tornado, with Vincent and the creatures inside, moved a few hundred feet away from the crew and time machine, then started slowing.

John tensed himself and held up his knife hand, prepared for the creatures to return and try to resume the battle. They didn't. When the tornado finally stopped spinning, it was gone, along with Vincent and the mutants.

The crew slowly emerged from the cave and stood in silence, not wanting to believe what Vincent's absence meant—that to save the rest of them from the creatures, he had sacrificed himself. They looked around for him, even going inside the cave to make sure he hadn't somehow ended up in there. But as they already knew in their hearts, he was gone, along with the creatures that had tried to kill them and had terrorized this planet for eons.

John looked up into the sky and saw the dusty remnants of the cosmic tornado.

"Vincent, you've gotten yourself out of worse scrapes," he whispered.

It was a faint hope, but at that moment, hope was all he had.

33

Out of danger for the moment, they turned their efforts to repairing the time machine. They discovered that the reason Vincent couldn't make the machine work was that the boulder thrown by the bear had severed some external wires. Soldering the wires together made the machine functional again.

"Well, it looks like we're ready to go," Suzie said as she squatted down to put the soldering iron away.

"Not yet."

She looked up, confused. "Why not? The machine should work just fine—"

"It's not that," John said. "I . . . Ever since I got these strange powers, it's like I'm more . . . sensitive to stuff. And I just keep feeling that we should hang around. I know it's risky, but . . . I just keep feeling like we should."

It was so fantastic, he couldn't tell her his specific intuition—if they could just stay and manage to survive a while longer, Vincent might be able to return to them. It was too unbelievable, even to him.

A day and a night was all John's conscience would allot for the wait. The rest of the crew was willing to wait longer, but John knew that each day that passed was another day that Earth's humanity was deprived of the chance to survive. Not to mention that his mother, still in suspended animation, deserved her chance to live.

They turned on the time machine and stopped time, then moved forward to escape the planet's gravitational pull. John looked at Suzie's hand on the controls, noticed that she was moving as slowly as possible, and understood why.

"It's okay, Suzie," he said. "Get us out of here. I was wrong, and . . . wherever he is, he'll understand."

Still, they crept forward slowly in time, all the while looking for any sign or message Vincent might have been able to send or sign that he might have left. "As smart as he is," John reasoned, "if anyone could find a way to leave us a message, Vincent could. And he still had his sat phone with him."

"He lost his sat phone, remember?" Suzie said, her voice gentle.

"But there was one we left in the cave. So maybe—"

He turned his head away from Suzie, not wanting her to see the desolation he was sure was on his face.

It was another lost cause, but he decided to check their e-mails. Unlike before, when Auyda's e-mails came during their journey, there wasn't one e-mail.

Soon they reached the tear in space. But there was no jubilance like before. This time, it was as though Vincent's loss had sucked them all into an emotional black hole. They had found the vial, but lost Vincent Goff . . . the kid no one thought would excel at anything. The brilliant young man who had triumphed over impossible odds.

"Belay my last order," John suddenly said. "We're going back to Peligroso. Right before we went into the planet's past."

"But, John," Suzie said, "don't you remember? Once a person dies, we can't go back and stop it. And we can't go back to the same timeline in the future twice. If we do we'll draw the time eliminators and—"

"I don't think Vincent is dead," he said quietly. He saw their shocked expressions and felt his face grow warm, but kept his eyes boring holes into theirs. "We've been dealing with theories all along. Here's my own theory. I think we'll be okay. We're not going back to change anything. We're going to the future, right before we left the future on Peligroso.

"And I have a plan. It's dangerous, but no more so than anything we've gone through so far. And we owe it to Vincent to try one last time. Even so, I need to know . . . are you behind me on this?"

Suzie reached out and placed her hand on his. Soon, the other crewmembers' hands layered on top of hers. "We're in," Feldman said, and the others quickly agreed.

"Okay. Now, I need everyone to put on their equilibrium-range detectors. . . ."

<hr />

Between Suzie and Charlene's careful navigation, they managed to return to the planet minutes before they left the first time, and landed on the mountain out of sight of themselves. They saw themselves running from the black-hole tornado and escaping into the time machine.

But then something happened that none of them could have predicted. After they left, the tornado changed course and headed straight their way.

"I have a hunch," John called to them over the growing noise. "I believe this is the same tornado Vincent created to save us from the mutants. I believe it's also the same tornado we encountered the first time we landed on the planet. And . . . I believe that each time, it was Vincent inside the tornadoes. I believe he knew of the danger and had traveled in time to warn us."

The others just looked at John, trying to absorb what he was telling them, but also trying to believe it was true.

"If I'm wrong, we're all dead," he said over the noise. "If I'm right . . ." His voice lowered. "I have to be right."

With frightening speed, the tornado drew closer. As it did, John left the time machine and walked in its direction. The terrified crew watched as the tornado seemed to lose its power and stop turning as rapidly, then grow weaker until it was gone. Just as the cloud of whirling dust vanished, Vincent fell out of it, along with six mutants of death, who landed in a heap about fifty feet away from him and were still.

They raced to him, and Charlene checked his vital signs. "He's alive!"

"Look!" Suzie pointed. The boca's arms were beginning to shift.

John grabbed Vincent and climbed the mountain to get back to the time machine. As the craft began to move, they saw the snakelike boca behind them, raising its great head in a frustrated bellow.

34

When they arrived in their own time, the machine was instantly surrounded by Time Travelers Academy staff. John carried Vincent, still unconscious, off the time machine, yelling, "Get this man a doctor."

Charlene and General Jones, accompanied by John, whisked the vial containing the cure from the time machine and hand-carried it to Dr. Huber, who led the team who would test, duplicate and administer the cure if the tests proved promising.

Next, Charlene and Jones led John down a hallway. "Hey, I've never been to this part of the Academy," John said.

"We have a hospital here," Jones said. "And some plague victims who volunteered to be tested for the cure. They're frozen, because we had no idea how long it would take you to recover the vial." He glanced at John out of the corner of his eye. "And yes, your mother's with them."

John's paced picked up a little more, hearing that.

The five patients were in a sealed room, but could be seen through a glass window.

"How do you know they'll wake up?" John said. "How did Mom wake up that first time and survive to be frozen again?

Jones smiled. "Let's just say that our Roswell visitors brought Earth lots of ideas we didn't have before. And they also gave us the means to make enough cure, right now, for the volunteers."

John looked at him, skeptical.

"How do you think we're able to create so many doses of flu vaccine when we need to?"

After a moment, John shrugged. "I never thought about it, but . . . whatever works."

⊹⫸⟡ ❈❖ ⟡⫷⊹

Within an hour, Dr. Huber gave the technician the order to bring the volunteer plague victims out of their frozen state. Minutes later, they awakened. They had been frozen for over a week, but to them, it was yesterday. Having just been brought back from a frozen state, the avian plague in their bodies weren't progressing. But within hours, as their bodies completed reanimating, that would change, with deadly results.

John, Charlene, General Jones and Dr. Huber donned protective gear and entered the room. John headed toward his mother like a shot, but General Jones reached out and held him back. "Not yet, son."

John glared at him but obeyed. His mother gave him a reassuring wave and a smile. "It's all right John," she called out. "I don't want you near me while I've still got this nasty bug."

Jones smiled at her, then turned to the row of beds. "We have good news and bad news. Which do you want to hear first?"

John's mom said, "Why, the good news first, General. Of course!"

"We've obtained a cure for the avian plague."

This brought cheers and hoots, if weak ones, from everyone in the group.

"Now the bad news. As you all know, you're here on a volunteer basis and this cure has never been tested. If we give it to you, we don't know if it will cure you. . . . It might even kill you."

One of the patients called out, "You told us that before, and I still signed the form. We all did. What do we have to lose? I say we get this over with!"

There were nods all around, and the first patient took the cure. Within moments, his skin returned to its original color, his visibly swollen lymph nodes shrank, and he said, "Hey, I don't feel weak anymore." Before anyone could stop him, he flung his legs off the bed and stood.

One by one, each of the others took the cure. Within minutes, it was clear that the second vial not only worked, but worked fast. The blood samples Charlene took showed that not only had the ML-20 been inactivated, but, as Auyda had predicted, the cure also killed the separated bubonic plague bacteria and the avian flu virus.

John raced back into the room and headed straight for the last bed in the row.

As soon as their embrace ended, he pulled back, and was stunned to see tears in his mother's eyes. "What's wrong?" he said, his words tripping over themselves. "Do you feel sick? Should I call Dr. Huber—?"

"No, dear, it's not that." She pointed to the curtain next to her bed. "Pull that curtain and then come sit with me."

He did as she instructed. The sadness had never left her face, and he was afraid to speak.

He didn't have to. After a moment, she took a deep breath and said, "I so want you to stay here with me." She reached up and caressed the side of his face.

"General Jones told me what you were trying to do, and you did it. It's such a miracle that both of us are alive right now. But . . . you have to go home."

"Back to Rockville? But why, Mom? You just said you wanted me to stay—"

She reached up and placed her forefinger on his lips. "Honey . . . something happened . . . to your friends, and . . . Bonita. Something terrible. I heard about it just before I got sick."

"What happened, Mom?" he said, panic coloring his voice. "Tell me—"

At that moment, her eyes glazed over and she turned deathly pale. "I'm so sorry, I . . . I don't feel so well. I . . ."

She began to fall backward, and he grabbed her and eased her head to the pillow, then hit the call button for the nurse.

But it was Charlene who appeared. She took one look John's mother and said, "John, we're still checking side effects. The antidote had this effect on the guy in Bed 1 too. Here." She handed him a pill. "You have to take this too. Anyone who might have been exposed to the plague or the ML-20 has to take it."

"But what's wrong with her?"

"She was already so sick when she took the cure, it hit her harder than it would have a healthier person. We believe it's temporary. Just until she's had more rest. But . . ."

He peered at her. "What is it?"

"We've tested it and tried to alter it, but . . . within six hours, all the enhanced abilities you gained on Peligroso will go away." She gave him an empathetic smile. "Bad side effect, huh? Kind of like going from Superman to Gilligan."

With a sigh, John took the antidote pill from her, placed it in his mouth, and drank the glass of water she gave him.

General Jones and Mike Adams entered the room, John turned his questions to them. "My mom said something terrible happened to Bonita. What happened to her, and why didn't either of you say something before now?"

"It was my suggestion," Jones said. "We didn't want you upset on your return trip to the planet."

"You mean you knew something bad had happened to them and didn't tell me right away? You *lied* to me?"

Jones reached for John's shoulder, "Come to my office and we'll—"

But John was on his way to the door, on his way back to Texas. He paused just long enough to say, "All along, I've been straight with you, and yet you lied to me. You *lied!*"

He pointed to his mother's unconscious form. "I'll be coming back. And if one hair on my mother's head is harmed, I'll be coming to *personally* kick both your asses."

"John, I don't think it's a good idea to—"

But the general could have saved his breath. John was already gone.

Jones had any number of options to have John detained and brought back. And perhaps he should. But John Richards was a man the general had come to admire, not only for his intelligence but also his internal strength. Without both, he would never have survived both journeys.

"You have to find out for yourself," he whispered at the open door. "Perhaps if you do, you'll discover your destiny."

35

John never took the antidote; he'd held it against his gumline while he was talking to Charlene. He headed for the nearest vending machine, bummed some change from the first nurse who passed, bought a pack of gum, took out a slice, and used the wrapper to wrap up the pill.

"Later," he muttered. "I'll take it later. Right now, I need my strength."

Once outside the hospital he began running, pleased that the incredible speed he'd gained on Peligroso had remained with him. At the gate, he jumped the fence, leaving only a dust-trail visible as he sped along at hundreds of miles per hour.

The hospital staff wasted no time. Within hours after John's departure, the cure was available in pills, with injections for those too sick to swallow the pills. The information was sent to drug corporations to manufacture the cure. By the next day, it was being shipped to every country in the world.

But had he known, John wouldn't have cared about any of that. He'd headed for the karate school first, and now stared, mute, at the parking lot it had become.

"Antonio would never let this happen," he muttered. "Never!"

But his words didn't change the facts. Antonio's house was deserted and locked up tight, with a for-sale sign in the overgrown front lawn.

A car pulled up to the house. John thought it was Antonio, but it was Antonio's twin brother.

"Mario, what happened?" he pleaded. "The school's gone, Antonio and Natasha aren't here—"

The man who looked so much like his childhood friend reached out a hand to steady him. "After you left, they all went back to the karate school after the curfew. They were all robbed and killed, and . . . the building was torched. There was some talk that the asshole next door had something to do with it, but . . . we

-176-

couldn't prove anything. I'm so sorry, John. I know Antonio never meant this to happen."

"I know," John whispered, knowing that if Antonio and Natasha were dead, then he had to believe that the rest of the story was true—that Bonita, the woman he had finally come to love, was also gone because of a cruel and senseless act of violence. And Chen Kahn likely died trying to defend the other three.

The rage that had propelled him home was gone. Distraught, he accompanied Mario to their burial site. "But wait, I want to stop there first," he said, indicating a florist's shop. Minutes later, they stood at four graves: graves that were still so new, the grass over them had barely turned green.

"I picked this spot because it was close to the school," Mario said, his face sad. "And the police couldn't find any family members for Mr. Kahn, so I told them I'd bury him next to . . ."

When Mario finished, he nodded, then thanked him for doing the same thing he would have done.

Holding the flowers, he talked to Bonita, Natasha, Kahn and Antonio for a while, then laid the flowers down.

"You might not have noticed it," Mario said, "but we set up a little memorial where the school used to be. Want to see it?"

John nodded. "Yeah. I'd like that."

The memorial was a simple wooden cross near the road, with the names of the dead inscribed upon it. "We wanted to do something nicer," Mario said. "More permanent. But as you can imagine, the new owner said no."

"That's okay," John said. "It doesn't have to be much. You and I know what it means."

He bowed his head to pray, and when he lifted his eyes again, he saw a group of men coming toward him. He could see what Mario couldn't—the laughing, cursing group was the Mal-A-Dies gang.

"When those men get here," he said to Mario, "let me handle it, okay?"

Mario looked. "Hey, that's the gang they think torched the school—"

"I know. Like I said, let me handle it."

It didn't take long for the gang leader to get on John's bad side.

"I guess your wedding plans are off," he taunted. "She should have ducked, and you should have paid us our money." The man smiled, showing his decayed teeth. "By the way, we haven't collected yet, where's our damn money!"

When John didn't reply, another of the gang spit on him.

"Oh, it must be raining," another one said.

John kept his stare on them but never moved, even though he knew he could easily kill them if he wanted. Taking his lack of reaction as weakness, one of the gang pulled a gun and aimed it at John's head.

But the punk pulled the gun away as soon as he heard the siren, and the entire gang turned and ran. The siren stopped as soon as the gang was out of sight, but the police car from which it had emanated continued in John and Mario's direction. When the driver emerged from it, John recognized Sergeant Kim, who'd

THE TIME TRAVELERS ACADEMY

responded before. Before. When Antonio was alive. When Bonita and Natasha were alive. Before everything had gone so horribly wrong.

John and Mario greeted Kim and accepted his condolences. "We've been looking for you," Kim said. "Can I speak with you alone for a minute?"

John glanced at Mario, who said, "It's okay. I'll wait here."

"I've been away," John replied as soon as they were alone. "The gang members killed them. So why are they still walking around free?"

"We don't have enough evidence . . . yet," Kim said. "But we know 100% that the gang members didn't kill Chen Lee Kahn. The ballistics test showed that the bullets that struck Mr. Kahn came from a gun that had Antonio Hernandez's fingerprints on it. That gun was registered to you."

For the first time, John met Kim's gaze directly. "I don't get it. Why would Antonio want to shoot Kahn? They weren't exactly friends. But Antonio respected him. We even trusted Kahn to look after the business while we went on a two-week trip to Russia!"

Kim looked at him for a long moment. "Perhaps you both trusted someone who wasn't honest with you. Chen Lee Kahn doesn't exist. We ran a check on him, and nothing came back. Nothing. We found his application for employment in the basement. Damaged by smoke, but legible. It was phony. It did lead us to finding out other names he's used. But when we ran a check on those names, we got nowhere. You should be careful who you hire."

"I . . . don't understand. I'm telling you, Antonio had no reason to kill him. Not one!"

Kim sighed. "Maybe Mr. Hernandez found out something about Mr. Kahn. Something Mr. Kahn didn't want anyone to find out. They both got into a fight and Antonio shot him."

John shook his head. "It doesn't make sense. If Antonio killed Kahn, then who killed Mr. Hernandez, his wife and her sister? Did Kahn kill Bonita?"

"We don't have enough evidence to know. We didn't find the gun."

John said, "So many questions and no answers. It doesn't make sense. Just that four people I knew and loved are dead."

"Correction. You didn't know Chen Lee Kahn. He doesn't exist."

Kim left, and John saw no reason to tell Antonio's grieving brother of Kim's suspicions about Antonio. What would be the point? With no witnesses, they'd never know who actually pulled the trigger.

John stared at the memorial, distraught. *Talk to me, Antonio. You never listen to me, and look where it got you! You always say some rules were meant to be broken, but look where it's gotten you. . . .*

Some rules were meant to be broken. . . .

Some laws are meant to be broken!

"Look, I have to go," he said to Mario. "Something Antonio would have wanted. Something I have to do . . ."

Before Mario could process what John was saying, John ran to and jumped over some cars, and left a befuddled Mario standing, alone, next to the makeshift marker.

When John reached the Academy, he slowed at the security fence, jumped over it, then proceeded to find Vincent. As he suspected, his friend had already returned to his room at the base housing. And his friend, at the moment, was sleeping . . . until John entered his room, grabbed a blanket from chair beside his bed, threw it over him, picked up the yelling, flailing bundle and raced out of the room.

Unlike John, Vincent had taken the antidote, which made him lose the powers he'd gained on Peligroso. Now, he was powerless to stop his abductor, whom he was certain was taking him for another blanket party. All his kicking and screaming did no good.

After a useless struggle, he felt himself rising in the air as John jumped over the same security fence. His only clue, had he been calm enough to notice it, was that they were traveling fast, much faster than a normal human could run.

John ran, carrying his struggling, blanket-wrapped burden, to a secluded place outside the barracks, roughly eight miles outside the base behind some nearby mountains.

"What got into you?" Vincent yelled as soon as John unwrapped him. "You could have just asked me to come outside, not grab me. I have two feet and I'm very capable of walking. What's your problem?"

John sighed. "I apologize for the surprise, but I couldn't risk anyone on the base hearing our conversation. And . . . I need your help."

Vincent stood up, a bit calmer now. "Whatever you need, you know you have it. And I know it has to be something serious. So I'll ask again . . . what's the problem?"

"The problem is, I know how to lead and command the time-machine crew, but you're the expert pilot and navigator on it."

"Okay, I'll avoid the obvious question for now," Vincent said. "But you're not entirely correct. You went through the same training I went through. You know how to pilot it just like I do. And now, to my first question. Why? The mission's over. No need to go back to Peligroso."

"I . . . I need your help," John said, not meeting Vincent's eyes. "This time, going backward . . . past the universal timeline. I need your help to go backward in Earth history."

Vincent walked away a few feet, then walked back to him, waving his hands in the air. "You know we can't do that, John. I'll do anything for you, but I can't do that. It's too dangerous. Do you remember in class about Einstein? That he might have already discovered time travel many years ago, but destroyed all his notes and records because even *he* thought it was too dangerous?"

"Something scared him into abandoning his work on time travel to the past. This time machine's like having the most powerful bomb in the universe. And what could be so important that you'd risk everything, *including your own life*, to go back in time?"

John walked to a nearby rock lying at the edge of the mountain. Sitting down, he explained what had happened to his friends and to Bonita. He finished by saying, "By the time I got there, everything was gone. Everything that mattered to me except my mom, I lost. My fiancée, my best friend and his wife and a co-worker I respected. All murdered. On top of that, my business was burned to the ground and foreclosed on, and purchased by one of the lowest, meanest men I've ever known."

A long moment passed, then Vincent said, "If it was me, I'd be pissed. Maybe if they'd told you when it happened, you could have held onto the land where the school used to be. But that's all. You couldn't have saved your friends, or the school building. If you go back in time and try to change a timeline that's already been set, you might create a paradox in time. The instructors weren't just saying that to hear themselves talk. Maybe this time, the time eliminators will show up and take both of us out."

"Yes, but the portal time travel shouldn't risk that—"

"Think, man! Think about when you told me this happened."

"Like I said, three weeks after I came to the Academy—"

"Right. So even if portal time travel was available—it's not, they disabled that feature—it's been over a month since the tragedy, and portal time travel can't go past one month."

Vincent flopped down on the rock next to John and put his head in his hand. "I'm sorry, man. I can't help you. It's against the rules of the Academy *and* the universal law of time travel. I'm so sorry, my friend. I just can't do this."

John stood slowly, his eyes to the ground, knowing that Vincent was right. Not only was his plan insane, but it risked killing both of them.

"I wish had never accepted this mission. Or that those time-recruiters never found me after they traveled to the past. If just one of those things hadn't happened, I'd have been there to stop what happened. Or at least, I could have tried."

Vincent looked up. "Can you repeat that? What you just said? About the time-recruiters?"

John shrugged. "Nothing that would change anything. I was approached by two time-recruiters who said they were from a month in the future. They gave me the same big yellow envelope I'm sure they gave you, I opened it, and just like you, my next stop was the TTA."

"But . . . why did they say they had to come from the future?" As Vincent spoke, he rose to stand and began pacing.

"They said they tried to contact me before I went to Russia, but couldn't—because they had to avoid contact with anyone except me. Later, I found out it was because they couldn't risk drawing the time eliminators to them."

Vincent shook his head as though trying to clear it. "Why was it so hard to find you?"

"Because I worked in Special Forces, in secret operations. Once I got out, all my records were destroyed. And I was under a different name in the military. By the time they found my real name and located me by my passport, the only way they could find me in time for the mission was to go back in time."

Vincent stopped pacing. "Look, I know you're not an expert in time-clause, time travel and time theories. So just trust me on this. . . . From what you're telling me, I think there's a chance you can save your friends. And I can help you."

"Thanks, Vin—"

"Not so fast. If I'm wrong, we might still sign our obituaries. Not only ours, but the universe and everyone who lives in it."

But then, a satisfied smirk transformed the young man's face. "That's if I'm wrong. But I'm seldom wrong when it comes to science. And anyway, if what you're telling me is true, then your family and friends shouldn't be dead and your business shouldn't be a parking lot."

To John's shocked look, he explained, "Simple. The agents that approached me were from my present. But the time-recruiters that approached *you* were from your future—about one month in your future. But that doesn't matter . . . they could have been from one day in your future. What does matter is that they were from your future, and anything they did, no matter how small, could have caused a change in the timeline—causing something to happen, good *or* bad, that wasn't supposed to happen in the first place. Like the deaths of your friends."

"But the time-recruiters didn't *do* anything," explained John. "They were very careful not to come in contact with anyone except me. In fact, our conversation only lasted seconds. Just enough time for them to hand me the envelope."

Vincent's smirk turned into a wide smile. "I guess you didn't study the chaos theory, Page 75, Section 2 in your Time Travelers Manual?"

"Well, maybe not as closely as you—"

"Okay, let me fill you in. Maybe they knew of the risk—because they avoided everyone except you. But maybe they didn't know that even a one-month backward skip in the universal timeline, *by itself*, could cause things to change. They probably didn't intend any harm. But . . . they unintentionally destroyed your life. Because anything those time-recruiters did to influence you in any way, form or fashion affected your future. You accepted a mission by reading an envelope that was from your future, and any action you took from reading that envelope changed your future."

John looked at him for a long moment. "Maybe I don't understand all that as well as you do, but I get the gist. . . . I think."

"Good enough. And I'll help you. But if we go back into your past, I can't get involved in your actions to save your friends. I'll remain on the time machine and wait for you. I'd be from the future, but *you're* going back to your own timeline. And . . . we might still trigger the time eliminators. So we have to be careful.

When I last saw the time machine, all eight equilibrium-range detectors were still in it. The wristwatch-looking things."

John smiled and nodded.

"And I need to get into the base's computer security to turn off the tampering alarms on the time machine. I know where they are, so it'll only take a few seconds. I'll also need a little time to reprogram the machine to go past the universal timeline—get past the blocks they put on it. But once we get through security, we can take the time machine and return it, and it'll be like we never left."

John thought a moment. "How do we get it outside the hangar it's in?"

"No problem there. Mike Adams filled me in on that one day. They only set up a separate launching pad because at first, they thought the machine would vibrate on takeoff. Turns out, it doesn't. So we just open the top of the hangar," he threw both arms toward the sky, "and away we go!"

"That's good. But . . . there's a roving patrol that goes around every sixty seconds. So if we're gone longer than sixty seconds, they'll notice the time machine missing. So we have to slide in and do this in between those 60 seconds. So out of those 60 seconds, we'll have maybe 15 seconds to get in and out. And that only leaves 45 seconds to do all the rest. And we'll have to return it to almost the same nanosecond or it'll be missed."

Vincent made a dusting-his-hands motion. "I might not have enhanced powers anymore, but I'm still fast. Don't worry about that part."

A long pause ensued, then John said, "Are you ready?"

"Yeah. Let's do this. I haven't had *nearly* enough excitement for a lifetime so far."

36

To traverse the eight miles as quickly as possible, Vincent allowed John to carry him piggyback. "But no blanket this time," he insisted, chuckling.

Back in his room at the base, Vincent tried to get into the base's security database. He managed to get into security, but the lack of the right password stopped him cold.

"Looks like they've got another level of access for remote computers," he said with a sigh. "I have to break the security code. It's normal for the pass codes to be assigned to the top person in charge, using his own password. Which is shared with only authorized persons. The top person in charge in General Jones, which will help."

"How so?" John asked.

"Because we know General Jones pretty well. Normally, the password is something a person can remember easily. So the person usually picks an important number or person or other term. Something important to them."

Vincent accessed General Jones's file.

"What's that link?" John said, and pointed to a line that said "Personal."

"Exactly what it looks like. Basically, everything about any computer user at TTA is stored on the central computer. Including what's stored on their own computer. That link is to the personal files on the general's computer."

Before John could stop him, Vincent clicked on the link.

Near the top of the listed files on the next screen was "FOXHOUND1," followed by a question mark.

Vincent looked up at John's gasp. "Everything okay?"

"Yeah. Yeah. I just saw something I thought I recognized. Hey, why not click on that one?"

Vincent's eyebrows rose. "John Richards, I never figured you for a hacker."

"Not a hacker, just curious."

"In case you don't know, my non-techie friend, they're one and the same."

The file contained a sketchy summary of the general's personal efforts to identify Foxhound1, but not why. So for some reason, General Jones knew of the mysterious Foxhound1, and like John, wanted to know the person's identity. Or perhaps Jones already knew who hid behind the codename, and chose not to commit that to the file for some reason. John supposed it didn't matter anymore whoever Foxhound1 turned out to be.

"Hey, come off the cloud, John. We've got a mission, remember?"

He shook his head and looked down at Vincent. "I'm not sure I feel good about this."

Vincent chuckled. "Considering what we just did and what we're *about* to do, you shouldn't feel guilty about a little snooping. I mean, now we know the General's hat size. That could come in handy at Christmas or his birthday."

John groaned. "I think I'll just sit here and let you work."

After numerous attempts to find the password to enter base security, Vincent said, "Man, I just remembered the general's favorite sport is golf. *Golf cart?* . . . Nope. . . . *Golf course?* . . . Nada. *Golf balls?* No way, Jose."

And then, he typed in *"Golf holes."* This was only a partial match, so he started plugging in numbers with it. "Voila!" he finally said. *"21golfholes.* Who would have thunk it?"

Two seconds later, he said, "I'm in."

John walked back over and looked at the screen over his shoulder. The display now showed the entire diagram of base security, then launch pad security, where Vincent created and superimposed an image of the time machine on the security cameras. "This will fool anyone watching the security monitors," he said. "Now, we don't have to worry about the guards making rounds while we're . . . uh, away."

Second, he disabled all the tampering alarms. "They'll be active again five minutes after we return. But now we can just walk in and take it, like taking candy from a baby."

John said, "No, that's stealing. We're only going to borrow this for a little while and return it."

+⊱—— ❦❧ ——⊰+

While everyone else slept, they snuck past the two boot-camp roving patrols with ease, yet were faced with another obstacle: how to get in the locked doors. "I have a plan," John whispered. Grabbing Vincent, he jumped over the launch-dome's wall, landing inside the building.

Vincent quickly changed the computer's programming to allow the time machine to go past the universal timeline. The console flashed a red danger sign, then accepted the change.

"It's ready," he whispered, and they took their seats. "Now, to create the rip in space we need to create the time portal."

He felt Vincent tense next to him, and understood why. What they were doing was dangerous, the consequences well described by Professor Rubiano in their classes—including meeting the time eliminators.

All that had seemed simple then, when they had confidence that they would never need to know it. But now, when he and Vincent both knew the risks, they knew a simple theory could lead to a complicated set of facts in a hurry. Nonetheless, he said nothing when Vincent pressed a red button on the console and within an instant, the clocks on the wall stopped. The ship moved into outer space, and into the future, and they watched the Earth rotate faster, then faster still, as they went forward in time. They went only three hours into the future to create the road in time, then rode that rip in space back to Earth, going backward in time along the way.

As though looking for a place to park his car in a parking lot, Vincent navigated the machine to John's house and parked it in his backyard.

Looking around, John said, "This is the day it all happened. This is the day I lost everyone and everything I loved. And I guarantee I'll make it right."

"Remember, you're not invincible," Vincent warned. "You could be killed in the same attack on your friends."

"What if I *am* killed? How will that affect time?"

"Theoretically, you're in your correct time. But there's another one of you at the Academy in training. And so you're safe. The other path you're on was caused by the time-recruiters."

"Speak English."

"Okay. If you're killed, and there was another one of you at the Academy in this same timeline, it might cause a severe paradox in time. You might destroy the universe."

"I'm curious what would happen if he did show up?"

"The time-equilibrium range would reach 100, and no more universe. But he's not going to show up." Vincent handed John the time-equilibrium range detector. "I'll monitor this from the time machine, too. Remember, once it reaches 90, time eliminators will appear. At 100, you can say goodbye to the universe."

"Then what's this?" John said, and pointed to the watch's display.

Vincent frowned. "It's your equilibrium range. It's growing. It's at 30 and growing. It's not supposed to do that."

John forced his eyes to meet Vincent's. "I want to save my friends, but not if I destroy this universe. Maybe it's the ML-20 that's causing it. I should have taken the antidote pill when Charlene first gave it to me."

He reached into his pocket and pulled out the antidote pill, and looked at it for a long moment before putting it in his mouth and swallowing it. The antidote took about six hours to work. Or, it was supposed to. But once he took it, the equilibrium range started dropping a little . . . then started rising again.

"It's not you, John," Vincent said. "It's me and the time machine. *We're* causing the equilibrium range to rise. It's like I'm from your future now, and anything I say or do will cause *your* future to change."

John looked at him, grasping for understanding.

"You have to leave and leave now," Vincent said quickly. "Get away from me. And do this as fast as you can. I'll be in contact with you by sat phone. Good luck."

John climbed over the fence and ran to the karate school, hoping to get there before Chen Lee Kahn or Antonio, Natasha and Bonita arrived, yet fearing that his very presence had already started the chaos theory, the grandfather clause and the equilibrium range on a collision course.

He checked the watch. The equilibrium range was at 86, and the closer he got to the school, the higher it rose. "At 90, eliminators appear," he whispered, remembering Vincent's warning, "and at 100, the universe will reset itself in the Big Bang."

He heard thunder. Even though the sky was cloudy, the thunder didn't seem to be coming from the clouds. He saw an octagonal-shaped entity appear in the sky right above him. It began to slowly grow. "A time eliminator," John said, looking at his equilibrium range, which had reached 92 and was climbing.

He stopped, unaware that he was already under their hypnotic effect, and the time eliminator started moving toward him. He snapped out of it and, using his powers, started running. He ran into the first place he could hide, a mountain cave. But hiding did no good. The time eliminators had caught up with him, and recognized him as a time bomb threatening the universal timeline. The only thing that had saved him thus far, he figured, was his super speed.

The time eliminators appeared and approached again, and again John ran. This time, he didn't stop running until he reached the Appalachian Mountains and ran into a mineshaft.

By the time he raced through the mine and began running back to the time machine, crossing three states to reach Texas, the time eliminators had detected his exit from the mountains and continued their pursuit.

Fearful of going back to the karate school, since they had first spotted him there, he headed for his house, trying to think of a way to loop around it and then back to the time machine. What he didn't realize is that, sensing that John wasn't going to be as easy as their usual prey, the single time eliminator had divided into two parts. Now, both sections were quickly approaching him and Vincent.

Frantically trying to get back to the time machine, he began jumping over entire buildings until he was on the street where he lived. Vincent, still waiting in the craft, heard the same thunder. He looked around and saw nothing, but when he looked over his shoulder, he saw John, saying, "Let's get the hell out of here while we still have time."

Suddenly another time eliminator appeared and approached. This one's target was Vincent Goff and the time machine.

Vincent heard John, but just stared at the time eliminator as it got closer. John didn't realize Vincent had been caught in the time eliminator's hypnotic trance. Only instinct guided his actions now. He jumped into the time machine and with one quick move, hit the stop-time button just before all three eliminators joined up to absorb both of them out of existence.

The hypnotic spell broken, Vincent looked at him and said with happy surprise, "It's you."

John leaned back in his chair, gasping, seeing the wind stop blowing and birds standing still, and taking as it as the sign that he had stopped time in time to avoid being absorbed by the eliminators that, until he saw one, he didn't believe existed.

But nowhere did the theory say that time eliminators were affected by the stopping of time. And now, they were approaching the time machine.

John lay back in the chair, trying to reconcile not being able to save his friends, not realizing that Vincent had once again been captured in the time eliminators' hypnotic trance.

"I never made it to the school," he gasped. "Never made it. If I could have seen them all one last time alive. But no, that wouldn't have been enough. I wanted to save them!"

In his frustration, he hit the machine's dashboard. Doing so broke Vincent's trance.

"Hey, John," he said. "How long have you been here? What happened?"

"Have you been listening? I failed. Instead of doing what I came here to do, I had to outrun the time eliminators and make it back here to stop time before they could absorb us."

Vincent didn't answer right away. But then he said, "If you stopped time, then why are they coming after us?"

John quickly looked in the direction Vincent was looking, then yelled, "Let's get the hell outta here."

With two button-punches, the time machine took flight and returned to the Time Travelers Academy. They were able to get past roving security and land the machine undetected.

"So what's next?" Vincent said.

"I think we need to get out of here."

Vincent grinned. "Let's head for the mountain. Obviously, it's where I do my best thinking."

On their way to the front gate, they bumped into Charlene.

"Oh, hi, John, I'm glad to see you. Last time I saw you, General Jones said you must find your destiny or something like that. How are you feeling?"

"I wish I could talk, but I can't," he said quickly. "We're going for a . . . a walk toward the mountains."

Before she could say anything else, they raced past her out the front gate.

"I built this machine, and I can look at it anytime I want!"

Mike Adams was an angry man, and the terrified sentry immediately allowed him into the hangar.

His hopes had soared after the first cure John brought back failed. Richards had earned that failure. Five years ago, Ivan Godunov's interference had almost ruined him, when he interfered with his dealings with the Russian officer who'd been happy to sell him and his business partner nuclear materials for resale. He'd looked for Godunov ever since, but all his efforts to find him had been worthless—it was only chance that led him to overhear Richards reveal his code-name his first day at the Academy.

Almost like it was meant to be, he thought now. It took some doing, but he was certain that when the crossed wires caused the mission to fail, Richards would get the blame. But not only had Richards overcome his attempt to sabotage the first mission, he'd actually gone on a second mission, also successful.

What galled worst was that, in the wake of the Academy's success in stopping the plague, he was certain that General Jones would get the Congressional approval he'd been campaigning for—to make the Time Travelers Academy the sixth branch of the Department of Defense. If that happened, any chance Ascendia had of taking full control of the Academy's operations was gone.

But that was all right—Richards, Jones, and a whole lot more people were about to get their comeuppance.

He walked into the hangar to look at his curse, the time machine, which he'd built so well, it seemed it could never be destroyed. When he got close enough, he slapped it, as though doing so would harm a machine built to travel billions of light-years.

That's when he noticed that the engines were warm.

That's it, he thought. *This is the last straw. Now Richards and his crew of misfits are taking it out on joyrides!*

The machine would have to be destroyed: what he had tried to do while it was on the mission, when there would have been fewer questions asked. The idea hurt. But if he couldn't use it for what he had created it for, no one should have the right to use it.

He looked quickly behind him, to make sure that his last bellow had frightened that snot-nosed boot-camper away for good, then set to work. It took only a few minutes to reverses the poles in the engine compartment. This would set an overload of the craft's nuclear-powered engines. The tampering alarms General Jones ordered him to install would sound soon. They would have fifteen minutes to either evacuate the students and staff or move the time machine to a safe distance.

"It'll be all right," he whispered. "And I'll start again, somewhere else."

⊹⊱ ⚙ ⊰⊹

General Jones woke abruptly at the alarm and threw on jeans, sneakers and a t-shirt and raced for the hangar.

When he arrived, he saw Adams standing next to the machine. "What's wrong with it, Mike?"

Adams smiled at him. "As you can hear, that's the overload alarm. Enough nuclear power to destroy a town of 5,000. Better get the evacuation started right away, don't you think?"

"The evacuation is already underway," Jones said. "I implemented it on my way here. The helicopter will be here any minute, per the emergency plan, to take the machine behind the mountains. They'll absorb its blast. You know that. Why aren't you trying to find out why the alarms tripped?"

Adams laughed. "Why would I want to do that, General? When I built this machine, it was to eventually have full control of it. Oh, I knew it would take a while. But as soon as the first mission failed, as soon as Congress realized that the military had screwed up—and made them look bad in the process—they'd throw the Academy off, order it privatized. And then Ascendia could take over."

Jones's eyes narrowed. "So it's you. *You're* Foxhound1. *You're* the one who's been interfering with the Academy since the day it was first funded." A long moment passed, and Jones added, "You're the one who planted the bomb in the stadium."

Adams nodded. "Right, General. One of many things I did to try to head this off. I even used our dear defense secretary whenever I could. He's a blundering blowhard, but considering how he feels about the Academy, I thought I could use his anger. And until the second mission, I thought I could do it without destroying the machine."

He shrugged. "Now, I realize that has to happen. No time machine, no reason for the Academy's existence."

He gave the machine another regretful glance. "Of course, doing it this way, the Academy will be destroyed too. No one will be able to use this site until the radiation's gone. But that's okay too. As soon as the hubbub dies down, I'll rebuild it somewhere else as a private operation. And I'll build a new time machine. This time, I'll have the funding on my own. Thanks to your obsession to keep the project going, the government's been very, very generous with Ascendia. And this time, I won't have you meddling in the plan."

The muted sounds of a nearing chopper came to them and the top of the hangar began to open.

"Looks like the emergency plan's working fine, General," he said. "When the helicopter lands, I'll be getting on it. I'll be far away by the time this place blows." He gave Jones a threatening smile. "Sorry I can't invite you along."

While Adams had spoken, Jones had edged closer, as close as he dared. There was little hope of it, but perhaps if he could restrain him, he could force Adams to undo whatever he'd done and prevent the explosion.

"You said you have a plan," he said. "And what's that?"

Adams chuckled. "You should know. Or at least guess. The person who controls this machine can literally control the world. But I don't need to control the world—just the United States. Think about it. Think about all the lowdown activities our leaders take part in. Affairs. Underhanded deals. Bribery and worse. Enron's only the tip of the iceberg. And think about how much power someone would have if they could travel forward in time, and then find out what that leader's done as soon as it hits the future's media. All they'd have to do is travel back to the present to, say, put a little pressure on the wrongdoer. Whoever held knowledge of the future could pretty much have their votes go their way every time."

"Not everyone will be blackmailed, Mike. Eventually, someone would fight you, expose you."

Adams shrugged. "Sure, there'd be some leaders who wouldn't go along. Ethics and all. But all I'd have to do is take whatever I find out and expose them a little sooner. They'll be voted out of office, and I'll have a handpicked candidate ready to take their place. With enough money, any number of votes can be bought."

He glared at Jones, who had managed to move a few precious feet closer. "I might have been able to gain control without having to do this. But you just had to keep TTA under military control, didn't you?" He sighed. "Well, in about fifteen minutes, you won't have anything left to control. And you only have yourself to thank. No time machine, no Time Travelers Academy. No more resources wasted by a lunatic."

Jones had all he could take. He lunged, grabbed Adams by the shoulders and shoved him away from the craft just as he helicopter pilot entered and said, "General, the helicopter is ready."

Jones let go of Adams and strode toward the pilot. "Proceed."

"Belay that order, Cadet."

Jones whipped his tall frame back to face Adams. "What?"

Adams ignored him and said to the pilot, "I'm ordering you to have the helicopter take me to a safe distance."

The pilot's eyes widened. "But, Mr. Adams—"

"Cadet, you're well aware that Congress has granted me authority equal to General Jones's when it comes to the time machine. I'm ordering you to take me off this base now."

Jones strode back toward Adams. "Have you ever heard of the Big Bang theory, Mike?"

"Yes, but—"

Jones coldcocked Adams, knocking him to the ground. "There's your Big Bang, and I hope you're seeing stars!" he barked. Then he told the pilot, "Carry on with the emergency plan."

Within minutes the helicopter lifted off, the time machine swaying underneath it. Soon, the machine was sweeping toward the mountain on its last journey.

Jones glanced down at the still-unconscious Adams, reluctantly picked him up and carried him to where everyone else had gathered in the underground bomb shelter. "He seems to have met with an accident," Jones said when the confused cadets saw him enter with Adams slung across his broad shoulders.

Once Jones was inside, the shelter's metal doors closed.

A rumor started that the nation was under attack. Panic rose among the cadets, for themselves, but also their families.

General Jones stood on a podium and shouted, "Quiet!"

With that, everyone stood at attention.

"You are safe and your families are safe," he said. "The reason you are here is because the time machine's nuclear reactor engine poles had been reversed, causing an overload. We couldn't turn it off, so I ordered our brave pilots to take it to a safe distance away from the Academy. This building will shield you from any radiation fallout and the explosion."

The tension let out of the group like a deflating balloon. But soon, Charlene came up to Jones with worry on her face. "I can't find Vincent and John."

Jones's gut clenched, and he said, "Are you sure, Dr. Vaughan?"

"Yes, I double-checked. I saw them earlier. Bumped into them, actually. They said they were going for a walk toward the mountain."

Jones gasped. "They'll be near the time machine when it explodes."

There was nothing he could do about it. The pilot reported that he'd just dropped the machine and was heading back. There wasn't enough time to rescue Vincent and John, or even locate them, before the craft exploded.

Vincent threw a rock down the face of the ledge they were sitting on, near the top of the mountain where John had carried him. "The rules stipulate you must have a time machine to go backward in time," he said. "But that goes against all the rules in your case. Some rules were meant to be broken."

"What's going on in that genius mind of yours again?" John asked.

"I'm just not ready to give up. Not yet—"

They heard the sound of rotating chopper blades and turned around.

"Holey moley, what's happening back at the Academy?" Vincent said, seeing what the helicopter was carrying.

They watched the time machine swing right over them, past the mountain, and then watched as the helicopter lowered it behind the mountain, in full view of them.

To better see what was going on, John picked Vincent up and they dashed toward the time machine.

"I can't believe it," Vincent said. "They dropped it on the ground, just like it was trash!"

As they got closer, they heard a beeping. Vincent stopped walking. "That's the overload alarm!"

"What does that mean?" John asked.

That beeps got faster, and Vincent said, "That means one minute before the engine blows."

John grabbed his shoulders. "You have to turn it off, then. It's a nuclear bomb!"

"That's why they brought it out here, John. It's imposs—"

"You can do this. The professor said you're one of the smartest people who ever lived. You can do this, I know you can!"

Vincent sucked in a deep breath, wondering if it would do any good to explain to John that there was no way to turn it off at this point, that by now, the heat had fused the rods together and there was only maybe 40 seconds left before it exploded.

John saw his face and understood. And he now understood what he had to do. "If you can't turn it off, then run."

Vincent began running, but stopped and turned around when he realized John wasn't following. "What about you? You can't just stay here and—"

"That wasn't a reply, or a request, that's an order. Now go!"

Vincent ran. And ran, and kept running until he was on top of the hill. He turned around, gasping, trying to find John in the darkness. He spotted him just as John yelled out, "Goodbye, my friend. I understand now! I understand about my destiny!"

Vincent watched as John's body started turning, faster, then faster still, creating a cosmic tornado. In less than five seconds, the cosmic storm engulfed him, then the time machine.

The storm carried both into outer space. Within seconds, Vincent saw the tiny dot of the explosion from the ground. A silent tear rolled down his face. "Goodbye, my friend."

37

Like any force greater than the natural, the storm seemed unstoppable. The twister continued picking up speed until it went far outside Earth's atmosphere, eventually making its way to Mars. Only then did it begin slowing, losing its strength. When it finally dissipated, John was thrown out of it.

He lay on the red planet motionless, then stood, amazed that breathing the Martian atmosphere wasn't lethal to him. The ML-20 organism, combined with his adaptation to the black hole near Peligroso, was enabling him to survive on the Martian planet.

He suspected that this power, as well as the other enhanced powers, would end when the antidote pill he'd taken took full effect. If that happened here, or on Earth, there was nothing he could do about it. His choice was to just experience his life as it came, without worrying about danger or consequences. He had vowed to never journey on the time machine again, and he intended to keep that vow. So these next few hours, before the antidote took his powers away, might be his last to jump past the constraints of time, speed, and space.

Suddenly weak, he got up slowly and stood. He looked back at Earth, then turned toward the west. Then, he started running, running around the Martian planet, faster and faster, approaching the speed of light. As he neared and reached the speed of light his clothes shed off him, unable to withstand the forces at that speed. Yet his time-equilibrium wristwatch could, because it was made out of trilasteverium.

In a split second, he had circled the entire Martian planet ten times. But still he didn't stop . . . until he heard the sudden loud boom.

He stopped and looked back, saw what looked like an oval hole. Through that hole, he saw only darkness. The hole resembled a miniature black hole. When he looked through it, he couldn't see any stars or planets.

"It's the rip in time," he muttered in wonder. Until now, he thought that only the time machine could create a rip in time going forward.

He ran to the black hole and jumped into it, not caring where he ended up, just grateful to be alive and doing something, anything, to end the painful saga that began when two men found him and handed him a yellow envelope and he said, *I do solemnly swear. . . .*

He glanced at his time-equilibrium watch as he ran, realized that his enhanced speed was taking him back farther than he imagined. Soon, he would be in the time before the date when his world fell apart—the day his friends and fiancé were brutally murdered and his school destroyed and taken from him. Not bearing to even hope that anything he did would change what had happened, he continued what comforted him right now, in this moment. He ran.

He allowed himself another look at the watch, and gasped when he realized that the right time and date—the time and date he never expected to return to—appeared on its display.

He stopped running and, not knowing why he should or even if he could, he began spinning again, creating another cosmic storm that engulfed him. This one, as his intuition told him, brought him back to Earth. But not in a place he expected or dared dream of. The cosmic twister had brought him to a spot within sight of the Great Wall of China.

He slowly stood, looking around, realized what country he was in . . . and then, that he was naked.

He looked toward the east. In a nearby village, he saw clothes hanging on a clothesline. He ran to it and grabbed everything off the line, then spotted a pair of well-worn slippers by the front door of the farmhouse. He grabbed up the shoes, still at a run, and later, in a secluded copse of trees, he tried the clothes on, finding only one garment that fit his large American frame.

Holding the shoes—he had more running to do, instinct had told him—he ran across the Pacific Ocean to California, then toward Rockville, Texas, reaching his house split-second after crossing into Texas. He sat on the front stoop of his house and put on the shoes.

When he looked up, he saw himself, back when he was running from the time eliminators, then escaping in the time machine. He held his breath. When he saw the time eliminators vanish, he knew he was safe in this time.

He ran toward the karate school, not caring what he found there. He glanced at his watch and was surprised to find it reading only 10, and that the indicator was stable, unmoving.

Vincent, you were right, he thought. *It wasn't you ... it was the time machine's presence that caused the indicator to go nuts.*

He smiled, and for the first time, allowed a bit of hope to creep into his heart.

Nothing could have prepared him for what he saw next: The building, his lucky find and the site of some of the best and happiest years of his life, was standing there, intact.

He tried the door and found it unlocked. A closer inspection told him it wasn't just unlocked. The door's lock had been forced.

He eased the door open, wincing when it creaked, then walked on quiet, slow feet to the office. He saw movement and almost stopped, but picked up his pace when he saw that it was Chen Lee Kahn.

What's he doing in my office? he wondered. *I never gave him the keys to the office!*

He mentally inventoried the talk he and Antonio had before he left for the Academy. Memory confirmed that only Antonio had keys to the office, and that Kahn had access to the doors he needed to do his cleaning and maintenance work.

And then, it hit him. What Sergeant Kim had said at the makeshift memorial. What he had said confirmed Antonio's suspicions about the quiet janitor and part-time instructor. But John had been too consumed by grief to make the connection. Then.

He strode to stand in front of the office door and watched Kahn for a moment. "So it's you," he said, his voice quiet but resolute. "You're behind all of this."

Chen Lee Kahn's body jerked when he saw John. "What are you doing here?"

He grabbed Kahn by the shoulders and slammed him onto the desk, fighting the urge to snap the traitor's neck. "Why are you surprised I'm here? I'm the owner, remember?"

"I, ah—"

"Don't even try. You killed my best friend, but that wasn't enough. So you killed his wife, and her sister, who was going to be my wife. Now I'm going to kill *you*."

He picked Kahn up, dragged him out of the office and into the main classroom, and threw him across the huge space. Kahn's body echoed when it thudded against the far wall.

With nothing but anger inside him, he crossed the room to stand over his enemy, who was bleeding from a cut on his head.

With difficulty, Kahn pushed himself upright. "What are you talking about? I didn't murder anyone. You don't understa—"

John stepped back. "You're mistaken. I understand plenty. More than you can even imagine."

Kahn sighed, whipped his body around to the wall behind him, retrieved two of the fighting-knives hanging there, and tossed them to John. Then, just as quickly, he retrieved two more and then turned around.

"If this is the way it must be," he said, "then let it be."

Kahn brandished the two 13-inch knives, then held them up in a defensive manner.

Seeing this, John did the same. "I never thought it would come down to this," he said, his heart plummeting. "I hired you eight months ago. I trusted you. And you did nothing but betray me and destroy my life."

They approached each other. Kahn swung his knives toward John's throat. John jumped backward. While in the air, he kicked Kahn 30 feet into a wall, causing his knives to fly out of his hands.

Moving slowly, since there was now no need to move fast, he ambled over to the fallen man and grabbed him up off the floor. The knife he held made a quick, ratcheting arc toward Khan's throat before stopping less than an inch from his bare skin.

Without flinching, Kahn said, "What are you doing here? You're supposed to be at the Academy."

He moved the knife another quarter-inch toward Kahn's throat. "How did you know that? That's top secret. How did you *know*?" Then his eyes narrowed. "Who *are* you?"

Sudden dizziness overcame him, and he dropped the knife and Kahn to the floor, then followed, landing with a heavy thud next to him.

Kahn rose up on his elbows. "You okay?"

After a moment, he was able to say. "Yes. A little weak. But I'm fine."

Kahn reached up, wiped at the blood trickling into his eyes from the cut on his forehead. "Eight months ago, my superiors told me to investigate you, your school and your neighbor next door . . . to find out if you might be connected to Gary Collins in some way. I'm with the FBI."

John listened because his sudden exhaustion wouldn't allow him to speak, to challenge the unbelievable admission he'd just heard, or what followed.

"The FBI found triggering devices for nuclear warheads in the Middle East," Kahn said. "The devices were traced to Twin Sky Electronics. Collins had no authority to make those devices. None at all."

John gave him a weak nod. He had suspected that Gary Collins was much more than a simple electronics dealer.

"We'll arrest him for it soon," Kahn continued. "As soon as the investigation's complete. The triggering devices were purchased by laundered military funds. At first, we thought the Secretary of Defense had something to do with it—V. Lanti has explosives experience. Plus, he's always pushing his nuclear defense platform on the President. We thought we had him when the bomb blew up the Academy's stadium. But turns out, it wasn't him. When we traced the money to its source, we found a big name—Ascendia Corporation. We believe its CEO, Mike Adams, is behind all of this. He's also ex-military, also with explosives experience."

"Is that enough to pin it on Adams?" John asked. "I mean, someone else could have just hired someone else to plant the bomb? I've met Adams. He doesn't seem the type. And he built the Academy. Why would he want to destroy something he built?"

"Our case is tight," Kahn said. "Our informant at Collins's business overheard several conversations between Collins and Adams. Except that we didn't know it was Adams at first. Collins kept using the name Foxhound1. It took a while to figure that out."

John nodded, feeling a ball of ice in his gut. "I'm a little familiar with the name. But I never imagined what else Foxhound1 was into."

He quickly filled Kahn in about what had happened to him in Special Forces, when the corrupt Russian general had screamed the name at him. Then later, when another Russian general had mentioned the name. And still later, when he'd found out that General Jones was conducting his own investigation into someone with that codename.

"All that time, Jones trusted Adams," he said, his voice bitter. "And all that time, he had a conniving murderer betraying him, and the Academy . . . and me."

"Yes, you," Kahn said. "He's arranged hits on Antonio, likely as retaliation for you . . . for screwing up his dealings in Russia."

John looked at Kahn, and whatever was in his face made Kahn reach out a stabilizing hand. "Look, it wasn't just him. It's something Collins already wanted. Something about wanting your building for a parking lot. But Adams wants you out of the way, too. He's concerned that you might find out about his deal with Collins."

Kahn chuckled. "He thinks you're an undercover agent at the Academy, investigating him. The dumbass."

He turned his gaze back to John. "I told my boss what I found out, but he didn't want to risk blowing the investigation by coming out here in force. But . . . that's why I was here by myself. We have an informant next door who told me that Collins hired the Mal-A-Dies gang to come here tonight. According to the informant, Collins knows Antonio does his accounting at night on this day of the week. They plan to ambush him and kill him. Maybe even torch the place."

He looked at the floor, then his eyes met John's again. "I . . . No matter what my superiors thought, I didn't want an innocent civilian caught in the crossfire. So I thought I'd get here early and warn Antonio if he showed up. Maybe try to head it off."

John found his voice with difficulty. "There's something I have to tell you. About tonight. You're going to need my help tonight."

"But after what you said . . . why would you help me?"

"Because I understand a lot more now. . . . Because you would do it for me. I know that now, and—"

The classroom door flew open and Antonio, Natasha and Bonita entered the room.

"John!" Bonita squealed, raced across the room and hugged him. But he'd just managed to get to a sitting position, and was almost knocked back to the floor by her enthusiastic embrace.

"I missed you and was worried about you," she said.

"I missed you, too," John said, and instinctively reached in his pocket to pull out the ring he purchased. It wasn't there, of course. He was still dressed in the simple clothing he'd taken from the clothesline in China. The ring was in his car's glove compartment.

There was no time to explain, even if he'd thought they could possibly understand. Collins and the gang could be here at any second. "Go into the basement," he said. "Kahn will stay with me. And lock the door behind you."

Bonita gasped. "But—"

"No buts. That's not a request, that's an order."

They raced for the door to the basement at the same instant Gary Collins and the Mal-A-Dies gang burst into the classroom. Some members brandished knives. And John knew that one of them had a concealed gun.

38

"Jackpot . . . we got 'em all in one place."

To buy time for the others to make it to the basement, Kahn rose from the floor and replied to Collins's remark. "You're at the end of your road, Collins. I'm with the FBI, and I have orders to arrest you all. It's your choice to come peacefully or by force."

Collins smiled and held up his hand to prevent the gang leader from answering. Then he smiled at Kahn. "You need to look around, my janitorial friend. It seems you're outnumbered. And don't bother calling the *real* police. We took the liberty to make sure the phone lines are cut. You see, I'm a businessman, that's all. This isn't personal, it's business. You all die tonight, and I get my payback starting tomorrow morning. Nothing personal, just business."

He snapped his fingers and said, "Kill them all. Then burn this place to the ground."

The gang reacted quickly, surrounding John and Kahn.

Knowing the past, John knew he wouldn't be able to bargain with them. He and Kahn still faced the gang leader. Still feeling the effect of the antidote, he wobbled slightly on his feet. Then he glanced at Kahn and mentally prepared for the fight of his life.

The gang rushed them, but between Kahn's expert kicks and knife defenses, one by one the gang members fell back, leaving only the best of the knife-wielding members to continue. At one point in the battle of dodging blows, lunging kicks and razor-edged knives, Kahn did a backward kick. Its momentum landed him outside the door. The gang members who'd already run outside met up with him, and his part of the fight resumed.

Some of the punks were easy to subdue, but six apparently were masters before they turned to crime. John fought four of them, but the other two rushed outside to help the other gang members subdue Kahn.

John hoped Kahn could hold out until help came. From the time he became dizzy, he'd been feeling weaker. Perhaps it was the ML-20 mutating in spite of the cure. Or perhaps the antidote was working faster than he expected. For whatever reason, he hoped Kahn could hold out if he couldn't. Judging from the grunts and screams he heard from outside, he was doing better than that, though. The realization made him smile.

Minutes later, it seemed that his time had run out. One of the gang had him in a headlock and was choking the life out of him. In his weakening state, he could do little but try to pull the man's arm away and grab what air he could drag through his compressed windpipe.

But then, he felt the man's grip suddenly loosen. He dropped to his elbows and knees, then twisted around, trying to see what had happened. Bonita stood there, wild-eyed, holding the iron meteorite she'd given him for good luck.

"We— We heard the fighting, and I . . . I found this on the podium," she sputtered. "He was trying to kill you—"

A sound behind him made him turn back, just in time to see one of the gang reaching behind his back, toward the waistband of his baggy jeans. At that instant, John knew this was the punk who had the gun.

Before he could react, he heard a guttural scream behind him and Bonita, blond hair flying, rushed past him. Before the man could withdraw his hand, the meteorite found its mark, and the punk toppled over and lay still.

Bonita whirled around, her face a mixture of triumph and savagery as she screamed, "Who wants to be next?"

Fighting the laughter that threatened to distract him, John saw another gang member approaching her, knife out. His strength had returned well enough that he was able to rush the man, spin and give him a power-kick. The knife sailed from his hand and with one final kick, the last gang member thudded against the mirrored classroom wall, splintering the mirror into an endless spider web.

Her eyes still wild, Bonita ran to him and hugged him, babbling, "I thought you were going to be gone forever, I miss you, never leave me again, never!"

By the time Antonio raced out of the same door Bonita had come from, only one of their enemies was left. Gary Collins, seeing his last hired thug defeated, bolted for the classroom's exit.

John saw, pulled Bonita's arms from around his neck, said, "I'll be right back," and raced outside.

Behind her, the gang member she had clobbered with the meteorite opened his eyes, shook his head from the pain . . . and saw his gun within reach.

At the sound of a gunshot, John ran back into the classroom right behind Kahn, who kicked the door off its hinges and threw a small knife with 100% accuracy toward the gunman. The knife struck the man's hand, stopping him from firing the gun again. Kahn finished him off with a karate punch in the upper neck, knocking him out. He whipped his head around, saw John holding Bonita and sobbing, then watched, stunned, as John lowered her to the floor and knelt over her.

Natasha emerged from the basement door in time to see Antonio and Kahn running toward her sister. She joined them, screaming her sister's name, her sobs already shaking the walls of the room.

But Bonita saw only John's eyes, heard only his voice. She had time to say, "I love you, don't leave me again," before closing her eyes. John's last kiss was for her, and for him.

The sirens came, but there was little for them to do except document the carnage and take statements. Except for Sergeant Kim, who dragged the gasping, purple-faced Collins back to the karate schoolyard and said to Kahn, in an exaggerated Texas drawl, "You looking for some trash? I found some on the side of the road." The out-of-shape, 300-pound wannabe cowboy had been spotted running down the street to his electronics store, which he wasn't likely to be returning to anytime soon.

Kahn smiled at Collins and tipped an imaginary Stetson his way. "This isn't personal, it's business, Mr. Collins. And I really hope you don't take this the wrong way."

Kim radioed for backup, and for ambulances to deal with the unconscious gang members in the front of the building.

John didn't hear any of this. He remained kneeling over Bonita's body, remembering the first time he'd ever seen her. How beautiful she looked, and how intelligent he discovered her to be. How she had looked the night of Antonio's wedding, and how hurt she must have been when he left for the Academy without even saying goodbye. How a woman like her should always have the best things in life. Things that he had wanted to give her. But he had decided too late. *Too late,* he thought, tears washing his face.

Too late . . .

He hadn't checked his watch since before the fight began. When he did now, his breath hitched in his throat. The reading was at 87.

Trying not to be obvious, he looked over all the police and ambulance personnel around him. Someone . . . someone coming near him . . . was a time bomb, whose interaction with him would change the future. He must avoid this person at all costs.

But even if he couldn't identify the person, which was likely impossible, he had to leave. Now. If he didn't, the time eliminators would appear, with devastating consequences.

He bent over, kissed Bonita's still face again, and whispered, "I'm sorry, I'm so sorry I failed you. But I have to leave. If I don't, I'll fail everyone."

He located Kahn, put one hand on Kahn's shoulder, said, "I know what I must do," then slipped from the room heading toward the back door of the school. It was best to avoid the police and medics, because one of them might be the time bomb.

The back door was locked. He muttered "Why the hell not?" and kicked it open. It exploded in hundreds of small pieces. When they settled, he stepped through the doorframe . . . and straight into the drawn guns of police who'd been searching the back of the school for stray gang members.

Moving with aching slowness to avoid alarming them, he eased the watch to where he could see it with a quick downward glance. The display read 88. Better, but nowhere near reassuring.

"I'd love to stay," he said to the officers, "but it seems like I'm running out of time."

Becoming a blur, he turned and ran right past the five gun-wielding men onto the street.

He heard "Stop or we'll shoot!" before the volley of bullets began. He looked back, saw them coming, turned forward, thought *Screw this*, and increased his speed, leaving the bullets on the dusty Texas ground behind him.

He jumped over entire lakes, rivers and city skylines, arriving in Oklahoma before exhaustion forced him to rest for a while. Alone on the endless prairie, he began to create another cosmic storm to return him to his own timeline.

But this time, the storm faded as fast as a Midwestern twister.

He tried again, and this one disappeared too. Fearing that was a sign the antidote was near the end of its action, he tried one last, desperate time. On the third try, the whirlwind formed and held, propelling him back to Mars. But time was definitely running out. Once on Mars, he tried to run at the speed of light, but couldn't.

Then he realized that he didn't need to create a rip in space to go into the future. All he had to do was run *close* to the speed of light. He began running again, going slowly forward in time. Once he reached the correct time, he rotated again, and was successful in creating a cosmic storm to take him back to Earth.

This time he landed in the Antarctic Ocean, surrounded by penguins that were soon to become dinner to a great white shark . . . unless the shark decided that John was meatier and tastier fare.

It apparently did. The shark attacked, forcing him to run again, this time north until he arrived in New Mexico. This time, it was easier to find clothes to fit him.

He appeared in the Academy's dining hall to shouts and surprised yells.

"Hey, we wondered where you've been," Feldman said. "You have no idea what happened here. . . ."

Everyone, to a person, had been convinced that he died in the explosion.

Vincent and Charlene were outside, at the back of the dining hall, looking up at the stars and crying for their lost friend.

"You two aren't planning my funeral, are you?" he said.

They jumped up and ran to greet him. As soon as he could, he asked, "How's my mother?"

"She's fine," Charlene said. "The cure worked. She's 100% better. We're still keeping her for a while, but just as a precaution."

John looked up at the star-filled sky and muttered a prayer of thanks. Then he said, "I have to see her."

They accompanied him to the Academy hospital. On the way, Charlene said, "We didn't tell her yet."

John slowed his pace a bit. "Tell her what?"

"That you died in the explosion. We just gave her your belongings—for safekeeping, we said. She asked us to store them in the hospital's storage room."

When they reached his mother's room, Charlene patted his arm. "We'll wait out here."

"Yeah," Vincent agreed. "As long as you promise not to disappear again."

John smiled. "Only if I must."

His mom was thrilled to see him, but after only a few minutes of hugs and kisses, she said, "You must go home, son. Something . . . terrible happened."

The words unnerved him. What else could have possibly gone wrong back in Rockville? The last thing he wanted to do was leave her again. Without truly understanding why, he found himself saying, "I have to go, Mom. I have to go back home now."

"But honey, wait till I tell you what happ—"

He placed a gentle finger on her lips. "You don't have to, Mom. Whatever it is, it's best if I find out about it myself. You've been through enough."

She reached up, grasped his hand and squeezed it. "I understand, son."

He retrieved his car keys from the storage area, then stopped at the front desk and got the phone number to the hospital and his mother's room number. Then, he began running to the airport to get his car. That's when the antidote finally began to kick in. He was still moving much faster than normal, but now, it seemed agonizingly slow.

Finally at his car, he flipped open the glove compartment, and there was the ring—the ring he'd never had a chance to give Bonita. He stared at it for a long moment, remembering the day he'd picked it out. When he was just a typical young man with typical dreams and aspirations, a fledging business owner whose only mission in life was to teach kids good values while teaching them how to take care of themselves and become successful at martial arts. But that was before he noticed the two men in dark clothes, waiting with a yellow envelope that would irrevocably change his life, and the lives of so many others.

With a sigh, he stuffed the ring, still in its tiny velvet box, into his pants pocket, and cranked the car.

+⊱⸺ ⚜ ⸻⊰+

While the man took his airport parking toll, the gate attendant asked, "Did you have a nice trip?"

John couldn't help smiling at the kid's innocent question. "Yes. I went where no one has ever gone before."

"Where on Earth did you go?"

"Mars."

The attendant started laughing.

John reached into his pocket and retrieved something he'd long forgotten about—a tiny red rock he'd risked picking up while on Mars. He gave it to the kid, saying, "Here's a souvenir."

The attendant looked at the red rock in amazement. "Hey, I've never seen anything like this before."

John felt the case holding Bonita's ring, then said, "Yeah, it's pretty unusual. Special. Rare. Hang onto it."

He drove toward Rockville, happy but fearful of what changes he caused and what he might find when he got there this time, wondering if his journey would ever end, but knowing that if it did, it would be he that must end it.

39

It didn't matter what he found out, he knew. When he put the pill in his mouth and swallowed, he'd only had a six-hour window before the antidote started working. He still cursed the loss of his powers, which necessitated a ten-hour drive back to Rockville. By the time he approached the main roads leading into Rockville, the sun was rising onto another hot, dusty Texas day.

He was relieved to see that the school still stood. But to his surprise, Twin Sky Electronics next door appeared deserted, the parking lot empty. He smiled and whispered, "Chen Lee Kahn, you did it. Somehow, you did it."

Bracing himself, he then drove by Antonio's place. The lawn was neatly clipped, and the for-sale sign wasn't there this time. Another smile came. At least he'd saved Antonio.

But now, he had to find out if his actions had saved anyone else. He had to face what his mother had meant when she said, *Something terrible happened.*

He knocked on the door and Antonio threw it open. "Oh . . . hi, John, good to see you. Your trip over with?"

There was no smile on his friend's face, or on his wife's when she entered from the kitchen, dishcloth in hand.

Seeing Natasha, his hopes soared. He took a deep breath, then said, "Is Bonita upstairs?"

A long moment passed, then Natasha burst into tears and fled back into the kitchen.

Antonio laid a firm hand on John's shoulder. "John, I'm so sorry, but . . . she's gone."

John hung his head, willing the tears that sprang to his eyes not to flow. But then anger at himself combined with his sudden grief, and he bolted from the house. Antonio yelled after him, but he couldn't go back, couldn't bear to listen that he had failed, yet again, to save her.

40

He made it home and to his bedroom before breaking down. But after a while, he knew he had to get up and get moving, or he never would.

On the way to the kitchen, he noticed the message light blinking on his phone. He hit play, and almost broke down again when Bonita's voice came through the speaker.

"I wasn't honest with you, John," she said. "When I told you I came to America to continue my education. In my heart . . . I hoped for more. For us. For our future. But that was not to be. There was a shooting. . . . I can't speak of it yet."

He found himself dropping into the chair next to the phone. "She's alive," he muttered. "Oh, thank you, God, she's alive!"

In his shock, he'd missed some of her message, so he hit the rewind button.

". . .when I was in the hospital recovering, I realized something. If you loved me as much as I love you, you wouldn't have just left. And without even telling me goodbye!"

His heart lurched, realizing how cruel he'd been, without meaning to be. "I'll make it up to you, I swear," he whispered, and continued listening.

The tears had left her voice, replaced by anger. "And that is when I realized that your . . . your *job* will always come first for you. I can't continue in a relationship with you for you play the worst games. What *is* your real name, anyway? What did you tell the girl you went out with the day before you came to see me in Russia? Did you tell her your name was Ivan, or John, or something else?"

She's jealous. He allowed himself a smile. *But she said she loves me. We can work this out.*

"I can live no more like this," she said. "But I have nowhere to go."

The gunshot came through the speaker so clearly, he clenched his own abdomen in response.

Shaking with the horror of the images in his mind, he called the number he knew so well. An operator said, "I am sorry, sir, that number is no longer active."

Devastated, he walked to the wall near his bed and pounded it, saying, "No, no it can't be."

But, it seemed it was. And once again, he had failed her.

⊹⟜ ❀ ⟝⊹

Now, he knew what his friend meant when he said, *She's gone.*

He couldn't bear to see Antonio again, not until he could confirm with his own eyes what his heart was screaming at him. The flight seemed to last forever, but at last, he stood on an early-morning Moscow street, knocking at the door of Bonita's vacant apartment, holding a hastily purchased bunch of the reddest roses the city could offer. As he knocked, petals fell from the bouquet, but he paid them no mind.

Bonita wasn't there. Even if the landlord hadn't already insisted that in his broken English, the yellow crime-scene tape across the door would have told him. But he didn't care; he had to believe that she was there in spirit, if not in presence.

Finally, his knuckles raw with the attempt of trying to resurrect something that was dead and gone, he laid the roses in front of the door, said a prayer, then walked away.

He walked until he found himself at the park where they had met, found an empty bench and thought of the first time he saw her there. *If only I could do it all over!* he kept thinking.

You had far more than a second chance, his mind responded, *and you failed each time.* And he knew, with the same certainty, that his prayer wouldn't be heard another time.

Still, he couldn't help muttering, "If I only had a second chance, I'd never leave her again."

"Is that a promise?"

He turned to the voice behind him. Bonita held the roses in her right hand. The cast on her left arm prevented her from supporting the bouquet, and he saw a few more petals fall. With a cry of disbelief he stood, ran around the wooden bench, picked her up and spun her around in his arms.

When he could finally bear to allow her feet to touch the ground again, she said, "My landlord saw the roses and gave them to me. I . . . I thought I might find you here."

"But . . . he told me you were gone—"

She placed her fingertips on his lips. "I was gone. No, I *am* gone. While I was leaving the message, someone shot into my apartment. I'm staying with a friend. And I . . . That was cruel of me not to call and leave another message, to tell you I was all right. But . . ." She glanced away. "The way you left me, I didn't know if you would care."

He grabbed her shoulders. "Not care?" he sputtered. "*Not care?* I care. I care a hell of a lot." He pulled her toward him and whispered, "I care so much, I can't live without you. And I can't lose you again. I can never lose you again."

He forced himself to let go and went to one knee, then felt around in his pocket. He retrieved the box, opened it with trembling fingers, and held it up to her. "Will you marry me?"

She gave him a skeptical smile. "Under one condition. You served in the military and gave that 100% of you. And that's great. But you're no longer in the military. If I say yes, I come first."

"I promise to put you first in my life forever," he said. "Will you marry me?"

The stern look on her face was impossible to maintain. She smiled and held out her hand. "Yes. Yes, John Richards, or Ivan, or whatever your name. Yes, I'll marry you."

He rose to stand and kissed her, knowing that he'd just been granted a new start in life. Again.

He was running again, but this time, Bonita was beside him as they dashed out of his mother's house after saying goodbye.

"But it'll only be for a few weeks," he'd told his mom. "And this time, you'll know where I am." He smiled at Bonita.

They had decided to wait about marrying until the much larger wedding Antonio and Natasha had planned for their second wedding. That way, Charlene and Vincent, still busy with the aftermath of the mission, would be able to attend.

For now, Bonita had whispered to him, *it is enough to be with you. Later, I want a biiiiiig wedding to celebrate!*

Today, their first stop would be the Time Travelers Academy, to keep the promise John made when he said he would return. They jumped into John's blue sports car after lowering its convertible top.

"Wow, you brought plenty of snacks," Bonita said, eyeing the overflowing bag in the car's tiny backseat.

"Hey, it's a ten-hour drive," he replied. "And most of that bag is filled with Mom's cookies."

Her eyes crinkled in delight. "Chocolate chip with those beautiful, tiny little walnut pieces?"

His grin came easily. "Yep. By now, she knows those are your favorite."

He'd called ahead, so their first sight after parking the car was Vincent and Charlene walking toward them.

"Bonita, you're as beautiful as John described you," Charlene said, her copper-hued face beaming. "And your English is wonderful!"

Bonita beamed right back. "Thanks to my job with the ambassador's children," she replied. "I not only had to learn good English, but all the curse words, too." She shrugged. "Otherwise, how would I know when to discipline them?"

There was laughter all around, and then tears, followed by more laughter.

Later, Vincent took him aside. "Look, I know you're out of the TTA now, but—"

"Yes, and that's the best decision I ever made. I promised Bonita she would be first, and I intend to keep that promise."

"Oh, no pressure, dude," Vincent said. "It's just that . . . now that they've made me mission commander—not that we actually *have* a mission yet—let's just say I might call on your expertise from time to time. An occasional opinion. After all, you were the first to have my job," he grinned, "and I like learning from a master."

John gave him a return smile, but a small one. "Opinions? I have plenty. But as far as ever getting on the time machine again?" He patted Vincent's shoulder. "I think I'll leave all the *real* risks to someone younger and with a smarter . . . mouth."

41

The double wedding held another celebration, since Antonio used his reception toast to announce, "We wanted a beautiful American wedding, and we sure got that today. But folks, we've been doubly blessed. In about eight months, we'll also have a beautiful American baby!"

Everybody held up their glasses, cheering at the news. Then the band they'd hired began playing, and the dancing began.

Two dances later, John whispered to Bonita, "I don't want to leave a woman as gorgeous as you, even for a second, but nature calls."

She giggled and held up her glass of champagne. "At least this time, there is no security checkpoint!"

He sighed. "For which I'm eternally grateful."

+ᚗ ᚗ+

There was someone in the last stall when he entered the men's room. Or at least, that's what he thought, until the stall door flew open and the two agents he never wanted to see again walked out of it, followed by someone else he suddenly had the urge to kill.

Mike Adams stopped ten feet from him, but only because one of the agents grabbed his elbow and said, "Mr. Adams, remember—"

"I know!" Adams barked and jerked his arm away. "I can say what I've got to say from here."

John, who'd watched the exchange, said quietly, "What a surprise, Mike. And how nice of you to . . . visit on my special day."

Adams gave him the smile that had terrified many. "How could we forget you, John? Or should I call you Ivan?"

"Let me guess. I've been drafted again."

Adams guffawed. "Relax, John, the world isn't in danger. Thanks to you, we can all sleep soundly. But," he tried to draw closer, but one of the agents said, "Sir?" and he stepped back one pace. Then he nodded at the agent on his left,

−210−

who reached into his jacket pocket. When his hand emerged, it held a yellow envelope.

"John, we need you again."

John glanced at the envelope the agent held. Something was off about it. There was no top-secret stamp on this one, and the envelope lacked the Presidential seal.

He stared at the envelope for a moment, trying to decide if he should confront Adams now, tell him that the envelope was clearly a phony.

After a moment, he looked up. "I thought you just said the world isn't in any danger. And I'm surprised they even let you near the Academy."

Adams shrugged. "Oh, Jones didn't like it, but once I pointed out to him that I'm the only one who knows how to rebuild and run the time machine, he went along with keeping my . . . indiscretions quiet for a while." He smirked at John. "You should know that he'll do anything . . . *anything* to keep the Academy going forward."

"Well, they might need you, but they surely don't need me. All I want now is to be left at peace and try to find some happiness."

Adams shook his head as though about to chastise an unruly child. "John, you're still officially in the reserves. Surely you know that you can be recalled to active duty."

"The *only* reason I'm still in the reserves is because my paperwork hasn't been finished. But go ahead, tell me why you need my help."

"We have a new concept. Actually, it's not new. It's actually the original concept of the Academy—going back in time. If we know the past, we can use portal time travel to change it to what I— what *we*, you and I, want it to be. That's what the mission was until a bunch of nerdy scientists scared Congress with their factless theories about time eliminators. So Congress banned it, the idiots!"

"What about the laws the Academy taught us?" John said. "About travel to the past being too dangerous?"

"Everything has danger to it," Adams said. "But everything I've ever done with Ascendia carried risks. You've taken plenty of risks, too. Your service in the military. Your missions. But the rewards of past-travel are great. So join us again."

"I'm married now," John replied. "And reserve status or not, I'll fight you if you force me to join. I'd even fight Jones on this. And even if I wanted to reenlist . . . I'm against corruption. You of all people should know that." He gave the men standing next to Adams a harsh glance.

"John, we're time-recruiters," the agent who held the yellow envelope said. "No different from the recruiter that brought you into the Navy. No one twisted your arm then, and we won't now. But . . . you know you're special. And we'll do whatever it takes to get you to join us."

John glared at him. "Whatever it takes? Like planting a bomb at the Academy? Or perhaps cutting the wires on the time machine? Or falsifying draft orders. Or maybe all three?" *And then allying with Gary Collins to destroy my life?*

Adams sighed, pulling John's eyes back to him. "Yes, it was me, John. I ordered those things. It was just business. Nothing personal."

A chill started in John's heart that went to his toes. "I've heard that before. Guy named Gary Collins. Know him? He's got that same philosophy. Exactly that philosophy, in fact."

"Gary Collins is in jail. I'm not. Thanks to Jones, there was no evidence against me. Which means no case. And even if there was, I'd be innocent until proven guilty. But that's not what I came to talk about." He pointed to the envelope.

"Not on your life, Adams. And not on mine, either, although you tried."

"You still don't get it, do you? You're a hero of a successful mission. If *you* go along with the idea of placing the Academy under private control, Congress will go along with it. And if they do that, you won't *have* to go back into the military. And you'll become rich. Like the proverbial beyond your wildest dreams. We need people like you to help us, John."

John allowed his anger to show. "Help you do what? You don't need me to run a mission. You've got everyone you need to do that."

"Weren't you listening? We have to motivate some members of Congress to make the right vote. To privatize the Academy, and choose Ascendia to run it. And when that happens, I want you to work with me."

"What makes you so certain I'd be willing? And how could I possibly influence Congress to do anything?" As he spoke, he tried to think of something he could use as a weapon if it came to that. "What if they say no?"

"Then we can do the same thing I tried to explain to General Jones. We can go back in time and find dirt on them. It shouldn't be hard to do. If they want to keep what we find out from the public, they'll have to vote the right way. Our way. For the good of the Academy. For the good of Ascendia. For your benefit."

"Your way is *not* the right way."

The agent held the yellow envelope out. "Look, we've already been here longer than we should. Here are your orders. You've been drafted pursuant to the laws governing the Selective Service. You have no choice."

John took the envelope and asked the agents, "I guess since you know my whereabouts this time, you're from my present?"

"No. Once again, we had to track you through Russia. But this time, we knew you'd be here because it's the day you got married—exactly one month back from our time via portal time travel."

"Isn't that dangerous? That goes against everything we were taught at the school."

The agent shrugged. "A theory is just a theory. But your actions proved that theory false."

John scratched his head. "How so?"

"Easy," Adams said. "When you went into your past and saved everyone, you changed the future. A huge disruption in the time-paradox. Yet no time eliminators appeared to stop you. Clearly, it's safe to go into the past. Time eliminators are just a bunch of theoretical hogwash."

"Sir, I beg to differ. Time Travelers Academy Manual, Chaos Theory Section, Page 118."

The answer had come from behind John, and he turned to see Vincent walking from the door of the men's room, where he'd heard most of the exchange.

The agent, suddenly nervous, said, "Mr. Adams, we should go—"

Adams threw up a hand to silence him, almost hitting him in the face.

"All right, Mr. Goff . . . and yes, I know your name. Fill us in on yet another brilliant theory."

"I won't do a direct quote, but John was able to go back into his past because it was actually his present . . . because his future was changed by you, the agents. Once you gave him the envelope, that started the changes. By going back in time and correcting his past, he didn't signal the eliminators because *he was supposed to be there in the first place.*

"But that doesn't apply to what you're planning. If you're from the future and using portal time travel, you're breaking the most serious rule in the universe."

The agent holding the envelope glanced at the other agent. John noticed that both their faces now held doubt.

John said, "If you want to continue this conversation, Adams, you'll have to do it at the reception. My new bride is waiting, and I have no intention of disappointing her."

He strode out, forcing Adams to follow. John could hear the agents protesting, but rather than loose track of Adams, they hurried after him.

Soon, they were mingling with the crowd, and John and Vincent were able to lose Adams and the agents when Lanti spotted Adams and headed for him.

⊰⊱ ⚜ ⊰⊱

As she walked toward Antonio, giving John an occasional sly smile, Vincent tapped John on the shoulder.

"What is it?" John said, but kept his eyes on Antonio and Natasha, who were about to have their first dance.

"Look at my watch, dude!"

At Vincent's harsh whisper, he looked down. The watch holding the equilibrium-range detector showed 70 on its display.

He looked back up to the smiling Natasha, watched her take a slow, teasing step toward her new husband.

The display now read 75.

He glanced back up, watched another slow step, then shifted his eyes back to the device.

80

He glanced at Vincent. "*She's* the time bomb?"

Vincent nodded. "'Fraid so."

He glanced back down, saw the display reading 85, then leaped toward Natasha, yelling, "No! Stop—"

At that instant, one of the agents bumped into him, knocking him against Natasha. John managed to remain upright, but the agent and Natasha fell to the floor, the agent on top of her.

Antonio and John scrambled to get Natasha off the floor. As soon as they were all upright, Vincent yelled, "95!"

The agent on the floor moved to stand. The other agent ran over to help him. Thunder sounded, and both agents turned toward the sound. They didn't know what the two objects were at first, but then one of them pointed and yelled, "It— It's true! They do exist! Run!"

Before the first agent could reach the men's room door, he was absorbed out of existence.

The second agent shouted, "I'm not going out like that," and grabbed the person nearest him—Vincent.

Holding Vincent like a bank robber taking a hostage, the agent shoved Vincent in the shape's direction. The shape moved away.

"You ass," Vincent said, trying to pull himself out of the agent's grasp. "You didn't believe in 'em, but you sure as hell believe they won't attack you as long as you're near another person."

"Shut up," the agent said, and began dragging him toward the men's room.

Vincent gave up struggling and tried reason. "Look, you don't know this will work. It's just a theory, remember?"

"Yeah, and so were those, those *things*!" the agent replied. Terror made his voice shake.

Inside the men's room, the time eliminator approached. Then a third one appeared. This one went directly to the time portal in the closed stall and absorbed it.

In spite of his fear, Vincent couldn't help muttering, "Wow, I didn't know they could do that!"

"It's gone," the agent gasped. The portal's gone. I can't go home!"

As he spoke, he let go of Vincent, lost his balance, and slipped and fell to the tiled floor. Vincent took his bid for freedom and ran to the other end of the long room.

The agent managed to stand, but the time eliminators quickly sandwiched him. In an instant, he shared the first agent's fate.

"NO!"

The stall next to Vincent flew open, and Adams emerged from the hiding place he'd taken when the melee began. He had only time to scream once before he vanished into the entity's gaping mouth.

Vincent watched as the time eliminators stopped moving, and for a moment, he thought they would disappear. They didn't; they headed straight for and then disappeared through the men's room door, back into the reception hall.

"Wha—?"

And then it hit him, and he raced after them.

⊰⊱ ❀❁ ⊰⊱

John had just heard the scream and was trying to fix its location when the time eliminators emerged, followed by Vincent, who was waving his arms.

"Drop the envelope!" Vincent screamed.

The time eliminators crept toward John.

"Throw it away," Vincent screamed. "It's from the future!"

Understanding came just in time. John threw the envelope in the air, and the winds that signaled the time eliminators' presence carried the envelope higher. They attacked the envelope now twirling above him, absorbed it, then vanished.

As quickly as it started, it ended. All that was left were the panicked sobs and shocked curses from the crowd, and the remnants of the wind, now blowing softly across everyone in the room.

42

"Go get 'em, tigress," Vincent mouthed to Charlene, who was sitting on the dais in front of them dressed in a dark green suit, waiting for her name to be called. John followed Vincent's silent remark by making a thumbs-up sign.

She smiled and smoothed the suit's tailored, calf-length skirt that she hoped looked trendy, but professional. Because of space restrictions, she'd only been able to invite a limited number of people to the ceremony. Her mother and father were the first. Feldman was there too, beaming at her, just like Suzie, Maria and the rest of her crewmates were. The last two were also easy choices. They had to be the pair who'd saved her life on a planet far away, in a time unimaginable to most.

When the speaker stopped rambling and finally told the group what they were there for—that Dr. Charlene Vaughn had been instrumental in discovering the cure for avian plague, thus saving humanity from destruction—she rose up to accept the Nobel Prize in Medicine.

As soon as the ceremony was over, she startled the group of scientists and dignitaries crowding around her when she raised her skirt above knee level so she could more easily run toward her mother and best friends. The talk of her passionate acceptance speech dominated the media, but for weeks, the elderly group's favorite topic was that they'd never seen a Nobel Prize winner who had such lovely calves.

One week later, all ten companies stood in their dress uniforms, at attention. In his keynote speech of the graduation ceremony, the new Secretary of Defense, General Jones, commended everyone, while V. Lanti, now retired, stood by, doing a poor job of hiding a scowl. The highest honors were given to Company 001, who had scored the most points in the Academy.

Admiral Suarez, the TTA's new director, stood nearby until Jones finished, then strode to the microphone.

"Before I release you," he said, "will Cadet Vincent Goff come to the stage?"

With the President of the United States looking on, Vincent marched onto the stage, saluted, then said, "Time Travel Cadet Goff reporting, Sirs."

He was saluted in turn, then Admiral Suarez was handed a box by General Jones.

Suarez smiled at Vincent. "For uncommon valor, for sacrificing yourself to save the lives of your crewmembers on Planet Peligroso, and for saving all cadets and staff by alerting them of a pending explosion, thus causing an evacuation that saved the lives of 815 people, you, Vincent Goff, are awarded the highest award given to members of all branches of the military service, the Congressional Medal of Honor."

The award stunned Vincent, but not as much as when he turned and saw his parents at the back of the audience. As soon as he could politely take leave of those on the stage, he ran to his mother and gave her a hug, then turned toward his father, who, at first, just stood and looked at him, wearing his full uniform, now with the Congressional Medal of Honor dangling proudly from the bright blue ribbon around his neck.

His dad didn't hug him. Rather, he saluted him, said, "Congratulations, Sir" . . . followed by, "I'm proud of you, son." Only then did he wrap his arms around the son he thought he'd lost for good.

A moment later, he heard someone yell, "Hey, there he is!"

Still hugging his father, Vincent winced. *Oh, no, they wouldn't. I'm a Medal of Honor recipient, they wouldn't dare—*

He felt himself being grabbed up. But this was no blanket party. This time, it was his entire cheering, yelling platoon who lifted him onto their shoulders and carried him around, yelling, "Vincent! Vincent! Vincent!" at the top of their lungs. Laughing and hooting with them, he threw his hat in the air, and the other cadets followed his lead.

+⟫⟫⟫— ⦅⁒⦆ —⟪⟪⟪+

Later that day, he stood with John on the deck of the newest time machine while John spoke to the crowd below.

"The universe is very large," John said, "but it has just been made smaller. Thanks to our Academy, the world now can travel to any planet in the universe and discover that planet's future. . . . As long as we obey the laws of the universe, the universe is ours. So let the journey begin!"

Leaving Vincent, he stepped off the time machine and walked over to Bonita and his mother, then turned back to look up at Vincent. "Captain Goff . . . see what's out there."

With a nod and a wave, Vincent followed his crew into the time machine.

Through his speaker, Vincent heard General Suarez order, "Stop time and proceed to Mission Two."

"Yes, sir," Vincent replied, and hit the stop-time button.

The time machine took off for its second mission, known only to those who would respect, honor and assist it to a successful end.

⊹⟩⟨⟩⊹

Later that year, Congress passed legislation that officially made the Time Travelers Academy the sixth branch of the United States Department of Defense. The new branch's motto?

The Journey Has Begun

Printed in the United States
132214LV00007B/93/A

9 781847 289261